GW01161426

Julie Grande Lund

The Snake in The Grass

Fantasy

© 2023 Julie Grande Lund

Illustrasjoner: Hoa Thu Hông

Forlag: BoD – Books on Demand, Oslo, Norge
Trykk: BoD – Books on Demand, Norderstedt, Tyskland

ISBN: 978-82-845-1029-3

Foreword

I dedicate this book to the people who supported me on this journey, through every and all my ups and downs.

I'd like to say a special thanks to my parents, my sister, and her partner and all of my friends, one of which read one of my works out loud in an overly dramatic manner in order to cheer me up (you know who you are). You all kept on cheering me on every day. Thank you so much for celebrating with me every time I passed a milestone while writing this, I am incredibly grateful for that.

You all truly took one for the team!

CHAPTER ONE

First, there was the Goddess. She had surrounded herself with the stars and suns, moons and light and darkness all by her lonesome. At some point, the comfort of the voiceless creations in the vast space no longer gave her any reprieve from her loneliness, and so she plucked out one of her eyes and pulled out a bone from her left wrist. From them she fashioned beings such as herself. They became her children, the two very first gods', her first creations, and she was very proud of them. While they did help her overcome her loneliness, she had felt pride in creating something, fashioning something from her mind with the help of her powers, and she fell for the temptation of creating something new again.

And that is how the world came to be. Her Children watched on as the Goddess chose one star as the center of her new creation. Then she drew together little pieces of dying stars. She gave them a new purpose as their light faded from existence. Together they were all bound together as a shell around the star at the center. All firmly stitched together into creating a world in which the Goddess could do much more. This world became her canvas. In it she encouraged her Children to explore their own powers, for she herself knew not what they were capable of. She created the world, their canvas, and then guided their hands while creating life.

Only the Goddess herself could create *life*. Sentient beings with minds of their own, that is. The other two gods were able to fashion much of everything else in the world. The Goddess may have created all the creatures of the world, but the two gods brought about the colours of the world. They fashioned the roaring rivers, silent creeks, bountiful fields. They formed the rocks of the ground into mountains reaching toward the sky. They planted seeds which grew into great forests and blooms in all manner of colours.

And while the gods created this hospitable world, the Goddess cut off more pieces of herself. She plucked out her second eye and created creatures later known as Cyclops. They were immortal in much the same way as herself and her first children, but not quite. Immortal in one way but bound by other laws than she and the gods. They had to feed to sustain their bodies, and the Goddess created animals to help them farm the lands. Then she moved on to experimenting with creations. Together with the other two, all kinds of animals found their homes in the forests, the mountains, the sky, beneath the ground, the fields, in the water.

Then came the faeries and spirits, who tended to the lands alongside the cyclopes. They then began the process of fashioning creatures who would be known as trolls and goblins, dragons, harpies, and unicorns. Then animals with the ability to speak, shapeshifters and humans and many more. But the more they created, the more they drew from the Goddess, there was no changing the fact that the creatures they made were weaker, lesser with each creation. Watching their creations be taken by death and decay, become one with the world they had created and fading from existence upon their passing hurt the Goddess. After only a few millennia after they found themselves satisfied with their work, they all retreated back to the vast space around their creation. They watched from afar as time passed, and the world changed.

And for a while, it seemed that the world they had created was a peaceful one, as all creatures coexisted, gave and received from each other, and kept on offering prayers and gratitude to the Goddess and her children. Everyone had been created by a piece of the Goddess, and so they were all a part of her, and this was the one thing that linked them all together.

Until it no longer did.

The more beings the Goddess made, the shorter their lifespan became. By the time she made humans, her creation's lifespans were so short it seemed like their lives passed in the blink of an eye. The cyclopes never aged, spirits and faeries had a different concept of time than others, and the rest could live for several centuries. At some point they would succumb to time and old age, however, and fall to rest as well. Humans were the beings with the shortest lifespan, and perhaps that is where the problem started. Because it did not take long after the Goddess disappeared that the humans started forgetting. Unlike a cyclops whose life was unending, alongside their memories staying true, humanity's memory was everchanging over the centuries. Whereas their memories and stories started out with all of creation being made from the Goddess and all of them being her creatures, it slowly started to twist into something else, something darker. Something cruel. No longer were they all creations by the Goddess, given a home on this world by her first Children, but rather twisted creatures who occupied the world she had given humanity, failures she wanted exorcised from her lands. Many creatures died out rather quickly, being no match for the sudden aggression from beings they once trusted and got along with, but most hid away before they were caught.

Now, that is not to say that all of humanity shared the belief that the world belonged to them and them only. While the part that believed the first truth did their best to spread peace, they were quickly overrun and called heretics and traitors to the Goddess by the others. And then suddenly, for several centuries, close to a millennia, there were three factions within humanity. One believed in and fought for peace with all creatures. Another believed that the world was theirs and theirs alone. The final group wanted nothing to do with either faction, and avoided them both as best they could, content to simply exist and live their lives.

There were some creations that fought back, like the cyclopes. They were far too mighty for humans to fight, trolls as well, and goblins were so many in number there was no end to them. There were those who tried to fight back, and succeeded, and those who failed. There were those who never got the chance to fight back, and there were those who realized that they stood no chance and hid from the moment aggression was turned on them.

There was even those who did not understand the sudden rejection, the hatred they had not done anything to deserve being directed at them. They tried to reason and understand, but gained nothing out of it, and decided to hide away anywhere they could.

Those were the shapeshifters, the ones who were the closest to humans in appearance, though that was also where the comparison ended. While humanity possessed magic of a kind, shapeshifters were more proficient at the art, more in tune with it, and their lifespan was much longer. Yet, while the shapeshifters were more powerful than humans, they were fewer in number, and thus whatever battle that could have been fought would have ended before it even began. The shapeshifters went into hiding as best as they could once they realized that any peace they wanted to broker would not be well-received. The humans taught their descendants to hate and hunt shapeshifters as monsters being a stain upon the Goddess' world. The shapeshifters taught their young to never trust and keep out of the way of any human they might encounter.

And as humans' memory of the Goddess, her children and their will became twisted, the shapeshifters lost faith in the Goddess and the gods', for they allowed all of this to happen, and did nothing to stop it. Never once did they put an effort into coming back. Not once did they declare that this was wrong, and so some of the shapeshifters began believing that this was the desired result that the three wanted.

For what kind of all-knowing, all-seeing, all-loving being that created all that they know, could be kind, *good,* and still allow such heinous atrocities to happen in their name? Who would want to believe in gods that cruel?

But there is hope, there is always hope. No matter how long one has to wait for it, good things do happen, even amidst all the pain, sorrow and horror. And when one thinks they are trapped in an endless cycle of lies and grief and fear, one must remember; there will always be someone to reach out their hand, a show of support, a promise of aid, proof of love.

And that is what makes it worth it.

CHAPTER TWO

There is a specific mountain in this world. This is where a village has been carved into the lowest part of the mountainside. It is a rather secluded village, far out into the outskirts. It is so far away that even the lords of the land sometimes forgets it exists. At the very least until the taxes are to be collected, and then the cycle repeats. In this specific mountain though, there lies a serpent. A humongous beast with the ability to speak the human language.

Or so the rumors say.

Of course, the rumors of the giant beast are ones spread by bandits mostly. And, truly, how much can you trust the words of thieves, rapist, liars and murderers? The villagers themselves have never once asked for any aid in liberating themselves of such a beast. If there is an animal like that so close to their homes, they would have requested aid in ridding themselves of it by now, would they not? It is only logical that they would, considering that serpents are rather dangerous creatures.

If there truly is a monstrous serpent in the mountain, which is highly unlikely, then it must be left well enough alone. If it isn't causing any trouble for anyone to complain about, that is.

Well, mostly alone.

"Andor!" It is supposed to be a shout, it can certainly be interpreted as one, but it sounds more like an annoyed, loud hiss than a yell. A scaly tail wraps around a young boy dangling off a rather frail-looking branch of an apple tree. The branch is rather high off the ground. Had the boy fallen, he would have hurt himself. The boy laughs loudly as he's brought down to safety, running his hands over the sun-warmed scales wrapped around him. Long and humongous. Black as the darkest night with a red underbelly and bright yellow eyes. The serpent is an intimidating creature to most people who lay their eyes on the beast.

"I've told you several times, don't climb too high up into my apple trees!" The boy, Andor, simply stares up into the slitted eyes of the serpent. Then he grins, lips stretching wide at the annoyance he is able to translate from the thin pupils and hissing breaths leaving the beast.

"You'll always bring me down to safety, snake!" Andor yells excitedly. The creature hisses in what is clear annoyance, tongue swiping the air in front of them. They lean closer, pupils thinning even more, if that is at all possible. A clear sign that the serpent themselves does not find this as amusing as the child does.

"Should just let you fall and hit your head, it would serve you right," the serpent mutters. Well, as much as a serpent is capable of muttering. Their forked tongue draws out the "s" like a hiss, making them appear much more intimidating than they mean to.

It doesn't make any difference to the child in the serpent's grasp. He grins wider, even as the snake coils tighter around the little body in a warning gesture, as if they are about to constrict him. An action which the boy will most definitively ignore later. Then the serpent lets the boy go. Andor, once free, runs over to his group of friends who are sniggering in the background. They huddle together, throwing the beast glances every now and again as they whisper quietly enough for the serpent not to pick up on. If such beasts had eyelids, the serpent would have narrowed their eyes in suspicion. The group of youngsters are plotting something, no doubt about it. It will most likely end in another headache for the serpent. It always does. It is an old game for them now. Thankfully, Andor's father, Gunvald, makes himself known before they can execute whatever trick they were planning. He climbs the hill up to the serpent's home with a sack thrown over his shoulder, calling on his son.

"Andor! It is time to come home!" The children slouch their backs, lower lips jutting out in sour pouts. The serpent, on the other hand, sighs in relief at the other human's well-timed appearance.

"But dad!" Andor whines, loud, and voice so high in pitch that the serpent winces and ducks their head, hissing in warning again. Gunvald though, used to this kind of pitch from his son, levels the group with a stern look and they give up. They know that there is no winning this. Sullenly, they turn to head back down to the village. Signy though, ever so defiant as the lone girl in the group glares first, reaches into one of the many berry-bushes. She grabs a fistful of them and crushes them against her face, ending up smearing more berries across her face than eating them, which just ends up with a color that unfortunately can be easily misunderstood. Or that might be her intention. At this point, the serpent has begun to give up on understanding her intentions. The serpent and Gunvald watches them stomp down the path, before the adult turns towards the serpent.

"They weren't too much trouble, I hope?" Gunvald asks with a humor laced voice as he carefully drops the sack onto the ground in front of the beast.

"No more than usual." The man chuckles nervously at the answer. He is not afraid of the serpent. It has never once been a threat to the villagers for the century it has lived in the mountain. Still, it is a bit unsettling to stand in front of a predator who can swallow you whole. Caution comes with age, even he had been as fearless as his own child when he was their age.

"Ah, well, children, you know," he says, as if that should explain everything as he wipes his hands on his shirt. The serpent flicks their tongue out.

"Indeed. I am used to it." It makes the days go by faster for the serpent, that much is true. And it is nice with company every now and then. While they do complain about being bothered by the children, they enjoy the company. All the complaining is just for show, it is just how they are. And children are fascinating, a great way of escaping solitude with the way they come up with the most fascinating games and stories. Their minds have yet to understand the limitations of the world.

"Right," Gunvald clears his throat, bouncing on the balls of his feet. "I'd best get back too., wouldn't want to offend the wife by not showing up for supper. Off I go, Master Snake." He waves a hand and turns around, following the path downwards again, whistling happily all the way.

"Off you go," the serpent echoes quietly. They watch the man disappear down the path before they bite into the sack. They bring it back towards the cave that has been their home for the last century. They hiss as they move past the mouth of the cave and the vines and bushes that frame it shivers and moves to block the entrance. The moment the greenery has blocked the entrance so no one can see or enter, the serpent begins to change.

They coil together, before their tail splits in two and grows feet. A lean upper body emerging from the scales, red and black scales melting into sun-kissed skin. Their head grows rounder, copper hair falling past their shoulders and down their back. Ears grow out of their skull, a nose taking the place of the snout. And the eye sockets narrowing from their big roundness from earlier. The beast melts away and a tall, lanky redhead stands in the abode, the sack in his hands. And there he stands for several moments, jaw working.

"It's Aske." The words are but a whisper, near on inaudible, but a vine reaches out and tugs on the man's hair in comfort. It pulls back as he waves it off. He's been here for a century, yet not a single human has ever used his name despite him giving them leave to do so. Several times. In an effort to not go mad, or even reaching the point of forgetting what his own name is, he mutters it to himself a few times each day. All simply to remember, just to remember that he is a person. It is not quite the same as someone else using it, saying it out loud. Yet he has long since accepted that as long as he stays here and plays the part of the monster serpent in the mountains, this is the only way he will ever hear it. As long as they only see him as an animal, that is. He can't show them what he truly is, however. Shapeshifters aren't safe amongst humans. The safest option for him is to just be a monster that grasps human speech. Centuries of memories has taught him that, centuries of pain, grief and loss has taught him that.

Maybe he should go find Saga. Go find his last remaining sibling and just, be beside someone who knows him. She is half a world away, though, according to their latest Dreams. She always was better at blending in with the humans, which is one of the reasons she dared to move closer to human civilization. Aske had not been willing to do so, and they had parted ways, which had put a strain on their relationship. It explains the walls in the Dreams, how she hides something from him. But… if she had come with him, if she had been here, maybe he would have been able to find the courage. The courage to walk amongst the humans, the courage to believe he could blend in. Maybe he would still feel like he is her brother, like they are still family.

He scoffs at himself. How utterly pathetic is he, living for centuries and still not trusting himself to be able to blend in? For not finding the courage to do anything but hide behind a lie, a façade, just to live?

Still, all that aside, it is not so bad here at this mountain. The villagers believe that as long as they're not hostile towards him, he'll be a non-hostile monster-serpent to them. Like that, they'll continue to bring him supplies. It is not so bad, it could be much worse. He could be actively hunted like an actual animal instead of living rather peacefully here on this mountainside. His mountain. He heads further into his home and drops onto his sleeping furs, eating the food Gunvald had brought with him. He focuses on feeding himself rather than being swarmed by the dark thoughts which always return with a vengeance whenever he is alone.

But it's hard to not feel lonely, when he is hiding like this, lying. Children come and play and cause a ruckus and liven things up. The adults come around with food and some pleasantries in exchange for the herbs or flowers or fruits that the shapeshifter grows in his garden. There is nothing more to it, though. No one he feels close to.

Not a single companion, not a single friend. No one that don't run the risk of disappearing in front of him like they never existed if he isn't careful. Slipping through his fingers like water.

He sits there in melancholy for a long while after finishing the food, eyes hazy, before he pulls himself back and shakes his head. One must do what one has to do to survive, and Aske is fond of living. So, what if he is lonely? This is a poor mountain village. Or rather, it used to be a poor mountain village with all the bandits that came through. But that was before Aske settled down here, and Aske isn't good with humans at the best of times. No matter how lonely he is, it is *safer* for him to keep to himself and trust no one, no matter how empty he feels with his way of life.

"Bandits," he murmurs, laying down and crossing his arms behind his head. It's been quite some time since any group came by lately. The numbers have been dwindling ever since he settled down here, but he'll have to prepare for the possibility that someone will come by soon. It is a tiny village which is periodically forgotten by their lords, after all. A defenseless village is always a sweet target, no matter the outlandish rumors surrounding it.

As the evening grows late, Aske finds himself unable to fight off sleep as it comes for him. Spending an entire day with children and entertaining them is, while enjoyable and never boring, also very taxing. Tomorrow will be no different, he will need all the energy he can muster. Aske sleeps well that night, and the next, and the night after that too. The hot summer air keeps his cold-blooded body warm, even in the cool mountains. There are no Dreams, and he makes none of his own, doesn't reach out to her, doesn't quite dare. The days pass by in a peaceful manner, even amongst the terror of the children running around his garden and making a mess he will have to clean up. But, of course, on that one day where Aske is all by himself, lounging on sun-warmed rocks and dozing in the sun is when it happens.

There's a faint trembling in the ground he only noticed because half his body is stretching across it. To confirm his suspicions, he moves to lay his head onto the ground as well. With an annoyed hiss of an exhale, he slithers down the path towards the village. The vibration in the ground grows ever stronger the closer he gets to the village. It grows to the point it is no longer simple vibrations. He can hear the actual sounds of thundering hooves.

The oncoming group force their way into the village, which doesn't take too much effort. The villagers just hurry out of the way and group together in the square. They watch the intruders shout, sneer, laugh and waving their swords and axes and causing a right ruckus. The bandits must have expected to see the villagers run and scream. Expected a widespread panic and the people begging for their lives and mercy as any man, woman or child would in such a situation. They realize rather quick that the people of this village are just staring at them, expressions conveying quite clearly that they are not impressed with this juvenile display. They stop their movements and wait, staring back at the people, just as dumbfounded. Gunvald takes this as his moment to get a clearer understanding of the situation. Not that it is all that hard to understand what is going on, but best to be on the safe side.

He takes a few steps forward, pipe in hand as he looks the bandits up and down. The bandits themselves finds it rather surprising to see someone who is not afraid when a group of armed men storm into a defenseless village. It is not what is common, after all.

"Might I inquire why you gentlemen have come here?" Gunvald is unfailingly polite. Though one can tell from one glance that this group is far from what anyone would ever describe as gentlemanly. Actually, this kind of group is truly what would make your heart race like a hummingbird in your chest. Fear either make you stand completely still or run screaming, to have you trample down others in an attempt at getting away to safety. They are not used to polite questions about their reasons for coming. Even so, the man who appears to be the chief of the group answers. He is a scraggly looking man with an amused smile stretching his thin lips wide.

"Your riches and your women." Gunvald turns his head to look at the people gathered behind him, pursing his lips and sighing, as if rather put out by this entire ordeal.

"Ah, a group of bandits." As if it isn't already quite obvious, and the villagers nod their heads sagely, chattering to each other as if this is a normal occurrence. "Well, riches we have got very little of, I'm afraid, and as for our womenfolk, that is a hard no from every one of us. I am sure it is quite the norm wherever you go. Now, we would all greatly appreciate it if you went on your merry way." There is a series of agreeable murmurs in the crowd behind him, and the bandits burst out laughing at the audacity.

"You're a real jester, old man."

"*Old*?" Gunvald looks highly offended by the remark and his face twists in annoyance, the most so far since the group had ridden into their home.

"But you don't get a say in this. We're not leaving empty-handed, and what, pray tell, can you do to stop us?" He looks to his men who all shout and raise their weapons in a show of intimidation. All the while the villagers are silent for a few moments as they do this. Then the air is filled with the shouts of children, doing their very best to be louder than the bandits. A few words get through the booming laughter of the bandits and catch their attention.

"The snake will teach you all a lesson!" It is Andor who breaks through the ruckus, and it causes the bandits to pause. He stands in front of his group of friends, arms spread wide and a defiant look on his young face, eyes narrowed with as much righteous anger as a ten-year-old can produce.

"The snake will chase you all away!" The bandits begin murmuring amongst each other, confused, and more than a little bit amused by the boy's courage.

"Snake?"

"There's a rumor," the bandit chief chuckles smugly as he moves his horse forward to tower over Gunvald and Andor. Gunvald moves to stand in front of his son as the bandit moved ever closer on his steed.

"Of a giant snake lurking in the mountains, but it isn't real. Monster snakes don't exist no more! Especially not here, where it ain't so warm!" He raises his voice, challenges anyone to refute him, but frowns when the children behind Gunvald grins widely as any happy child can, and points behind him. The villagers cover their mouths to muffle their mirth as they take a few steps back, and then;

Then there is a loud hissing sound behind the bandits.

The chief turns around in his seat. The sight makes him pale and lose all his bravado. He has never once encountered such a creature for as long as he has been raiding and plundering. The enormous black and red serpent towers over all of them, staring unblinkingly. The beast hovers unmoving for several long, painful seconds in which the bandits' hearts beat so loud in their ears that any other noise is drowned out.

Then the beast opens their jaws wide, showing off four long fangs, as long and thick as the bandit chief's arm, if not longer. And then, then the beast lunge.

CHAPTER THREE

Aske has never found the task of scaring off groups of rag-tag bandits particularly difficult whenever he changes his shape into that of a serpent. Most humans *do* panic when a beast several times their size appear and hovers over them. Aske only needs to open his jaws as wide as he can, and they'll scatter, and this time is no different. To be fair, the horrified horses do help when they try to toss off their riders and run away. Some of the men run after the horses, trying to recapture them, mount them anew. Some raise their weapons and try to wound the beast, but the scales are old, thick and hard. The beast writhes and slithers about in such a manner they don't get a clear hit in. As such they only end up managing to numb their own hands while doing so, if they ever get any contact. Despite his massive size, the serpent is quick.

Aske lashes out and sends them flying. They will most likely be scared out of their minds for a very long time. Bruised and hurting for a while as well. The shapeshifter has no intention of taking any of their lives, though. He's just going to impart a very important message.

Get out and do not return.

He snaps after them, manages to snag one of the bandits by his shoddy leather armour and tosses the man high into the air. He watches him scream and flail before he crashes into someone with enough courage to charge towards Aske. He lashes out with his tail again, sending several falling over as he wraps it around one and hoists him up in the air. The bandit flails and screams when Aske dangles him above him, opening his jaw wide again. For all intents and purposes he acts as if he is about to swallow him whole. Aske swipes his tongue out menacingly, before he throws this one away too. They smell atrocious, he won't have them near his mouth like this again, he might just hurl.

The bandits quickly realize that there is nothing they can do against this beast, as their weapons have little to no effect at all. And so they give up and call a retreat while they can. They limp their escape as Aske follows, hissing loudly yet again to drive the point in. Just loud enough to make sure that they keep the hurried pace all the way out of the territory. He finally stops at the edge of the village, watching them hobble down the paths and disappearing, before he returns to the villagers. They are all chatting amongst themselves happily and applauding him for the splendid display of terror when he comes back into sight.

There's a sting somewhere, Aske feels, insistent and burning. He must have moved in the wrong direction upon someone attacking him for that to have happened. With every movement he feels whatever it is digging deeper beneath his scales. Twisting, burrowing deeper, doing more damage to the vulnerable flesh beneath. The children cheer and chatters with much excitement amongst themselves. Their next game will be a somewhat proper re-enactment of this very situation. They will be the mighty warriors chasing bandits away. The serpent must be a part of it by any means necessary when they have fleshed out the rules properly.

"Splendid, Master Snake, thank you for the timely rescue!" Gunvald calls out as he claps his hands enthusiastically. He glances back over his shoulder to get nods of agreement from his fellow villagers.

"Very well done indeed. You do have a habit of arriving just in time!" Not that there have been any bandit attacks for years now. For Andor and his friends, this is the very first attack they have ever witnessed.

"It's nothing," Aske answers before hissing in pain and moving over to the human, who graces the serpent with a worried look.

"What's the matter?"

"There's something between my scales. Pull it out." He lowers himself down, hears the horrified gasps of the humans around and sees Gunvald's queasy expression as he reaches over. The man grabs hold of whatever it is that is causing Aske discomfort. The shapeshifter is grateful for the man's careful movements as he does his best to minimize the pain of pulling out what turns out to be a dagger lodged between some of his scales. Not a single one of the villagers recall the serpent ever having been injured for as long as they've lived. The unprecedented situation worries them all a great deal, as anything unusual usually worries people.

"Thanks." Aske then turns and slithers away, wanting to get back to the comforts of his cave. He's feeling exhausted. All he wants is to burrow beneath his worn furs and sleep.

"Oh, um, you, er, don't you need any help with that?" Gunvald calls after him, already looking around for the village doctor while holding the dagger as far away from him as he is able. The serpent merely hisses, saying it is not necessary. Aske knows that it will be a hassle to reach the wounded area on his own. Yet it is also not the first time that he's tended to a wound on his own body. He'd rather struggle a bit than let a human put their hands on him when he's vulnerable ever again. As he slithers up the path, he curses himself for having been so careless. A century of peace can make one soft and Aske hates to admit that he celebrated his victory too early, lay down his defences too fast. He literally offered up his soft underbelly. An infant's mistake.

After this heroic act, Aske believes he very much deserves a long nap. He's going to need it, allow his body the rest it needs to recuperate. The moment he is past the greenery framing the cave, the vines begin covering the mouth of it. He shifts back once most of the sunlight is blocked out, searches for the wound, finds it right beneath his right shoulder blade. A tricky spot, but he manages to bind it securely and pulls his tunic back on before he flops down onto his furs. He falls asleep, but it is not a peaceful rest. The wound throbs, plagues him even while unconscious. Hours later he jolts awake by the sensation of his blood feeling like liquid fire, and his foggy mind pieces together the puzzle.

He snarls to himself, wrenching his shirt off with weak hands. His body is heavy, he's burning both on the inside and outside, and he struggles to breathe, it feels like someone has dropped a boulder on his chest.

'*Poison!*' His mind supplies. The dagger had been coated in poison, and Aske hadn't considered that possibility because poison is not usually much part of a bandit's trade. It does not change the fact that he has poison in his veins, which is not good. Aske is no healer. He can turn into a serpent and a half-snake, a hybrid between a humanoid and beastly appearance. He can conjure fire and control greenery, but healing is a skill in which he is sorely lacking. And this fever haze that has taken root in his head won't leave him any more capable of healing than he was before.

"Fuck!" Now, Aske has never come across a poison or venom that his body has not been able to resist thanks to his nature and experimenting while young. Yet it always slows down the healing process to some varying degree. He has a sneaking suspicion that he'll be taking a long while to recover from this, and it will be far from pleasant.

"From such a shallow wound, how laughable!" It is infuriating, but what he truly fears are not the pain and discomfort which he will be experiencing during his recovery. He fears that someone from the village will come looking for him. They will most likely become suspicious of his prolonged absence. He prays to anyone who'll hear him that no one comes. A hundred years of peace will *not* be ruined by one measly poisoned dagger. He won't let that happen. His life may be lonely, but it is as safe as can be, and he will not be chased off. He mutters a spell, glancing towards the cave opening. The greenery shifts, completely blocking out any light.

No one will enter before he is ready for it, and with that done, he allows himself to fall unconscious again.

Aske is quite fortunate that the villagers are hesitant to come close to a wounded animal, much less sending their children to play with one. Yet, they are indeed worried about his well-being. The cave has stayed sealed since the day of the bandit attack. They are wondering if everything will be alright, because in the long memory of the village itself, the serpent has never been wounded. The village doctor wants to go up, even though she knows very little of how to treat a monster serpent. At the same time lies the problem of their ancestors' old promise to never enter the serpent's home without being invited. A promise the serpent had insisted on upon their arrival. Gunvald uses this argument, and they all agree to wait.

Two more days pass, and Gunvald stand with three others and the doctor, discussing the situation yet again. Though with much more frustration and vigour this time.

"I'm willing to brave the cave, to ensure that he is alright!" the doctor insist, but Gunvald frowns, hesitant.

"We swore an oath-"

"Our *ancestors* swore an oath!" She's worried and frustrated, and Gunvald can understand because he is equally as frustrated. The difference is that he, as the village chief, must be the one to make the final decision.

"They swore an oath that *none of the people born and living* in this village shall ever intrude upon his home without invitation! We broke it once, and we're lucky he didn't find out then. I will not risk a repeat with a different outcome! We will *not* break it again, and that is my decision!" Their heated discussion has caught the attention of a lone traveller. A traveller so inconspicuous no one took much notice of him when he entered the village days prior. This man, broad shouldered but soft around the middle, has been in the village for two days, resting in a proper bed for the first time in weeks. While he'd love nothing more than to mind his own business and regain his strength so he can journey on, his curiosity won't allow it. So, he heads over, clearing his throat in a bid at getting the arguing group's attention.

"Excuse me?" They turn towards him and he clears his throat again, a nervous habit.

"Right, my name is Bragi, and I'm a healer, as in, I use healing magics. If someone needs healing, I might be able to help?" The group turn away and talk quietly amongst themselves. They keep shooting him looks that tells him that they're not sure if they can trust him or not, which is fair. He is an outsider, after all. Rural little villages out in the far reaches of a territory are always a bit closed off to strangers. He offers them a second option.

"Or you can explain to me what kind of wound or ailment it is and maybe I can help by figuring out how to treat if? If that makes you more comfortable?" This seems to ease their worries, if only a little, but they're all startled when a group of children burst forward. All four of them look stricken and shouting out before the adults can do or say anything.

"It's the snake!" Andor exclaims, and Bragi blinks, not sure if he's hearing correctly.

"The snake- *it's real*? The monster snake of the mountain actually exists?" His eyes nearly bug out of his skull as his mind wraps around this revelation.

"Yes." Gunvald fixes the children with a stern look, harsh enough that they look away in shame. He had not wanted any strangers to know that their guardian is wounded and unable to come to their aid or defend himself until he is well again. Unfortunately, what has been done is done, there is no undoing that.

"We recently suffered a bandit attack, and Master Snake became injured in the skirmish. We haven't seen him since." The words force themselves through gritted teeth, and Gunvald does not look away from the children as he speaks. They take a few hesitant steps back, shoulders up to their ears as they wring their hands behind their backs. They are used to receiving a scolding for their tricks and pranks, but this is something completely different. None of the adults are looking at them with forgiving eyes this time.

"Oh!" Bragi gasps. To learn that not only is the beast from the rumours real, but it is also the protector of the little mountain village, is a lot.

"If we bring you to him, will you heal him?" He blinks, as Gunvald turns to him, a steely glint in his eyes, watching. As if waiting for the traveller to retract his offer now that he knows that it is a beast and not a human that requires aid.

"Well, I, er, I offered, didn't I?" Bragi stammers, before clearing his throat yet again and straightening up properly.

"I had indeed thought it to be a person, but my offer still stands. If I can help, I will." Gunvald scrutinizes him for many moments, before he nods. Broad shouldered he may be, but the rest of him is soft, his hazel eyes bright and honest, and though his ash-brown hair and beard seem a little unkept and scraggly and streaked with grey, his appearance can be blamed on travelling and age. He appears to be a rather respectable man, all in all. The sword at his hip makes the man a bit uneasy, but still, when travelling it is sometimes necessary to carry a weapon. Gunvald, in his well-hidden desperation, decides to trust this man. And if he is wrong, the responsibility will rest solely on his shoulders.

"Right then. I will lead you to his home and entrust him in your care."
The group he had been standing with starts to argue, but he holds up a hand
to silence them. They quiet down, though they don't look at all happy about
it. They stare after the two as Gunvald leads Bragi away, first to gather
whatever he might need to help, and then they are off.

Bragi admits to himself, as they walk up the steep path, that he worries
that he's being led like a lamb to a slaughter. It would hardly be the first
time, he remembers one time when he was younger, much more naïve- no,
best not to dwell on that now. All he got out of that experience is that he
now always has his sword within reach when he travels.

They reach the top, and the brunet is in awe at the greenery he sees. Large
apple trees the healer is sure shouldn't be able to grow so high up and the
soft green grass. The many different berry bushes and several types of herbs
growing, bountifully. Not to mention all the colourful flowers. It is simply
amazing. Then there is a green-covered part of the mountain wall, indented
slightly inwards, obviously covering the entrance to a cave.

The serpent's den.

"Master Snake dwells in there. I can't go any further, because he doesn't
want us in there, and I'd rather not violate his privacy any more than what
I am already doing by sending you in there." Gunvald hesitates before he
adds; "If you should be put in danger because we asked this of you, turn
and run." Bragi blinks.

"Pardon?"

"Master Snake has never once harmed any of us, but he is hurt, and might
act just like any other wounded animal. So, if you find yourself in any
danger, please run and forget we asked any aid of you." Bragi nods,
thankful for the out should it come down to it. He watches Gunvald
disappear down the path, before heading for the wall of vines. He wonders
how he should proceed from here, how to get inside because the wall of
vines appear pretty solid, impenetrable. He reaches out for it, searching for
a weakness, an opening. It is such a lovely covering, he'd rather not have to
cut it, especially since it appears to have been meticulously grown and cared
for.

"Now, how do I- oh!" The moment he touches it, it parts and opens the
way for him, as if they are all connected to one sentient mind.

"Why, thank you?" He ventures inside and finds that there are plants and flowers inside as well, with a spring big enough for a person to bathe in should they wish. There are a few cracks in the mountain roof to bring about enough light that he can see once the vines covers the opening behind him again. It is rather lovely, the man thinks as he looks around, trying to locate the beast.

He never comes across any serpent. He does, however, find a pale, feverish man with long red hair in a tangled mess of undone braids, his long, scrawny, shivering form curled up onto a bed of furs. He is suffering a dark and festering wound beneath his shoulder blade, visible beneath a loose mess of bandages.

"Oh dear."

CHAPTER FOUR

If Aske ever were to be asked what it feels like being poisoned and unconscious, he'd liken it to a hellish nightmare like no other. His mind is his own prison while the rest of him is on fire. The absolute worst part is beneath his shoulder blade, where the knife had dug in. It is concentrated, his skin is melting off his bones, leaving him bare and vulnerable. Even trapped deep within his subconscious as he is, Aske knows his situation is worse than he first thought it to be. His body isn't fighting the poison, at least not as quick or as well as it should. And then there is that nagging fear that he will be found, and have his life be ended. Brought to an end without him being able to defend himself, like a defenceless child.

But then, sometime later, Aske isn't sure how long, there is a cool feeling near the wound. It is gone as sudden as it appears and Aske wants to weep, because as fleeting as it was, it had brought some relief. His body is not fighting, it is succumbing, and it is terrifying and all he wants is that cool relief again. He just wants that slight touch of comfort again. Nothing is more terrifying than being aware of every single part of your body and in how much pain you're in, but unable to do anything but *feel* it.

But then the sensation returns, feels that cooling relief return, on his forehead this time, trailing down his cheek. It is not something he imagined, even if it disappears again. He didn't imagine it. And perhaps that is his descent into madness, but he will take it, anything to get out of this endless spiral of fire and heat and agony.

And it returns, again and again, and this time it *stays.* Aske welcomes it. The wound throbs less and the fire, while still there, isn't as painful as it has been for who knows how long. It gives him something else to focus on, and he latches onto it, hoping and praying in his fever-addled mind that it won't disappear again. It's almost enough to shatter him into so many tiny pieces, to know that there might be relief at the end of it all. The sensation stays, clears his mind, brings him enough strength at some point to claw himself back to consciousness.

His eyes flutter open, and he finds himself on his stomach, which isn't right. He hadn't laid down on his stomach. He blinks his eyes several times, the crust making it hard but the haze clears. Aske realizes several things at once; his throat is dry, like someone poured sand into his mouth while he slept. It hurts as well, like someone forced him to swallow needles in his sleep. He is in desperate need of water. His shoulder is still throbbing in agony and his entire body is stiff and heavy, but it is not as bad as before.

There's also a sword by his bedding which he's never seen before, and he is not alone in his cave. The sword is proof enough that someone has intruded into his home, but he can hear something being crushed and ground into dust. With a flick of his serpent tongue, he catches a whiff of the strong smell of herbs. Alongside the scent of an unknown person. He turns his head, moving as quietly as he is able, and sees the back of a person he has never seen before. Broad shouldered, and clothes worn from travelling, two things that are never a good mix for his kind.

Panic seizes him, and Aske bites his lower lip hard to avoid making any sound to alert the intruder. He can't let the stranger know that he is awake, he can't, and Aske moves his arms beneath himself to see if he can move about. His body feels heavy, and not quite like his own. It is more like that of a puppet whose strings he is struggling to control. Still, he crawls to his feet with the sort of silent grace only centuries as a snake can grant him and unsheathes the sword. Aske knows that the only thing that can save him now is to strike the stranger down from behind and bury his body in his garden, leaving no one none the wiser. He's done something similar many times before, and he can and will do it again. It'll be simple enough, if his body cooperates.

Humans can't be trusted, he knows this better than most. Humans are cruel, fearful of what they don't understand, and justifies every little cruel action with any foolish reason they can come up with. Aske won't make the same mistake twice. His skin is covered in reminders, of scars large and small, he will not add another. And Aske won't come up with a holier-than-thou justification for this either. It is just for the sake of survival. He just wants to keep this peaceful, and lonely, life he's leading. He's suffered enough, it's not too much to demand.

But before he can do anything, the human turns around, dropping the mortar and pestle in his hands. The man has a kind face partly hidden behind a scraggly beard.

"Ah, you're awake!" The relief in the man's expression surprises the shapeshifter long enough to make him hesitate. Then clarity comes upon the human, and Aske can see exactly when it happens. The man understands, knows what Aske is attempting.

Aske lunges.

CHAPTER FIVE

On Bragi's end, before his patient managed to crawl back into consciousness, things have been much different during his time in the cave. He has yet to see the monster serpent, despite having been in his den for the last two days. The only living being he's come across is the incapacitated redhead resting on a pile of furs, trapped in a fever-induced sleep. For all Bragi knows, this poor man is the serpent's next meal. The man might be unconscious because of the dangerous amounts of poison in his veins is most likely injected in him from the beast.

For all Bragi knows, his action in helping this man is counterproductive, but Bragi simply can't turn his back on anyone in need of help. It is just not in his nature, as that of a healer. So, the moment he came upon the man, he had examined him, drawn blood to analyse with his magic and begun making an antidote that he fed him. He cleans the wound properly several times, redressing it each time. During this time, he is making sure that the man's body is accepting the broth and medicine he makes, and the water he draws from the spring.

The poor dear will have a better chance at recuperating if his body regains strength, after all. And then several more days pass, and the fever is finally slipping, and the brunet notes with relief that colour is finally returning to the man's cheeks. He is also pondering the absence of the serpent yet again, since they have yet to show up. This makes Bragi grow complacent, and he leaves his sword close by the furs as he goes outside to gather fruits and herbs to aid the man. He is running out of his own supply, but the garden outside has some of what he needs.

While gathering what he needs and concocting potions and meals, he wonders who planted and cares for said garden. He has seen none of the villagers come up and tend to it, yet it doesn't lose any of its splendour. It cannot be a natural occurrence, and Bragi hopes that whoever tends to it won't mind him gathering some herbs to help the man in the cave.

The healer doesn't expect the redhead to wake up anytime soon, and thus he sits with his back towards his patient as he grinds the herbs into fine powder. By doing this, he has a view of the entrance of the cave, and won't be surprised if someone passes through. Yet even over the sound of him grinding the herbs in the stone bowl, he's made aware of something behind him. He puts down the mortar and pestle and turns around.

"Ah, you're awake!" He is surprised to see that his patient is up on his feet already, and a bit wary of the man holding his sword. The man is surprisingly tall, much taller than Bragi thought he was when he was curled up on the furs. He must be pushing past two meters at the very least, maybe even more. Along with noticing how tall the man is, Bragi also notes that the man is afraid, that much is clear, but the healer doesn't understand why. The serpent is nowhere near here as far as the other is aware, haven't even shown up at all during the days Bragi's been here. Which is quite odd considering the cave is supposed to be their home and the serpent had clearly been wounded according to-

His train of thought comes to a startling halt when he sees the redhead's eyes, and it becomes clear to him why the beast has not shown itself. With a bright yellow colour covering his entire sclera and with pupils which are the thinnest slits of fear and sharper teeth than is normal poking out of the open mouth, it becomes rather clear that the man *is* the serpent.

"You're… the snake? *Shapeshifter?*" It is a bit of a leap, because even though the man's eyes are a complete yellow, and the pupils are anything but human-like, it doesn't mean he is truly a shapeshifter. Shapeshifters have not been spotted in well over a century, thought to be extinct. Yet, with the way the man's eyes widen with fear, and how he moves to lunge forward, sword raised, Bragi fears he might have hit the nail on the head. He does not need to fear the redhead though, for as he lunges forward, his legs buckle beneath him, unable to carry his weight anymore. Bragi catches him before he crashes to the ground, and wrestles the sword out of his hands, tossing it away.

The redhead fights, claws at Bragi like a wounded and frightened animal, whining in fear. The brunet is quite used to having patients try and break free however, either out of stubbornness or pain, and hauls his weakened patient back to his furs with a grunt. He is as careful as he can afford to be as he tries to lay the man down, and the other man releases a whimper when he finally realizes he has been overpowered, exhausted as what little strength he had fizzles out of him. Bragi feels like he is staring down at a terrified child, and he feels bad for the use of force.

"I'm not here to harm you," he offers, though it does very little to inspire confidence in the wounded man. He's wriggling backwards away from his touch despite the fact that the action should cause him quite an amount of discomfort. Bragi pulls back, holding his hands up where the other can see them.

"The villagers asked me to help you. I'm a healer, I came to help." The redhead's movements and wriggles slow, and his brows furrow in confusion.

"You're not a hunter?" He croaks, voice rough and quiet from disuse. Bragi should give him more water, especially now that he's woken up. He sorely needs it.

"Heavens, no!" The brunet exclaims as the pieces begin to fall in place in his mind. "I'm not exactly fighter material, now am I?" He pats his rounded middle with a chuckle.

"Now, get some rest, and I'll have food prepared for when you wake up again." The man opens his mouth to speak again, probably a rebuttal, but only falls into a coughing fit. His throat is far too dry to allow him to speak for a longer period of time. Bragi quickly pulls out his waterskin and helps the man soothe his parched throat.

"Don't tell them!" It is more of a plea than a demand, but the healer nods, nonetheless.

"I won't tell a soul." Once the man has finally drifted off again, unable to fight off the exhaustion his actions brought him, Bragi moves back to the mortar and continues to grind the herbs, this time facing the bed. No longer worrying about when the serpent might slither through the cave opening, Bragi keeps his eyes on his patient.

The monstrous beast of the mountain is a shapeshifter, a real, honest to the Goddess and her Children, shapeshifter! Bragi has heard stories of them from his brother and his teacher, but he's believed them to be extinct for a long time. Here, in this cave, he is watching living proof that they still exist. At least one of them. No wonder the man had been terrified. He'd spotted the sword and thought Bragi was here to kill him. The brown-haired man is not a fan of killing, he prefers to help people.

And according to the rumours, the serpent of the mountain, now revealed to be a shapeshifter, has been here for a century at the very least. Now, Bragi knows that it is impossible for this man to have lived that long. Especially considering he looks very young compared to the age of the rumours. Logically, that means that at some point, he had been a part of a family here, and that family has been guarding the area for a hundred years. The villagers seem quite fond of their current guardian as well. He is not evil, certainly. He has a set of skills, magical attributes he was born with, a gift. As far as Bragi knows, shapeshifters aren't all that different from humans, other than perhaps being a bit more robust than them. They are more attuned to the world around them, and magic. Whenever the healer thought of this when he was younger, he'd always ponder about the reason humanity, or groups of humans as it turns out, had turned on the other species.

He has yet to find any reason for it. Not that there's much lore to find about the shapeshifters as whole, which is a curious thing of its own. To have coexisted from the beginning of time, but knowing nothing, it is just not right. And what had caused the fall out? The man's heavily scarred body, the torso in particular, and the way he had reacted to Bragi's presence had told the healer more than enough about the cruelty he must have experienced.

"I promised him food." The brunet shakes his head and begins to gather what he needs to make some more of that broth.

CHAPTER SIX

Hours later, the shapeshifter awakens again. He no longer appears terrified at the sight of Bragi, but he is no less wary of him now than when he woke the first time, if the way he keeps his narrow eyes on him the whole time is any indication.

"Here, this should help you feel better," the healer tells him, handing a bowl over to the other man. The redhead sniffs it cautiously, trying to find any fault with it, before taking a sip. Whether he actually finds the taste of the broth good or not, Bragi cannot tell. His expression betrays nothing. It is quite uncomfortable because it almost appears like the man doesn't blink. Which is very unnerving in the silence when he keeps on watching the human for any sudden movement that might not be benign in nature.

"My name is Bragi," the healer begins in an attempt at forging some friendly ground. Introductions, he has learned, almost always makes it easier to gain common ground. A way in which a conversation might flow naturally, and not be stilted and awkward. Which the situation certainly is now.

"I was passing through the village when I heard the inhabitants discuss how they could help you. They were quite worried, you see, especially a group of children. Why, one of them threatened me with a terrible prank if I should fail to save you. I think his name was-"

"Andor," the shapeshifter cuts him off, voice still quite rough. It almost sounds like he is forcing the words out with no small amount of discomfort.

"That's right!" Bragi exclaims, relieved that the other is humouring him with conversation. While not being friendly, at the very least Bragi's patient isn't directly hostile, either. And he is sitting still on his bed, dutifully eating and being, well, compliant.

"Well, I am quite sure in my assessment that I can soon go back and tell them that you will make a full recovery." The shapeshifter hasn't looked away for even a moment since he woke up. Thankfully, he *is* blinking his eyes now, albeit in a slow manner, as if he must consciously execute the action. Bragi does wonder if the shapeshifter had been born with those eyes, or if they're a result of him being in the shape of a serpent for extended periods of time. There is much to learn here, if the other is willing to teach. Oh, how Bragi hopes he'll be willing to teach.

"May I ask your name?" That's the only way to learn more, since the other has not offered his name up on his own volution. He needs to have the redhead understand that Bragi is not a threat to him, and then he might be able to safely ask questions without offending him. Bragi has the distinct feeling that he can very easily offend this man without meaning to.

"I can't very well call you Master Snake, unless that is your name." He lets slip a chuckle, until he realizes that the other man is not laughing with him.

"It, er… it isn't, is it?" If it is, then Bragi have really stuck his foot in it already. The shapeshifter stares for many long, painful moments and it makes the brunet begin to squirm in his seat.

"Aske." It takes Bragi a second to understand what it is that the shapeshifter has offered up, but when it does dawn on him, he grabs the opportunity with both hands eagerly.

"A pleasure to meet you, Aske." Bragi just barely manages to avoid sighing too loudly in relief at having received an answer. At least the man is no longer scared, the healer thinks as he looks the shapeshifter over. Weakened, but much better. Much better than he should be, at this point, actually. His skin is less pale than it was the day before, the cluster of freckles on his face and body no longer such a stark contrast to the rest of him.

"May I take a look at your wound once you're done eating?" Aske narrows his serpentine eyes at Bragi, and the brunet plasters on a friendly smile, even though it doesn't seem like it has much effect on this fellow. The hackles have been raised.

"I swear I won't hurt you. What good would that do, considering the effort I've put into healing you?" Maybe rational logic might help the situation a bit? Putting a lot of effort into something only to unravel it is a wasted effort, a useless effort. Who in their right mind would do that? Who would waste valuable time like that?

"How would I know how you humans think?" Aske growls, and the human falters. He understands rather quickly that even though the shapeshifter has lived near a human settlement for quite some time, he harbours no trust or love for them. Nor does he seem to understand them. It makes Bragi wonder if the redhaired man ever felt safe in his own home. Bragi comes to realize that a hands-on approach might not work here, and that in order to not aggravate his patient, he'll have to do this a different way.

"Can you, er, undo the wrapping yourself then? And I can look from over here if that makes you feel more at ease?" Aske just stares at him for a few moments. He seems to have a habit of doing that when people try to converse with him. At least while Bragi is attempting at conversing with him. While regarding the human, his mind is working to come to the safest conclusion. He finishes his food, and turns to sit sideways, enough to be able to see every move Bragi will make as he motions for the man to come closer. It seems like the man has decided it would be easier for the both of them if he just lets Bragi do it himself.

"*Don't* try anything!" Aske hisses a warning, and Bragi nods as he cautiously moves closer to his patient.

"I would never," he answers as he carefully peels the wrappings away, eyes rowing over the wound. It is healing rather well, closing very nicely and quickly. The festering, rotting skin tissue he had seen on the first day is all but gone. Well, he had cut away most of it, but never gotten rid of all of it. It seems like the healthy tissue has gotten rid of it all on its own though. Curiouser and curiouser.

"It seems to be healing well," he tells Aske happily, applying ointment before rewrapping it, careful not to make any sudden movements.

"It will leave a small scar, though."

"Got plenty of those," Aske mutters over his shoulder, watching each one of Bragi's movements. Bragi nods, pursing his lips. As he's been treating the man, he's catalogued a great deal many scars. Old, deep, jagged. It is also terribly obvious that they were all inflicted on purpose, and were not mere accidents. They must have been painful.

"In just a few days it should close up completely, and we can forgo the wrappings. But you *must* keep from exerting yourself, so you don't reopen your wound." Aske makes a small, conflicted sound, like he is unwilling to agree with the healer, yet knowing that Bragi is most likely right. The healer wonders if Aske is going to be the kind of patient who insists they know better than him, that they'll be fine. A patient who will then end up making their situation several times worse for themselves out of either stubbornness or pride.

"Shapeshifters heal quicker than humans," Aske mutters tersely, barely audible. So, pride it is. Yet his words spark Bragi's curiosity, because whenever there is knowledge to be acquired, he is quick on the uptake. Especially medical knowledge about different species.

"You do? How much quicker?" He asks, excited, and the shapeshifter pulls slightly away, suddenly again so wary of the brunet. For a moment Bragi fears he has overstepped, but then Aske leans back and allows the other man to finish wrapping his wound.

"I don't know, quicker," he mumbles and Bragi treads the waters, pushing a little bit more.

"Will you turning into a serpent cause any strain on your body?" Again, Aske jerks away, this time turning to fully face him, eyes narrowed and lips curled back. Upon the first time Aske woke and Bragi felt like he was staring down at a wounded and scared child. Now he feels like he's staring down a cornered animal. A beast about to either lunge at him, or bolt. Bragi hopes he does neither. After another few strained moments, he shakes his head.

"Good, good. Once you've regained some of your strength, perhaps you can change back into a snake, and we'll head down into the village? It will do you good to stretch, er, stretch your tail, as it were." Bragi falters, a bit embarrassed at his own wordplay when their short interaction has shown that it doesn't go over well. Especially when the other man stares at Bragi like he's mad. But then, with a curt nod and without letting Bragi stew in his own awkwardness for too long, he agrees and lays back down. That is the end of that conversation.

The rest of the day is quiet, their next meal shared in a tense silence, until night falls. The greenery shudders and moves to cover the entrance of the cave with a glance and mutter from Aske, so that the only light that lights up the cave comes from the few cracks amongst the mountain roof. And that, Bragi realizes, is the end of their day, and rightly so. Aske needs rest, and Bragi doesn't feel all that chipper anymore either. He lays down on his sleeping mat after telling the other man to wake him up if something should happen. A non-committal grunt is his answer. The human doesn't feel too put out though. As long as the human healer stays, the shapeshifter will most likely never feel comfortable. Best help the man heal as quickly as possible, and then be on his way.

Aske waits until the human's breath evens out, then waits a while longer before he slips out from beneath his furs. He moves around the sleeping man as quietly as possible on heavy legs, before he heads towards the cave entrance. He glares at the greenery for several seconds before growling from deep within his chest.

"*Come out.*" At first there is nothing, but then a few leaves rustle, and a tiny figure, no bigger than the length of the size of Aske's palm, climbs out. The little creature hangs onto a vine, and pointedly keeps their eyes away from Aske's burning orbs.

"What were you *thinking*?" He hisses, and the little spirit speaks. The spirit's words are something that can be best described as sounding like whistling to mortals. Aske, however, understands the little one well enough after having spent quite some time sharing a living space with them, and answers in kind, displeasure clear, in his voice.

"*Of course* I understand you were worried!" The little creature gestures wildly with their hands, not willing to give up their point of view just yet.

"Yes, I needed some help- no, don't you look smug about this, how could you have known it would end well?" Again, the spirit gestures, pointing over their shoulder and out, and Aske shakes his head, very nearly snarling out his next words.

"No, don't you dare drag Tulip into this, they care for the flowerbeds, only you and Daffodil can move the coverings at your will, Orchid." The whistling grows in volume as the spirit grows distressed and the shapeshifter hushes them, holding a hand out.

"Alright, fine, hush, I forgive you, calm down." Orchid leaps out and curls into the redhead's rough skin, trembling slightly. Aske feels a stab of guilt. The little spirit has been so worried, they had just wanted to help, and he can't fault them for that. His garden spirits only know the humans of the village, they don't truly understand the cruelty of mankind. They had simply seen a kind looking human and thought he could help.

And he did. A man who takes his duty as a healer seriously. But maybe that is only because Aske is in his human shape, and the human can somehow relate to the appearance. Aske won't take that chance with the spirits. They're so tiny and frail, and their warm glow makes them easy targets. They have few ways to properly defend themselves from a man of Bragi's size. He could cause a whole lot of damage to them by just flicking them with a finger.

"Just promise me you won't let him see you, alright? Not all humans are good and kind. I can defend myself, you're much more fragile." Orchid nods, and Aske holds out his hand up to the vines, allowing the spirit to climb back in.

"Tell that to Tulip, Daffodil and Dewdrop as well. Keep out of sight, the lot of you." Orchid disappears into the foliage, and the greens move and shudder as the spirit disappears further in. Aske sighs, one hand moving up to grasp at his shoulder, rolling it carefully. His wound still hurts, but not so much that it takes up all his attention anymore. He can ignore it well enough. He glances towards Bragi, sleeping soundly. Asleep, any human appears unassuming, harmless.

Awake, however, they hide their true nature behind pleasant smiles and hollow eyes, wolves in sheep's clothing. Harbingers of pain, grief, destruction, and death upon those they don't understand, and themselves.

Violent and ugly creatures. When they're children, young and free-spirited, they can be understood. The moment they grow older however, the shapeshifter thinks as he moves silently to hover over the sleeping man, the moment they lose their free spirits and are stuck in their ways, that is when the change happens. That is when humans are no longer safe.

Aske stares down at Bragi.

He should just end the human now, he thinks, as his nails grow into claws. End him and be done with him, as was the original plan. He no longer needs the human, after all.

CHAPTER SEVEN

Andor, Birger, Signy and Halfdan are bored. Transcendentally, utterly bored. So far, their little village has avoided most of the mischief this group can conjure up because they spend most of their free time with the serpent. However, since the beast is now injured and healing, the children have no one to turn to but their own people. They play their games, their pranks, they climb and scare their parents and the other adults in the village out of their wits, and if a few pieces of fruit and other kinds of snacks disappear suddenly out of nowhere, it is obvious where to look.

The amount of chaos the four have wrought made Gunvald incensed enough to banish them to the outskirts of the village, right by the path leading up to the serpent's home. So here the group lie on their backs, staring at the sky and counting clouds, pointing out when they find a particularly funny shape. And they are so very, very bored. Perhaps they shouldn't have made a mess in the stables by scaring the donkeys in there out into the open causing a right havoc in the square? Oh well, lesson learned.

"What if he can't help the snake?" Halfdan suddenly asks, and Andor sits up abruptly, scowling at his friend. They've all silently agreed to not talk about what will happen if the traveller cannot help their playmate. They never spoke the words out loud, it was just an understanding cemented by grim looks, and Halfdan just broke it. That is an unforgiveable offense that demands retribution.

"He has to," Andor says, gritting his teeth. "He knows magic, after all." It is a flat argument, even for children their age, and Birger, ever the voice of unwanted reason, points that out, which, really, is a greater offense than what Halfdan just did.

"That just means he knows magic, not that he can help the snake." Signy glares and punches the boy's arm, hard. The other two boys collectively wince at the sight and at the other boy's yelp as he rolls away and out of her reach. Birger rubs the offended appendage, pouting as he does so. Well, at least she has taken care of the punishment.

"Be quiet, Birger! The snake has been here since forever, he *must* get better!" While they all want that to be the truth, the lot of them are also worried that the opposite might become their reality soon. The healer had left well over eight days ago, and there's been no news at all. Whether it was good or bad news that awaited them, they should have been told by now, right? Andor wants to climb the path and play in the serpent's garden, he wants to climb the trees and be pulled down to safety by the animal. He wants to play and talk with their guardian, but he's not allowed to. All the adults have stressed to keep away until the healer sends word. Gunvald had mentioned something about privacy. Never enter the serpent's cave without his permission.

"Isn't that the sorcerer, though?" Birger has climbed to his feet as he rolled away from Signy, and is pointing up the hill, and all of them, following his line of sight, sees that indeed, it is. The healer is descending the path, with the serpent right beside him! His hulking form seem smaller than they remember, and he moves a slight bit different than they can remember too, but that hardly registers at all, because the excitement they feel upon seeing him drowns those concerns out. They leap to their feet and cheer so loudly the entire village hears them and come running. By the time the two are at the bottom, everyone is there, and Bragi thinks that it is obvious how surprised Aske is by the gathering. Yet he answers any question thrown at him the best he can. The villagers wonder about his health, if it'll take long before he has recovered completely. They ask if he needs anything they can provide, if they can help. Then the children chime in.

"Let us ride you, snake!" And that is when Bragi steps in, saving Aske from answering.

"Absolutely not!" He shakes his head. "Aske has yet to recover completely. Once he is fully healed, then you can play." Being told that they can't have something they really want, is not what the group wants to hear, and they tell Bragi so, loudly.

"You can't decide that!" They stomp their feet petulantly, but Bragi does not falter, only furrowing his brow and crossing his arms across his broad chest in a stern manner.

"You want him to reopen his wound? Do you want to risk him being hurt yet again and having to rest to heal even longer than he already has?" The children blink, before scuffing the tips of their worn shoes into the dirt, shaking their heads. They certainly don't want that, and they mutter quietly amongst themselves. They are far from pleased but must concede defeat. If them playing with him risks him being hurt again, then they'll have to wait even longer, and they do not want that.

"Then you'll simply have to wait," Bragi tells them as a villager comes up to them and hands over a heavy sack.

"For a speedy recovery," the man tells them, and the healer glances inside at the contents before smiling in gratitude.

"Oh, yes, this will help immensely, won't it, Aske?" Bragi turns his head to the left, only to notice that the serpent is no longer beside him. He turns from right to left again, before realizing Aske is already halfway up the hill, having left him behind silently. According to the villagers' reactions, this is not something they are unfamiliar with.

"Oh, er, well, off I go!" Bragi waves nervously to the villagers before he hurries up the hill as fast as his legs can carry him. Once he catches up, he takes one look at the serpent and frowns. Aske's massive head hangs low, and his movements seem sluggish, certainly slower than when they descended, and the healer's suspicions prove true when Aske changes back into his human form by the cave entrance. He collapses onto the ground with a groan, but when Bragi reaches out to help him back up on his feet, the redhead snarls at him, yanking his arm away and out of reach. The scowl is firmly planted on Aske's face for the many moments it takes for him to gather enough strength to push himself to his feet and stagger inside.

The greenery rustles as he moves past the entrance, despite the man not being even remotely close to touching it when he enters. It is an odd sight, since there is no wind either, but Bragi brushes that off and worries more about the way his patient falls over onto his furs. It is by no means a graceful collapse, and it looks painful. For a moment he thinks that Aske has aggravated his wound, that what he warned the children might happen have already happened by just going outside, but the redhead shifts, facing Bragi, and the tension seems to seep out of him from where he lays, eyes distant, thoughtful.

There is a long silence between them, though not an uncomfortable one, thankfully, as Bragi prepares the food given to them. It is only when a couple of rabbit's legs are roasting over the fire that Aske speaks up.

"You called me Aske."

"Well, what else would I call you?" The other man asks, not even looking up from his preparations, a small yet sincere smile gracing his lips. Aske just stares, eyes wide, before he closes them tight and turns his back to Bragi, curling together. The brunet wonders if he has overstepped in some way, again, but then he hears whistling and settles back in his seat. He cannot have caused any offense if the man has started whistling, but when he thinks about it, no one back in the village had used the shapeshifter's name. They just call him snake. Perhaps it is upsetting for him, to be called by his name? Or is it that no one knows his name? He obviously doesn't trust the villagers with the truth, perhaps he did not trust them with his name either? But then, why would he have told Bragi?

"Shut up," Aske whispers to Orchid, who has snuck inside while they were out, hiding until Aske and Bragi returned, and is now petting the shapeshifter's cheek from where they have nestled themselves in his hair. They ignore his demand and continues to reassure him that everything is alright, that they and the other three are there for him. It does help him swallow the lump in his throat.

"No one calls me by my name," he says a bit louder, and there's movement behind him. He spins around as Orchid hides further into his hair, heart in his throat and wincing in pain as he lands on his wounded shoulder blade. Then he blinks at the roasted leg which is held out for him to take from the other man.

"Do you want me to call you differently?" The question is framed gently, but the look on Bragi's face clamours for an answer.

"No," Aske says after a few tense moments, accepting the food.

"Then I'll call you Aske. Though, no worries, my friend, I'll be out of your hair by tomorrow. Your wound is nearly healed if you didn't reopen it now with your acrobatics." Aske feels no small amount of relief at these news, shoulders untensing as he bites into the meat. His wound no longer bothers him, other than his shoulder being stiff and the wounded area still being a bit tender, and his body exhausted by the extreme toll the poison had taken. But worst of all, his recuperation has taken longer than needed because of the human healer being in his home. He never felt safe enough to properly relax like this. The human may have gone good on his promise to not harm Aske while he was healing, but who knows what will happen when the shapeshifter is healthy again?

There is a part of Aske's mind that tells him that he is being ridiculous. Why would a human heal him, then kill him? Had the man truly been a hunter, Aske would have been killed the moment the human realized his patient was a shapeshifter, while he was weak and vulnerable, unable to defend himself. That is what the rational part of his mind is screaming at him, yet the part of him that remembers being on the run for most of his life, the part that remembers the screams, the loss, the pain, the causes of his scars, both on his body and in his heart, tells him to be wary. To not trust this unassuming man. The part of him that remembers how he now hides in a cave and call it a living, all alone.

Because that is how their mother died, that is how Inge, Alv and Gunnar died. Trusting humans brings nothing but pain and suffering, and Aske will not fall for it again. No matter how lonely he feels at times, no matter how nice it is to have felt a calming and gentle touch, no matter how desperate he is to experience more like it, he will not falter. Therefore, he looks forward to it, he looks forward to when the new dawn rises.

Even if Orchid is whistling worriedly in his hair when he lays down to rest for the night, unblinking eyes trained on Bragi's back, he tells himself he looks forward to it.

"It'll be fine, Orchid," he says as he watches Bragi sleep.

"He'll be gone soon, and everything will go back to how it used to be." Orchid quiets down and nests themselves comfortably in his hair, watching over their friend as he sleeps.

And when morning breaks, they watch the healer descend the path, perched on Aske's shoulder and feeling all the tension drain from him.

"Finally."

CHAPTER EIGHT

When Bragi left the shapeshifter's cave, he had every intention of leaving the modest little mountain village and continue in his journey, but Gunvald and the village doctor had happened upon him before he could. They had inquired about the serpent's health, obviously on the forefront of their minds, and then they had said something about them never being able to properly repay him for his aid in their time of need. Now, Bragi has never much cared for a reward for helping someone in dire need of it and tells them so. Of course, monetary rewards do help when one is constantly on the move, to pay for lodgings and food and other necessities, but he is not in need of it right now.

"Money we're not made of, my good fellow, but if you'd be interested, we do have a rather extensive collection of tomes in our town hall," Gunvald offers and Bragi pauses. He tries not to show it, though it is obvious that the thought of being surrounded by written treasure is very appealing to him.

"Not only does it have texts of medicine and history, but there are also quite a lot of lore of all the creatures in our land, all gathered before our predecessors happened to settle here." The man preens, prideful over the collection within the village, and finally, he reels the healer in.

"Oh, well, if it wouldn't be too much of an imposition?" Texts of creatures usually contain a little bit about their biology as well, and that, well, to a healer that is quite interesting.

"None at all." Gunvald waves his hand, pleased that they'll be able to repay the man, somehow, for his kindness. It is terribly rude and impolite to not give a reward for someone's hard work, after all. Especially so when it was a task both dangerous and important to the village. So Bragi finds himself spending days in the town hall, with Gunvald coming by with delicious meals prepared by his wife. The village doctor sometimes sits with him, and they have some very interesting conversations. Bragi rather likes her. She's older than him, but not so set in her ways that she's not willing to learn what knowledge he has to offer that she lacks from before, and vice versa. It is quite pleasant, and it's been quite some time since he felt so, well, at home, at any place he has stopped at. He's always felt so uprooted, for decades now. There is no urge to get a move on now, he feels quite settled. He hasn't felt like this for such a long time he is not sure what to do with it.

It is on the fifth day after leaving the shapeshifter's cave that it happens. Bragi is sitting by the window, engrossed in a tome about Livwyrms when a shadow falls over him. He frowns, wondering if the sky is turning cloudy, and looks up, only to jump startled and nearly fall out of his seat when he sees the cause of the shadow.

Aske's humongous serpent form is glaring at him from the outside. Or rather, as such reptiles don't have much of a facial expression, he can only conclude that it is a glare based on the heat in Aske's thin-slitted eyes. The angry glower nearly pins him in place for a moment.

"Oh, good grief," Bragi sighs heavily, patting his chest in an attempt at calming his racing heart before he moves over to open the window. The air is warm, the breeze caressing his cheeks. It is a lovely day for travelling.

"Hello there, Aske, how are you feeling?" Aske doesn't answer at first-, and as time passes, Bragi begins feeling awkward.

"Why are you still here?" The serpent demands suddenly, and the healer gestures to the texts on the table he had been sitting by.

"Oh, I was offered access to your library, and I accepted. It is very extensive, especially considering that your home is so isolated. Truly marvellous, I must say!" Aske doesn't answer, but instead he ducks his head and slithers forward, causing the human to stumble back, watching as the serpent advances inside the building.

"You really *are* large, huh. Marvellous, really." Now, the human thought Aske's animal shape was big from before, but perceptive changes when the beast is inside a small room, and not outside with unlimited space around him.

"What do you want?" The serpent hisses and Bragi blinks as he takes his seat again, surprised by the question.

"Pardon?" Aske looms over him, opening his mouth enough to show off his four sharp fangs. With a great deal of fascination, the human notes that if the serpent bites into him, those fangs will skewer him. He'd be much like the roasted rabbit legs they ate in the cave. How delightfully terrifying.

"What do you want? So that you can leave." If any outsider were to look in, they would think that the poor human is about to be the newest prey of the serpent, severely outpowered. After all, what can an unarmed man do against such a massive beast, huge enough to swallow him whole? Bragi quickly understands, though, that right now, he is the one with all the power. If Aske attacks him, the villagers might shun him and drive him out. His peaceful life here will come to an end. But Aske is obviously uncomfortable with Bragi staying in the village for any duration of time, and the reason is quite clear; Bragi knows Aske's secret, and Aske does not feel safe with him staying here because of it.

He doesn't trust Bragi to keep this knowledge to himself. Now, Bragi accepted that he would receive no gratitude from Aske for treating him, and that is fine, it is quite alright, because Bragi didn't learn medicine and magic to have people thank him for every little thing he did for them. All of that is quite alright, but he will *not* be called a liar and betrayer. He levels Aske with a glare, which causes the serpent to pull back a bit, not quite having anticipated such a reaction to his demand.

"I promised you I wouldn't tell anyone. I *do* keep my promises," he tells the serpent, slowly, more than just a hint of irritation colouring his voice, not backing down when Aske draws closer again, as it trying to intimidate him into telling him otherwise, to justify the frankly unnecessary suspicion the shapeshifter feels. Bragi won't, instead he stares resolutely back into the unblinking yellow eyes, shoulders set, feet firmly planted on the ground, hands in his lap.

Aske gives in first, and with a final hiss he slithers back out the way he came.

"I won't be staying long!" Bragi calls after him, but whether the other heard him or not, he is uncertain.

Bragi notices that the serpent is down in the village every day now. It is unusual, according to Gunvald, when he comes by with a meal. With a sigh, Bragi watches Aske play with the children and concludes that despite the fact that he has assured the redhead that he is no threat to his home or life, the other doesn't trust him. It is a little bit insulting, and sad at the same time. It is depressing that the man lives in constant fear, it must be very exhausting.

Bragi takes another look around the library, sighing. It is a treasure throve of knowledge, in the outskirts of the border of the world. It is such a shame to leave it, but he's not comfortable being monitored every day either.

'Two days,' he thinks, and goes back to the text in front of him. He'll leave in two days; therefore, it is vital that he manages to read as much as possible before he continues his journey. Maybe this new task he has set himself is the reason why he is being prodded awake by irritable children the next morning. He finds himself still in the library, his face crumpling pages containing texts about fairies.

"You can't sleep here! On *texts*!" Signy, rightly indignant, crosses her arms. Andor appears more energized than Bragi thinks the boy has any right to be so early in the morning, but he remembers a time when he was much the same, decades ago. When he himself was a wide-eyed naïve child. He groans as he sits up properly, his back being quite unimpressed with his sleeping arrangement. He's grown too old for this.

"Right you are, young lady." His spine pops in several places, and he feels relief as he sags in his seat.

"Did you come to wake me?"

"Actually, we came to deliver this," Birger explains, and only then does Bragi notice the four small leather pouches the children are carrying. They present them to him, and he accepts them somewhat reluctantly, not sure what is going on, or if he is being set up for a prank. One can never know with a group of children as mischievous as these four.

"The snake says thank you for all your help!" The group exclaim, and Bragi peeks inside. Medicinal herbs in the first three, going by the smell. The last one is spices, having a soothing aroma. He had not expected this, but it makes him smile. It truly is wonderful to be acknowledged. It might not seem like much to most, but considering Aske's reservations about him, this is a grand gesture. Even words of gratitude, how wonderful. Bragi can't deny that it makes warmth spread through his chest cavity as he offers the children a small smile.

"Oh dear. That is awfully nice of him. Where *is* Aske, if I may ask?" The children laugh at the wordplay, before telling him that the serpent is in his garden, tending to it. He stands up, straightens his clothing as best he can before he walks out of the town house and heads for the hill leading up to the cave and garden. It is on his way up that his stomach reminds him that he has yet to eat breakfast through a loud grumble, and he sighs. He'd best thank Aske for his generosity, and head back down for some food. When he crests the top of the hill, he sees Aske, ever still in his animal form, hunched over a bed of yellow and red flowers, hissing. The plants tremble. Everything about this place is odd, in the most curious of ways.

"It makes no difference, Tulip, that's just the way it isssss-"

"Why hello there, Aske. The children handed the pouches of herbs to me just now. I want to thank you for the gift, they will undoubtedly help me when I continue my journey tomorrow." Aske turns towards him, tongue flickering out for a second, hovering in the air before being pulled back inside the safety of his mouth.

"Leaving?" It is odd, how Aske who had been eager to see him leave just not too long ago, sounding confused at the concept now.

"Yes, I leave tomorrow." Aske is quiet for a few moments, his enormous head tilting, like that of a curious cat. Then Bragi's stomach grumbles loudly, again, and the brunet flushes bright red behind his beard, cheeks warming, lips pressing together. Well, that broke the tension rather well, he thinks, and makes the move to bow his head and leave. Aske moves quicker. His tail lashes out and slams against one of the apple trees with considerable force, and several pieces of fruit fall as the tree shakes hard enough that leaves fall like snow around it. With that very same tail he lobs an apple at the human, who fumbles to catch it.

"You don't need to leave just yet if you don't want to," the serpent says, staring straight at him and Bragi is quite baffled. Then he understands the implications and smiles grateful as he bites into the apple. The freshness of the fruit surprising him.

"Thank you. For your hospitality, Aske." The shapeshifter hisses, an annoyed sound, before going back to his flowerbeds. There's some rustling happening, and Bragi wonders if the shapeshifter is scaring some poor animal hiding in the shrubbery. He almost wonders if the plants themselves are shaking in fear of the intimidating beast but shakes his head. Plants shaking in fear, absolutely ridiculous, he thinks as he takes a seat by the trunk of the tree.

There is a whistling sound above him, and Bragi looks up, expecting to find a bird of some type. Instead, he finds a very small creature clutching to the bark just above his head, grinning mischievously.

CHAPTER NINE

"Oh, this is absolutely astonishing!" Bragi holds Daffodil gently in his palm, holding them close to his face, and chuckling when they tug on his beard playfully.

"Is it a spirit?" he asks the other man, who has changed back to his human form, and is right now hosting the remaining three in his hair, his locks braided into several braids and bound back to keep out of his face. Whether the braids are the work of Aske himself or the spirits, Bragi doesn't know. It suits the other man, though. All three of the spirits twisting in the red strands are whistling excitedly. Aske appears more and more disgruntled with each passing moment with the way his mouth twists, eyes narrow, though he seems perfectly at ease with having the little beings climbing all over him.

"Yeah, earth spirits."

"How did they end up here? I've never seen or heard about them before."

"They came into being because I tended to this garden with care. It took me, what, over thirty years or something like that to bring them about." Aske shrugs, catching Orchid as they tumble down from his shoulder.

"Marvellous." Bragi looks away from Daffodil and stares at Aske. "Yes, thirty years, yes, that would coincide with your appearance. We must be very close in age." Aske raises a brow as he lifts Orchid back up, the corners of his mouth tugging upwards in a barely-there smirk. It is the closest to mirth the human has ever seen him exhibit.

"Close in age? How old are the rumours about this place?" The shapeshifter wonders aloud, almost teasingly, and Bragi tilts his head.

"Around a century old, but you cannot be that old," Bragi replies with a shrug and the smile stretches wider across Aske's freckled face.

"You *cannot* be a century old!" Yellow eyes crinkle, and the spirits break out into loud whistling laughter, and Bragi's jaw drops.

"You look *younger* than me!" he calls out, affronted. "And you mean to tell me- no, that is impossible! To live that long is inhuman!" And then Aske crosses his arms, his smirk turning challenging as he raises a brow, one shoulder rising a bit as he turns half a step away from him.

"Makes perfect sense then, seeing as I am not human at all, am I?" Bragi pauses. Even though Aske mostly parades about as a beast, his human appearance has made Bragi look at him as a human, even though he knows for a fact that he isn't. It is just that perhaps since he saw him first in a frail human shape, that is what he associates Aske with. But knowledge is a treasure, and Bragi has a weakness for it, and when it is offered up so playfully in front of him, he cannot do anything but reach out for it.

"So, shapeshifters heal faster than humans and lives longer than us. How old are you then, if I may ask?" Aske ponders for a moment, turning his eyes heavenward as he counts quietly to himself.

"Over three hundred-"

"*Three hundred?!*" Bragi cuts him off, gaping. Another round of whistling occurs, and Daffodil yanks on his beard to get his attention.

"Right, yes, of course, it is rude to interrupt, but *three hundred?!*"

"You can let go of that anytime now." It is obvious how amusing Aske finds this whole situation and Bragi huffs and finds that he wants to erase that smirk from the other man's face. If Aske finds amusement in Bragi's disbelief of his age, well, fine, Bragi can play that game too. He will not be laughed at for being surprised about something he did not have any prior knowledge of.

"My *deepest* apologies, friend," he offers with a far too saccharine voice, "I didn't think you were *ancient*." The smirk is abruptly replaced with a scowl.

"Hey!" This time it is Bragi who is gloating, and Aske narrows his eyes, rising to the childish bait.

"Not my fault you're no older than a babe." He retorts, and Bragi colours.

"I am nearly forty!" Aske guffaws, the spirits with him, and once the indignation fades, so does Bragi. It doesn't take long before he's wiping tears of mirth from his eyes as he catches his breath. It has been quite some time since he's laughed this much.

"I imagine that to you we must seem like children, hm?"

"Not really," Aske admits. "Besides our magics, abilities and longevity, our bodies are built up pretty much the same." Bragi leans in closer, perhaps seeming too eager, because Aske suddenly seem to remember himself and pulls back, a wary expression on his face yet again. And there's that wall again, the fortress the shapeshifter carries around himself. He'd begun to lower the drawbridge, but Bragi had made one wrong move and it had been abruptly yanked back up. Bragi sits back, dejected.

"I won't hurt you, Aske. I am a healer, I've taken an oath."

"You're not the first human healer to have touched me," Aske mutters, but his voice is laced with such venom and barely repressed fury that the brunet can't help but wonder what had happened. He knows better than to ask, he really does, but the question rolls off his tongue before he can stop himself. If the shapeshifter appeared tense before, he's frozen like a statue now, the only sight of life being the slow rise and fall of his chest. Then, in one fluid and furious movement, he yanks his shirt off and turns around halfway, pulling braids aside in a forceful enough movement it must have hurt, pointing his thumb over his shoulder.

"See my spine?" The healer does, of course he does, he saw it when he was treating the redhead in his cave while he was unconscious. On both sides of the man's knobby spine is a trail of scar tissue, from his tailbone and up to his neck. Like several cuts had been made systematically, deeply, with intention.

"He tried to take my spine out while I was alive." Horror floods through Bragi at the mere imagining.

"And *conscious*." Aske isn't even looking at him as he speaks again. "Leave." The moment of camaraderie, if one can even call it that, is over. With one single sentence from Bragi, it ended, and he mourns the moment. It had been such a nice moment.

"I understand," Bragi says as he stands up. "I am well aware what kind of monsters' humans can be, Aske. I'm sorry you've had to experience it yourself." Aske says nothing as Bragi leaves, but he accepts the comfort the spirits give him as he curls up under the apple tree.

"What does he know?" the redhead mutters, nails digging deep into his forearms, leaving indents and bruises. "He's one of them."

As Bragi descends the hill, he can't help but feel sick to his stomach. To imagine that someone who had taken the same oath as he has, had done such a heinous act to another living being, it... it is not all that difficult to imagine. And that is the worst part of it. Just because the oath is sacred to him, it does not mean that it is just as important to another of the profession. There are those who would pick and choose who and what are protected by the sanctity of their oaths. He thinks back to the many old and deep scars he had seen when he had treated Aske, and shivers. He thought they were proof of a perilous life before. Now he is beginning to think, with dread, that they're memories and proof of something else. And if they are, his displeasure with Bragi staying and his distrust, they are well and truly justified. Such wounds, such terrible and horrible acts leave scars on not just the physical body, but on someone's heart, soul and mind as well. There is no way that Aske can just discard all those feelings just because Bragi has said that he holds his oath sacred.

Therefore, Bragi decides to leave the village soon anyways. Aske said he could stay, had even opened up a little bit about himself, but the human knows he pried too much. For the sake of the man who has suffered much by the hands of humans but still dedicates time to keep a settlement of their kind safe, Bragi will leave soon. The brunet hadn't really planned on staying for as long as he did anyways, and there is still much to see. There is no shortage of people who need skills like his, after all.

It had been nice with a short break, that is all. Bragi enters the village again, sees the villagers mill about doing their daily chores, and he's hit with a wave of nostalgia. His own home used to be just like this. He should probably return there someday soon, pay his respects to his brother. It has truly been too long. His spiralling into his own mind is abruptly, and quite rudely, interrupted by Andor hitting the back of his knee with a stick. The boy did not put much force into the blow, but Bragi is so surprised he stumbles anyway.

"What the he-"

"Tag, you're it!" He gapes, then frowns, opens his mouth, but the children have already spread out, laughing all the while. Bragi breathes in deeply through his nose, tilting his head back. Then he releases a dark chuckle.

"Oho, so the youngsters think that just because I'm soft around the middle and well-mannered, that I'm also mild-tempered?" He chases them all over the village, and Birger is the first to be caught, followed by Andor and Signy. Halfdan lasts the longest, thanks to his long legs, but in the end, even he is caught, and they're all treated to a scolding over how to *not* engage others in games.

"No wonder Aske is so thin, if he has to do this every day," the healer huffs, wiping sweat from his brow.

"The snake isn't thin, though? He is really huge." Signy raises a brow and Bragi blanches.

"Ah, well, you are right about that, er, well, at least he gets his exercise." What had he promised the shapeshifter on the very first day they spoke? *Not* to give away the fact that he is a shapeshifter. By the Goddess maybe it is best that he gets a move on, before he inadvertently breaks his promise.

'Three days,' he tells himself. He'll leave in three days. He spends the rest of his time buried deep in tomes, enjoying the hearty meals he is served, and on the last night, he enjoys a soft bed and a peaceful rest.

The afternoon on the third day, he stands at the outskirts of the village, shaking hands with Gunvald as he, his wife, the group of children and even Aske in his beast form, has come to say their goodbyes.

"Now, there was no need to come see me off." Bragi smiles, but Gunvald shakes his head.

"You've done a lot for us, so seeing you off is the least we can do. Know that you'll always be welcome here." The way Aske's humongous head shifts a bit to the side tells Bragi that he truly is not, but he just smiles in thanks and nods his head. The children each give him a hug, before he waves and makes to turn around and continue his journey, only to turn back around when he hears Gunvald speak up. Bragi turns a half-step around, blinking.

"Master Snake?" Aske is trembling all over, and then he releases a wail that has them all hurrying to cover their ears. His tail lashes out, narrowly missing the group in front of him, and he falls to the ground, his writhing body shrinking, his tail splitting and scales sinking into skin and hair sprouting from a head that is rapidly turning human. Aske claws at the ground as another cry is wrenched from his throat, body convulsing. The sound is heart wrenching, it makes the children start crying in distress as they pull away, not wanting to look at what is happening and hiding behind the adults. Bragi jumps into action, rushing over and trying to turn him over so he can assess the situation. Aske lashes out, most likely on instinct, nearly hitting the healer square in the chin when he does his best to restrain the other.

"What's happening?" Birger shouts. "You said you fixed him!"

"This is something else!" Bragi snaps harshly, finally managing to turn Aske around as all fight leaves him. He's muttering something beneath his breath, finally going limp and sporting a vacant look in his eyes that worries the human greatly.

"No… no…. *not you, no…*"

What on earth just happened?

CHAPTER TEN

The way Aske had just suddenly up and left the village had been jarring for the people there. Even more so when Andor had grabbed a hold of Aske's cloak and asked with a tearful voice if he would ever come back. Aske's face had become pinched, and he had appeared very conflicted for a moment, before he had yanked himself free and marched away quickly, giving the boy no real answer.

Bragi followed, searching for something to say before thinking better of it. Obviously, something is very wrong, there must be a good reason as to why he would suddenly leave the place he has called home for a century now. This person whose name he had muttered the day upon his collapse, Saga, is most likely the very reason for the sudden departure. And the importance of this person… Bragi isn't sure he'll get the image of a weeping, heartbroken Aske out of his head any time soon. He had appeared as if his entire world had been reduced to rubble, and it had been horrifying to watch how his eyes hollowed, dulled, became *lifeless*, but then he had pulled himself together, with many a deep breath, and stormed away. He returned with some travelling gear and had marched past everyone and to the village border. In human form. Not that his breakdown had not been witnessed by the many who had come running at the sounds of his wailing.

Bragi isn't sure why he's following him, and not quite sure if he's welcomed either. He's worried, of course, but they are not friends, whatever chance they had at that had been burned to ashes beneath Aske's apple trees, and he owes the shapeshifter nothing, but he is following, nonetheless. The world is dangerous, doubly so for Aske, because he is a shapeshifter-

"Master Snake!" Aske stops and turns to see Bragi behind him, and Gunvald nearly jogging in his attempt at catching up to them.

"Master Snake, wait! I have something for you!" Aske waits, and watches as the human stops to catch his breath. Gunvald holds something out for the redhead to take. Aske cautiously accepts the object, turning it around in his hands. It appears like coloured glass, fastened to three thin metal poles.

"What's this?"

"Coloured lenses, to hide your eyes." The shapeshifter snaps his gaze up at Gunvald, who offers him a kind smile

"We have known all along. Know that you'll always be welcomed home, Master Snake." And with nothing more to say, the head of the village turns and heads back to his home, leaving Aske dumbstruck. Bragi nearly smiles, but then Aske is moving again, and he scrambles to follow, only to stop short.

Why is he following the shapeshifter? He pulls his map out of his pack and tries to locate himself. Now, there is a village in the direction of which Aske is heading, and Bragi nods to himself. That is where he'll head next. So, he puts away his map and hurries to catch up to Aske, who has already created quite the distance between them. Suddenly Bragi regrets not acquiring a mount at the last village as he feels his knees object to the exercise. He's not as young as he once was, and Aske does have much longer legs than him.

Not that he is *too* out of shape, he's just softer around the middle, and lately, it's been nice to stay for some time in each village he passes through. He would very much like to settle down somewhere, maybe it is time? To belong somewhere again, it'll be nice, won't it?

"Why are you following me?" He looks up, nearly walking into Aske who has stopped and is regarding him with suspicion written clear across his features.

"Oh, sorry-"

"Why are you following me?" He demands again and Bragi huffs, drawing himself up into his full height, chest puffing out. It doesn't have the desired effect, with Aske still having to look down at him because the shapeshifter is absurdly tall.

"I am not! Your path just happens to align with mine for now!" Aske doesn't lose that suspicion he carries so easily, but he does turn around and just keeps on walking. He keeps a hurried pace on his long legs and Bragi struggles to keep up, as for each single step of Aske's, Bragi needs to take three. There are some things he notices as evening comes and even Aske must take a break. The shapeshifter is very restless, he looks more haggard for each day that passes and he sleeps very little, which is odd. He is in a hurry, something grave is plaguing him and tearing at his frayed patience.

It is disheartening to watch, truly. It is as if he's being hunted or is afraid to lose something precious, something that means more to him than anything else in the world. He refuses to speak of anything.

A week later they arrive at the village on Bragi's map, and while the human stops and decides to rest here for a while, explore the thriving and populated area, the shapeshifter marches straight through, with Gunvald's spectacles hiding his serpentine eyes. He disappears without as much as a backwards glance, or a goodbye.

And that's the end of that. It is not as if Bragi had not been expecting this outcome during their short travel considering the redhead's anxiousness and restlessness, but he finds himself mourning, nonetheless. Mourning a friendship that never actually existed, a friendship that was rejected even before it managed to take root. It would have been laughable if it wasn't so saddening.

Who knows where the shapeshifter is headed, or what prompted this rushed journey of his, but Bragi knows this; he is not welcome to follow, and he respects that. He also has his own journey, and who knows how long he'll stay in this village? Maybe he'll stay for good? It's quaint but lively, the man thinks as he passes the days comfortably. He wants a place to settle, has searched for such a place for some time, and this village is as good as any other, isn't it? And the people are very welcoming, it reminds him of his old home. And he enjoys that feeling.

"Yes," he says to himself, taking a deep breath and feeling his bones settle into the inn's bed a week later, when Aske must have managed to put a reasonable distance between them, when there is no chance of catching up to him, most likely. Not with the way he had moved so quickly, not with those legs whose one step was three or four steps of a man of Bragi's stature. Less chance if the other had changed shape along the way and moved as an animal. Alas, there is no need to dwell on such things, as following the redhead was never an option in the first place. The shapeshifter will not welcome his company, but this village, they will.

"I think I'll stay here."

CHAPTER ELEVEN

Saga jolts awake by the sound of children, *her children*, screaming. She scrambles to her feet to address the danger, only to realize that there are none. There are no enemies, no screams but an eerie silence, and she is not at their home, but out in the open, and not in the safety of her nest. Her throat constricts and tears well up in her eyes, because no, no, no, this isn't-

"Mam?" She blinks and looks down, sees Runa rub her own eyes, exhausted, scared, and sad. Saga takes a deep breath, forcing the lump in her throat down and blinking away the gathering tears in the dark before her daughter can see them.

"It's nothing, sweetling," she tells the girl as she slumps back down to the ground and hugs her daughter close, fingers threading through short red curls.

"Just a bad dream, it's nothing dangerous." Whether or not she is telling Runa this, or to herself in an effort to calm herself and her rapidly beating and aching heart, Saga isn't quite sure. No matter how many times she says it though, even after Runa's fallen asleep again, it does not change the fact that her nightmare is now their reality. And just because she is now awake, it doesn't mean that she doesn't still hear the crying and shouting and screaming, that she isn't haunted by the horrifying sounds. They've rooted themselves deeply into her soul, rattling her with every step she takes, chills her to the bones with every breath she takes.

She sleeps no more that night.

When dawn comes, Saga awakens the little girl, and they climb down from the tree they sought refuge in during the night. The thick, overgrown, and twisting branches did a good job of hiding them from any unwanted attention during the night.

"Come now, Runa. We've got to hurry." Saga coaxes the girl once they are down on solid ground. They move at a fast pace, which ends with Saga having to carry her daughter most of the day. The little girl is unable to keep up with her mother on her short legs without exhausting herself from the very start of the day, thus she transform herself into a tiny animal and lets her mother carry her. It suits Saga better anyway. She can carry on at her own pace like this, without worrying too much about Runa keeping up.

"Mam?" Runa grabs her attention when the sky is darkening at the end of the day and Saga is looking for a suitable place to spend the night.

"Where are we going?"

"To find my brother," Saga tells her, frowning. It doesn't tell the girl much, not really. She's never met him, she doesn't know him, doesn't know what he can do. Saga doesn't know what he can do to help either, but he is the only one she can rely on now.

"How will we find him?"

"The same way you-" Saga cuts herself off before she can complete the sentence, even though she already knows that the damage is done, that Runa knows what she had been about to say. Runa can't do that anymore, the reason being that all her siblings are dead. All Runa can feel is an aching emptiness, and Saga is quite familiar with that feeling. Whenever she lost a sibling, someone was physically carving a hole in her chest with a dull and rusted dagger.

"He's coming, he'll meet us on the way," she says instead as they come upon a steep rocky hill. She feels along it, and just barely within reach, she finds a ledge. She takes a few steps back, sees the ledge goes further into the rock wall, and exhales.

"Runa, if I help you up, can you see if we both fit?" Runa nods, wanting to help, and crawls carefully over the ledge when her mother lifts her up. She decrees that it is both safe and big enough for the both of them to fit, and that there is a tiny section of stone roofing they can huddle under, thankfully. Saga follows quickly, and ushers her daughter as far in as they can go. There, she takes off her cloak and wraps the both of them in it as comfortably as she can, pulling her daughter close and curling into a ball around her. Her much taller and lankier form makes it easy to completely encompass her daughter, and it gives her some relief to know that should they be caught unaware, she is able to cover her completely, from any direction. Runa seems to take comfort in being embraced like this as well, with the way she burrows as far into her mother's arms as she can. It might also be from the cold as the sun set. They cannot chance a fire, as such Saga is relieved that the weather is still warm in the south. It makes the journey just a little more bearable, as long as she tries *not* to think about the reason why they are on the run. Thankfully, with the direction they are heading, it should only become warmer.

"I miss Da." Runa suddenly whimpers, and Saga tightens her hold on her, understanding where this is coming from. It's not sudden, not really, she's held out well so far for a child no more than eight summers.

"I miss Aina, Alv, Ebba and Halle too."

"I know, I do too." With all the broken pieces of her heart, she misses her lifemate and children. But there's nothing to be done about it, so she clasps the girl's cheeks and gently makes the sniffling child look at her.

"I know you want to cry, and I do too, so much. But we can't stop running, okay? We can't stop because it isn't safe, not yet, alright?" The girl nods.

"You can cry, now that we have stopped for rest, if you need to, it's alright. I'll hold you, and protect you, I will always protect you, I promise." Runa can cry, but Saga needs to stay strong. They don't have much of a lead on their pursuers, so she can't allow herself to break down yet. Runa can cry now, Saga knows she shouldn't stop her daughter from getting it out of her system, it can do more harm than good, but… she must try and encourage her to keep it for when they have stopped for the day and found a safe place to hide. She'll support her through the crying then, but Saga herself must wait, wait until they've reached complete safety. Then she'll scream and cry and rage, but until then she must keep these harrowing emotions buried deep. Even if it feels like she's moments away from splintering into thousands of pieces, from just the thought alone, she must stay strong.

Runa seem unconvinced by this, as if she can see her mother's conflicted emotions on her face as clearly as the bottom of a clear river, but she tucks her head beneath her mother's chin and exhales shakily. Other than that, she doesn't make a sound before she drifts off to sleep. Saga feels horrible about it.

"It'll be alright," the adult whispers.

"Everything will be alright, I promise. We'll be safe, I won't ever let them touch you." If Saga believed that the Goddess or her Children ever listened and acted upon any prayers of desperate and lost souls, she would have offered a thousand prayers, just to ensure her last remaining child would reach safety, at the very least. But she doesn't believe they'll listen, she doesn't believe that they care, so she can only rely on herself to get them to her last remaining family, whose presence is moving as well, even now at the late hour where the sun has completely disappeared in the horizon. Searching for them, even now, and she lets a wet laugh escape her. He doesn't rest, not much, constantly on the move, so she opens her mind, lets herself become a beacon for him to follow. Find us, find us, she begs quietly to herself, hoping against all hope that he hears her.

'Because I do not possess the strength to do this myself anymore." She's startled by the sound of an owl hooting, and she looks up to see one standing at the mouth of their little cave, just a few scant steps between them. It is a curious little thing, and she holds her hand out, beckoning it to come just a little bit closer. It is perfect, absolutely perfect, she thinks as the animal comes closer, just within reach, and that's when Saga strikes. She digs her fingers into its feathers, and while the owl jerks as if to escape, it quickly grows docile. Her hand crackles with energy and light.

"I'm sorry," she tells the owl, whose eyes grow rather blank, and it turns on its legs and hops out of the cave, flying off. Saga lies back down, closing her eyes. She doesn't enjoy using her magic for this, but right now she can't be considerate of anyone or anything else but their own safety. She can't take another loss like that; she'll crumble if she does. With that reality settled, she rubs a hand up and down her daughters back as she presses a kiss to the top of her short curls. If this trick words, and they continue at the pace they've gone at so far, they should be fine. For a little while.

And that is how it is for weeks. Saga has Runa shift into something light and tiny, and she carries her great distances, but of course, the little girl understands the urgency of reaching their destination quickly, and therefore she asks her mother why she's the only one shifting her shape.

"Why don't we fly, Mam?" Saga is quiet as she hands her daughter their waterskin. When she doesn't immediately answer, the girl grows worried, uneasiness churning her stomach.

"Mam?" Saga sighs in resignation, shoulders slumping as she knows that not answering will make the child even more worried. She holds her hands out in front of her. They're trembling, and Saga makes a grunt of effort. The skin of her fingers melts together as down and feathers grow, but then Saga jerks as if hit, and they all flutter to the ground. Her hands are human again. The child watches in horror. Her mother's strength is gone, and that is when she realizes just how perilous their situation truly is. She was frightened before, of course, but she believed her mother had the strength to protect her. Now she is terrified, considering their greatest attribute is out of their reach. Saga notices her daughter's sudden quietness and terror and hastens to reassure her.

"I promise I'll protect you, Runa." While it is true, it is also bravado. Saga is terrified herself, as a part of her that's been with her for her entire life is out of her reach. She cannot shift and being a shapeshifter unable to change her shape is the equivalent of being a fish on land.

"My brother comes ever closer each day. I promise, we'll be safe again. So, you must listen to me, alright? No matter what, you must listen to everything I say until then, do you understand?"

"I promise, Mam."

"Good." Saga manages a weak smile, but even that fades away when Runa speaks up again.

"They're not coming back, are they?" Runa knows what death is, she has seen it first hand, yet connecting it to her own family at such a tender age, she must have tried to keep up hope, even though reality has proven to be less merciful. Maybe her young mind has tried to protect itself? Or maybe Saga's mumbling after each horrible nightmare that has plagued the adult since the beginning of their journey has influenced Runa to a point? Made her believe their waking nightmare wasn't real.

Even though she witnessed it with her own eyes, that day.

"No, sweetling," Saga admits, voice cracking. "They're not. I'm so sorry." And Runa, after weeks of running form their home and all its memories, both good and bad, finally breaks down. Sunset coloured eyes swimming with tears. It's as if a dam broke with the truth, and she collapses against her mother, who lets her cry her young heart out while simultaneously keeping her own tears from falling. Listening to her child's wails is tearing at her, but she cannot cry. The child cries herself to sleep, and Saga stands vigil. She's too full of emotions she has bottled up with no idea or desire to process just yet. Her priority is their lives and safety.

"Soon." She promises herself, brushing her hair back and tying it up in a knot.

"Soon." They must keep moving, and not stop. That is a fact, but nothing is ever that easy. The next morning, Runa's face is flushed, she's sweating and whimpering and entirely too warm. Saga curses as she reaches a road, her daughter a heavy weight on her back. From the very beginning, this journey has been too much for the young girl, and Saga knew that. Now that everything has caught up with her, now that her body and mind both understand how much she's been through and what she has suffered, it demands time to rest. Time they simply do not have. Carrying her like this takes a toll on Saga as well, and she can hear each and every one of her daughter's laboured breaths over her shoulder. At some point blind panic washes over her when she realizes that she cannot go on like this. It is too dangerous.

She is desperate and doesn't know what to do. She needs to find a place to hide until the fever breaks, carrying the girl like this is dangerous for her weakened body, she needs rest, food, water, she needs-

"You alright there?" She spins around, coming face to face with a giant of a horse, a cart, and its rider. She curses herself, that she is so out of it that she wandered near a road without noticing, for not hearing their approach, for *stopping*-

"What's wrong, shapeshifter?" Saga freezes, blood turning to ice in her veins. They know, they know, *they know* and panic begins to set in, her own breathing growing as short and rapid as her daughter's, but then she gets a proper look at the person on the cart, and she sees to her relief that it is not a human riding it, a human knowing what she is. A cyclops sits there, reins connected to the six-legged horse, a Sleipr, a beast subservient only to giants, she realizes, held in one huge hand while the other is resting casually over his knee. The cyclops is twice as big as her, but his kind is not hostile towards hers, nor any people, really. With the one eye the Goddess bestowed them, they can see through anyone, to their very core. There is no hiding from them, and even if they weren't all-seeing in such a way, Saga and Runa's condition explains more than enough, doesn't it?

"Hunters." The redhead says, and his lone eye widens a slight bit, understanding dawning on him.

"Please, my daughter is sick, I can't- I can't carry her!"

"Get on then." Without hesitation he reaches down, and Saga allows him to pull them both up and into his cart. Being that it is made to carry a being twice as big as her and his supplies and wares and whatnot, even she with her abnormal height can just barely see over the edges when she sits up properly, she notes. They can hide here.

"Which way are you heading?" He asks, snapping his reins, and the hulking beast of a horse begins pulling the cart again. With its six legs, it moves quite a lot faster than a normal horse.

"South." The cyclops grumbles and Saga bites her lip, afraid he might toss them off.

"Please, just until her fever breaks, and we'll be out of your hair."

"What hair?" The cyclops guffaws, slapping his bald head and her face flush red in mortification. It is just an expression, but still. The cyclops just continues to laugh, and points to the crates near the front.

"There's food and water there, shapeshifter. My Sleipr here and I will carry you for as long as you need, it's no hardship on our part." The Sleipr grunts, tossing its head, but makes no noise of disagreement.

"I'm sorry for endangering you as well for taking in me and my daughter." She feels like she should offer him that much at least and show that she is grateful for the assistance. The cyclops tosses her a dark smirk over his shoulder, an action full of violent promises.

"If your pursuers catch up while you're with me, we're not the ones who'll be in danger, girl." Saga is most grateful for the help as she begins finding what she needs to aid her child. Water and food, and blankets to rest in, then Saga will allow herself a breather as well.

CHAPTER TWELVE

An ear-shattering scream rings in the air. Aske jolts up with a gasp, the dream digging its claws into his mind and refusing to let go. With a sound a mix between a sob and a curse, he rubs his face viciously, hoping to dispel the nightmare's hold on him. He is only partly successful. His body is trembling as he gets up on his feet, his hands fumbling when packing up his bag, his feet barely keeping from buckling as he takes his first steps of the day. It is still dark outside, dawn is some time away yet, but he won't find any rest now after that terror.

He begins the new day's trek across the colourful yet barren tundra, his mind still too shaken to understand just how exhausted his body is. That is not the important part right now. What is important is that now Saga's presence seem panicked. Aske knows that he is too far away to be of any help yet, so all he can do is press forward and hurry as much as he can. He's already been on the road for weeks, nine weeks, to be exact. And he is exhausted.

Days and nights have blurred together because of the nightmares, but one thing is for certain; he *is* getting closer. That is the last thought Aske remembers as the sun begins to light up the sky, to peek over the horizon, and his eyes roll up into the back of his head. His body crumbles unceremoniously to the ground, and there he lays until the sun has moved high into the sky and is beginning to ponder about descending yet again.

He jolts awake and clumsily leaps to his feet when he is alerted by the crackling of a fire and feels its warmth. His lips pull back into a snarl as he rounds on the person by the fire, pupils dilated and scales breaking out across his body as he instinctively begins to transform.

He stops short at the sight of Bragi blinking up at him, first in surprise, then his expression melts into that of a person who is utterly unimpressed as he stares at the shapeshifter.

"Well good afternoon to you too." He delivers the words with a rather flat voice and Aske just stares back at him, dumbstruck.

"I- you, what, *when?*" He stumbles over his words as he straightens up, undoing his transformation. Bragi doesn't answer, though that might be because he doesn't quite understand what Aske tries to ask, or because he simply doesn't want to. Either way, he silently fills a small bowl with stew and hands it over to the shapeshifter with an expectant raise of his brow. Aske accepts, but makes no other move than that, his head still a jumbled mess of questions. He finally sits when Bragi gestures for him to do so, his body moving on its own, and that's fine. It gives Aske time to gather himself.

"Why are you here?" It is a coherent sentence, straight to the point, and he only sounds mildly suspicious.

"I merely came upon you as I continued my own journey." Aske stares at him disbelievingly, and Bragi points his thumb over his shoulder. There's a horse tethered to a dried up, old barren log.

"Oh." A mount would explain how he managed to catch up to him, but not why Bragi was going in the same direction as him.

"Eat, you look ghastly." Well, that is just rude, so Aske scowls at him. Then he eats because his stomach is demanding nutrition, and he won't let himself be embarrassed even more by having the blasted thing announce to the whole bloody world how famished he is. So, he empties his bowl, then a second, and half of a third. Aske hasn't paid much attention to how famished he had been until he got some proper food in him.

Grudgingly, he thanks Bragi for the meal, and looks heavenward. It is already growing dark; he's been out all day. He's wasted so much time, he needs to get a move on. The redhead has barely got his feet under him to push himself up when Bragi puts a hand on his shoulder and yanks him back down. Immediately he raises his hackles at the brunet.

"What are you-"

"Do you think you'll get far on those shaky legs? You'll fall over again if you try." Aske wants to argue, to tell Bragi to remove his hand unless he'd like to lose it, but he doesn't have the energy to. Bragi is right, however much he hates to admit it, he's not going anywhere. The shapeshifter sags, all fight leaving him. For now.

"How did you catch up to me? I've been travelling without pause for weeks." Bragi frowns as he pulls his hand back, assessing Aske's state of being. His clothes look baggy on him now, compared to when they left the village, the sockets around his eyes sunken in, cheekbones stretching his skin thin. He appears gaunt, ghastly.

"I probably caught up precisely because you've been moving without stop. You've quite well run yourself into the gorund, going at the pace you've been going. I stayed in that village you passed through for ten days. Whatever it is that you need to hurry for, you're not going to find it if you pass out for whole days." Aske is shocked to learn that Bragi managed to catch up with him so easily after having stayed so long, mount or no mount. Still, he is loath to admit that Bragi is right about this. It has already happened once, and Aske do feel dreadfully drowsy with a full stomach, so he sits quietly, waiting.

Bragi, after a long silence, heaves a heavy sigh, before turning fully towards Aske again. He looks weary, the shapeshifter thinks. He hadn't back at the mountain village, he'd appeared quite upbeat back then. Now Aske can clearly see his age in the crow's feet by his eyes, the greying strands of his brown hair and beard.

"You do not trust me, and that is fine. It is understandable even, but you need to know that you've been travelling for two moons after we parted ways. I stayed in that village for ten days before acquiring my horse, and I did not try to catch up with you. Obviously, you've exhausted yourself, and your speed has dropped. Now, I won't ask what makes you run yourself ragged, but I *will* tell you that all you've done is become a liability to yourself. So, I will propose an arrangement." The redhead glowers, but Bragi keeps quiet, waiting for Aske to take the hint.

"Tell me, then. What is your so-called *arrangement*?" Aske tosses his hands in the air when it becomes apparent that Bragi will say no more until Aske gives him the lead to do so. Which is ridiculous, considering how the human has already insulted him and carried on without asking permission earlier.

Several times, in fact. Aske has punched people for less.

"I propose that we journey together." Even before the words are all fully out the shapeshifter protest.

"No." He deadpans.

"Hear me out, first, please."

"No, you're right, I don't trust you. You helped me back then, I'll acknowledge that, but this is different. There is absolutely no reason you can come up with that will make me lead you *anywhere near* my destination, and that's final." Bragi sighs again, rubbing a hand over his weary eyes. Old the shapeshifter may be, but he is acting like a stubborn child, and frankly, Bragi is in no mood for it. His patience with this man is wearing rather thin after the last few horrendous days he has experienced.

"I'm not telling you to bring me with you to *where* you're heading. I'm proposing that we travel together for parts of the journey, and then part ways when we're close to wherever you're going, as close as you're comfortable with, of course."

"How am I to trust that you won't try anything in the meantime? Or follow when we part ways?" Bragi understands, he truly does, that Aske is naturally suspicious of humans after everything he has gone through in his life. The scars are proof of many crimes committed against him, but at this point, Bragi does feel like he has proven that he means no harm. He is out of patience with this.

"For goodness's sake, you impossible man!" he snaps. "I'm neither out to trick you nor hurt you! I helped nurse you back to health, and it is quite aggravating to see you *waste away all my efforts with your recklessness*! Finding you passed out on the tundra where anyone could find you and where wild animals could attack you was mortifying! You're over three hundred years old, or so you claim, *act like it!*"

"Are you *scolding* me?" The redhead snaps back in disbelief. "As if I am a child? *You?*"

"If you don't like it, try acting like an adult and you'll be spared from my scolding!" Bragi huffs, annoyance clear on his face. Aske pauses. The complacent human has a fiery streak to him. Still…

"Do you worry and fuss over *all* of your former patients, or are you just sticking your nose into *my* affairs?" Bragi rears back at the accusation, face flushing and avoiding looking at the redhead.

"I, well, no, but- oh, really, that is to say!" Aske quirks a brow, waiting.

"No." The human admits. "Because I usually never stay at one place for too long. And most of my former patients *listen* to my advice."

"I listened." And Bragi can't *truly* argue with that, because even though Aske had been reluctant and avoidant back at the mountain, he *had* listened to Bragi's advice for his recovery. He had been stubborn about it, complained about it and shot daggers with his eyes at the human which could almost be physically felt, but he had kept from aggravating his injury in any shape or form.

"Well, you're obviously not taking care of yourself out here! When was the last time you allowed your body proper rest? Food? *Water?*" Now it's Aske who purse his lips and looking away because the human is right. Again. He's anxious, considering more than just one thing is wrong. He hadn't expected to be travelling for as long as he has. And the fact that he still feels so far away is worrying, because it shouldn't take this long, not with her ability. By all reason, she should already have caught up to him by now. He looks towards Bragi again. He has yet to *do* or even just *say* something that makes the hair on the back of his neck rise, but Aske also can't remember the last time anyone knew what he is and didn't attempt at killing him in some way.

Except for the villagers. He had thought he had hidden it from them for so long, but they had known about him from the start. A terrifying thought, had they been the kind to hate the other species.

Yet they hadn't cared at all. The redhead eyes the horse. It will make travelling easier, quicker too when his burdens are carried by the beast and not himself. He'll be lighter, they'll move quicker. It has been well over a hundred years since Aske did any travelling, but Bragi has been doing it for decades now, it has been his way of life for most of his life, apparently. The world has changed while the shapeshifter hid in his mountain, that much is clear. As much as he is against it, there are more perks than cons when it comes to travelling together with another person.

And should it come to it, Aske thinks as he looks back at Bragi who is waiting for an answer, he can always kill the human. Fighting, at the very least, is not something Aske has forgotten. He'll take the risk, another life on his conscience is nothing in the grand scheme of things.

"Alright. On the condition that when I tell you to fuck off, you won't argue. You'll leave, without any fuss." Bragi nods, curtly, but appears somewhat pleased nonetheless as he smiles.

"You have my word, friend." Aske doesn't return the smile. He has agreed, for the sake of his goal, but the human shall never be allowed anywhere near it.

CHAPTER THIRTEEN

During their first few days of travelling together, Bragi learns that not only is Aske skilled in manipulating all kinds of plant life with his magic, but he is also able to conjure fire. His curiosity has led to Aske begrudgingly telling him about a time when he was known as a fire breathing serpent, from a time much less peaceful than now. From before shapeshifters seemed to disappear from the face of the earth. Of course, a lot of careful needling had to be done before Aske even considered telling him this.

Of course, he only became known as such a beast because he fought humans to protect his family, friends, allies, and Bragi can understand the sentiment. It still doesn't change the fact that Aske has killed people, both to protect, and to avenge fallen loved ones. The end doesn't justify the means, not always, and while the brunet understands that Aske has suffered horribly at the hands of humans, many humans suffered due to Aske's actions also. He keeps that to himself though, as he is sure Aske won't take kindly to Bragi pointing that out. Their comradeship is on fragile enough ground as it is, it won't survive Bragi pointing out that Aske brought suffering upon humans, when Aske fosters little fondness for humanity. But there is something interesting he can gleam more information from.

"So, you can mingle your shapeshifting abilities to your other magical attributes? I thought you'd need to use your hands to cast magic?" Aske blinks, caught a bit off guard by the question.

"Well, I don't have hands while in my serpent form, so fire comes out of my mouth? I can still do magic, yes. It's not like my affinity disappears just because I take on another shape. Magic is my will, it is not connected to my physical appearance." Bragi nods along. It makes sense, what Aske is telling him. His animal form is a part of him, just as truly him as his human shape is, so it makes perfect sense that he should be able to use his magic as he pleases in both forms. Of course, he cannot use an overabundance of magic, there is a limit to how much he can use, just like any other being in this world who possesses an affinity for magic. Magic is indeed will, and it takes a toll on one's body and mind if used too much.

"The spirits, Tulip, Daffodil, Orchid and Dewdrop, you said they came into being by all the work and care you put into your garden… They won't disappear if you're gone for too long, will they?" The mere thought alone is a sad one, especially since, at the time, it seemed like only they knew of Aske's true identity, that he only trusted them and no one else. They are his friends, companions in the mountain, helping him maintain and love his garden. Aske is quiet for a while before looking away with a shrug.

"They might." The words are seemingly spoken with nonchalance, but the way he had paused before answering is telling enough that the thought bothers the shapeshifter. The thought of the little spirits disappearing out of existence nearly breaks Bragi's heart. He'd become quite fond of them despite not having known them for very long. They were adorable, kind, playful. Innocent.

"They're willed into being by emotions, or convictions, and when the source disappears, they do too, most of the time. But the villagers are aware of them, the children often play with them, so they might last a little while. As long as they're remembered and cared for, they'll exist. Once forgotten, they'll disappear, and humans tend to forget, so by the time I return, they might be gone."

"Oh, the poor dears." Aske regards him for a few moments before pulling his hair back from his face properly and begins braiding it as they walk. Bragi has noted that he favours having his hair pulled back in tight braids, at least sections of it so he can keep it out of his face, and wonders where the habit came from, why he doesn't just cut it off. That does seem like a much more personalized question than the shapeshifter will be comfortable with answering though, so he keeps it to himself.

"You could probably manage to will your own spirits into being, if you try hard enough." Aske is rather nonchalant about his way of speaking now, yet there is no hiding the way his shoulders are set, the tenseness of his entire being.

"How? I am afraid I don't have much skill with anything else than healing magic, and I have nothing I'm passionate about, like your garden. I am a travelling man, after all." The redhead sighs, though he sounds rather annoyed now, as if he regrets bringing it up, but feels like he must finish explaining even though he obviously finds it a hassle.

"Spirits don't ultimately come from magic, they come from emotions, yeah? The care you put into something, so to speak, so if you feel particularly affectionate for an object you've got on you or around you, a spirit might be born from that. They don't have to be tied to an element. Their abilities and personalities come from what they're tied to. Tulip, Daffodil, Dewdrop and Orchid came into being from my passion for my garden, therefore they are earth spirits. If you put effort into it, you could probably bring one out from your sword, equipment, or even your tomes." It's a test, to see if Bragi will take up his sword, to see if that is the tool in which he'll create a spirit from if he truly does desire one. And if he'll do as Aske expects him to, to try and make a spirit out of a weapon.

"Oh!" Bragi claps his hands together, quite excited. Aske's eyes narrow.

"That would have been lovely! I'll try when I have the opportunity! Do you think I could make one out of my bag? It would be practical to have one tending to my herbs and warning me before they go bad." The shapeshifter seems a bit taken aback, blinking several times before he catches himself as he steps on a dry branch which noticeably cracks beneath his feet.

"Suit yourself, but just because it is possible, it doesn't mean you actually will succeed." Bragi pouts, which looks rather ridiculous on a man his age, if Aske is honest.

"Must you give me hope and then shatter it in the same conversation?" He demands mournfully, and Aske tosses his arms in the air with an exasperated growl.

"I thought you liked knowledge? Thought you ought to know."

"Of course I love knowledge, it is wonderful and it is a never ending venture, but you do have a nasty habit of ruining it before I even begin!"

"A nasty habit?" Aske crows. "We haven't known each other long enough for you to say that."

"Well, we are certainly getting there!" Bragi huffs, but despite the other's attitude, the human does want to try and will one into existence one day. When his life is more stable, perhaps. When he has a place to call home, again.

He has yet to gather the courage to ask the other man about the reason for his impromptu leaving of his home, because it is as the shapeshifter has said, they don't know each other well enough. Asking might result in an unnecessary argument. In the worst case scenario it might end up in a physical fight. And it isn't any of Bragi's business anyhow, especially since they will part ways when the time comes.

And even if Aske is rather brusque, to the point of being quite rude, to be quite honest, and suspicious and wary of anyone they cross paths with, he's not the worst person Bragi could be travelling with.

"Hey, healer!" Though at this point, Bragi is finding it hard to think of worse people to travel with. Why can't Aske just use his name, he has yet to properly use his name. Sometimes Bragi wishes he had the ability to strangle the redhead, just to have him shut up for just a moment, though he's quite sure that it will end with Aske shifting shape and strangling Bragi to death himself, or crushing him in his coils. Besides, Bragi swore an oath, and that oath means a great deal to him, so instead, he just breathes in deep and tries to hold onto his patience. It is only temporary, he keeps reminding himself. This part of his journey is only temporary.

"Yes, Aske?" He grinds out through a clenched jaw.

"Why are you travelling? Why aren't you with your family? Pretty sure they'd be better off with you than I am." Aske tries for a nonchalant question ending in an insult, just to keep the spirit of their every day arguments going, and Bragi would have welcomed any question other than this one. The horse yanks on the reins, sensing the shift in the mood from the human. Aske glances back when he realizes that Bragi has stopped walking, and frowns, about to point out that they are on a very tight schedule when he notices the human's expression.

"What?" Bragi blinks, before shaking his head, smiling brightly. Too brightly, considering what Aske just saw in his eyes, a look he's seen far too many times.

"Nothing." Aske mutters, turning away and moving on. It is disconcerting, the way the human hid everything behind a smile so quickly, it makes goosebumps prickle the shapeshifter's skin. It is unnatural. It is terrifying. Not even Aske with centuries of practice can do that.

"No, you asked a question, did you not?" Bragi trots to catch up to the redhead who adamantly shakes his head.

"Wasn't important."

"No one asks questions unless they're curious as to what the-"

"It's not bloody important!" The taller man turns to glare at the other, and the horse whinnies as it is startled by Aske's exclamation. The redhead feels bad enough, for some reason or another, that the question got such a reaction out of the human, and he is also kind of angry that Bragi won't let it go when he is giving him an out. Bragi just keeps the smile, not undeterred at all.

"I have no home." It's practiced, practiced so well that Aske would have missed all the signs if he wasn't watching so closely, unblinking. The slight quiver at the corner of his mouth, the overly controlled rise and fall of his chest, the tight hold on the reins causing his knuckles to whiten, the unnatural brightness in his hazel eyes, how they widen with each second to the point the shapeshifter almost worries they'll pop out of his skull.

"I'm sorry to hear that." The words taste bitter on his tongue, even if he means them. He knows the pain of not having anywhere to go, somewhere he can call safe. He's lived a good portion of his life like that, and it makes bile rise in his throat that he had nearly forced Bragi out of the mountain village when he seemed to be so comfortable there. It is sympathy because he knows the pain, Aske knows it is nothing more than that, but he doesn't want to feel it. It's disgusting, feeling sympathy for a human he barely knows.

"Oh, it happened a long time ago," Bragi says with false cheeriness, a false bravado of nonchalance, a shield against the hurt he is obviously still struggling with.

"Still, I'm sorry I brought it up." The redhead offers an apologetic shrug. "I know how it feels, how it hurts, so… I'm sorry." Bragi smiles in thanks, this time much more genuine.

"It's alright, you didn't know. I have no home, and my only family died when I was very young, alongside my teacher." Aske winces. This doesn't make him feel any better at all. Not only has he, unknowingly, picked at an old wound, it went even deeper than what he originally thought.

"Parent?" And why, oh *why* is he picking even more at it? Is he trying to pick and prod at a scabbed over wound to cause it to bleed again?

"Brother, actually. He was a devout servant of both the Goddess, her Children, and our people."

"Right." The Goddess and her Children. It has been quite some time since he's thought of them, prayed to them. He doesn't feel like starting that up again anytime soon. Not until he finds his mark, maybe not even then. It depends a lot on how he finds them.

"So, he was some kind of priest?" Bragi nods and Aske watches him from the corner of his eye as the human smiles almost wistfully.

"Yes. He didn't hold many sermons, as many are wont to do. He read the scripts, of course, that was his task after all, and worked the fields and taught children how to read, write and control their magic if they had any. He was fast friends with a cyclops who passed through our village once or twice a year."

"Didn't think humans liked the cyclops?" Aske raises a brow. It unsettles the mortals to have a creature who can see straight through them hanging around. No amount of lies or acting can deceive a cyclops, who, through the eyes gifted to them by the Goddess, see into their target's very soul. Even Aske would find that kind of scrutiny uncomfortable.

"Most don't, I imagine, but my brother admired the cyclops greatly. I wish I had remembered his name, he was a very kind fellow, gentle, despite towering over us. He had a Sleipr with him if I recall correctly." Aske whistles, impressed. A Sleipr, not many of those left in the world. He's never seen one himself, despite his old age. The cyclops don't share those beasts with anyone anymore, for good reason.

"Maybe you'll meet him again, someday?" Aske offers, a kindness he didn't think himself capable of offering a human. The conversation had started out awkwardly, but it has evolved into something that is almost pleasant.

"Oh, come now, Aske! I've been journeying for twenty-three years and I've yet to come across him since I left home. I doubt I will by the time my end comes." Bragi may say this, but he does have this wistful look on his face still.

"You never know, Bragi." Aske shrugs, not knowing when his tone changed from hostile to indifferent to slightly encouraging, though he doesn't put in an effort to revert back to his original attitude.

"The world isn't as big as everyone seem to think."

CHAPTER FOURTEEN

It takes a full week before Runa's fever breaks, and when it finally does, Saga nearly crumples in relief. She scolds herself for not having paid proper attention to how much of a toll the journey has taken on the little girl. The trauma itself rattled her a lot, but on top of that she had to push herself and even see her mother terrified each day.

'I'll have to be more careful in the future,' she thinks as she runs a hand through her daughter's hair. It's matted to her skull with sweat, the curls falling out.

"How is she?" Hildingr's voice breaks through her thoughts. She throws a tired smile at the back of the cyclops's head.

"Her fever is gone. She's just exhausted now."

"Then you'll be riding with me for a few more days," Hildingr laughs, and Saga exhales tiredly. In the cyclops's wagon they've been able to cover a lot of ground, even more than she thought they would, but a Sleipr is a true beast, always moving at a good pace, and apparently never growing tired. They've only stopped a few short times since they got aboard, so the rumours about the giant horses have been proven true here. Her brother's presence grows ever closer every day, and unless their pursuers have followed without rest, they won't be able to catch up anytime soon.

"I am truly grateful, Hildingr. If it weren't for you, I'm not sure we would have lasted much longer. Not like this."

"Think nothing of it!" The cyclops booms. "It is only natural to help someone in need." Not everyone believes that, Saga knows. The world would have been a better place if people did believe this, but they don't. And it is because of this that tragedies happen. Tragedies like her own.

"Our pursuers believe the opposite."

"*BAH!*" Hildingr scoffs so loudly that Runa stirs in her mother's lap. "Humans think they're the favourites of the Goddess and her Children, for some unthinkable reason. They have a strong dislike towards anything and anyone who is more blessed than them, which is ridiculous. The Goddess created us all, and she loves us all equally. And when our lives are over, we'll all either be praised by our choices or punished for them. There is no arguing with her once our physical lives are over."

"So, you think hunters will be punished after their souls leave their mortal bodies?" Saga finds it hard to believe. The world has been horrible for many centuries, even long before she was born. Nothing has changed yet, so on what basis should she believe there is retribution for evil?

"I know they will." Hildingr replies darkly. "I'm old enough to remember when the Goddess and her Children walked the earth. I know their laws and promises, whether they were light or dark. Humans are so short-lived, so desperate to be superior, that they've contorted the truth with a belief that suits them better, scares them less." Saga looks down at Runa, frowning.

"With all the violence the humans have unleashed upon my kind, I don't even see them as my equal, much less superior. I do understand that not all humans are like the hunters, but that does not mean that I trust them any further than I can throw them."

"And that's not very far, with those spindly arms of yours." Hildingr chuckles smugly, causing Saga to roll her eyes.

"Everyone looks spindly to you. I assure you; I am quite physically fit. I just look spindly and gangly because of my height." Hildingr barks another laugh, and Runa does jolt awake this time, momentarily panicking as she's quite disoriented. Saga pulls her close, keeps her from unwittingly harming herself as she works to calm her down.

"Mam?" She's so tense, so scared, but Saga smiles reassuringly and combs her fingers through her daughter's hair, speaking;

"We're safe, sweetling." And Runa sags in her mother's embrace, closing her eyes and taking a few deep breaths, nearly falling asleep again before she realizes they are in motion, and that she had been startled awake by the sound of something sharp and loud. She struggles to sit up properly as she looks around, stopping short when she sees the hulking giant turned towards her in his seat, the lone green eye watching her closely. She falls back with a startled yelp, to which he again laughs.

"Scary am I, Tiny?" Saga chuckles as she soothes the girl again, showing that there is nothing to fear. If her mother is not afraid, there is no reason for Runa to be either.

"She's barely eight summers, and this is the first time she's gotten a look at the world outside our nesting area. She's never seen one of your kind before." Runa looks up to her mother, who gestures to the cyclops.

"This is Hildingr, a cyclops. He's been helping us since you fell sick."

"I fell sick?"

"Yes. We've been riding in his cart for some time now. Once you're healthy again, we'll be moving on." Runa nods, feeling better hearing that, and snuggles into her mother, already drifting off. She is still weakened and tired, and her mother is warm. Saga smiles fondly as her daughter's breathing evens out.

"So much excitement when she woke up, huh. Little ones sure like to sleep a lot." The tone is teasing, fond, not in any way meant to ridicule the child, but the shapeshifter raises to the bait anyways.

"Who can expect them to keep up with the ways of a full-grown adult when their bodies are so small and frail? Not to mention their young minds, so innocent and naïve." Runa isn't so naïve anymore though, it doesn't much apply to her anymore, and it saddens Saga.

"Is she still, though? Possessing an innocent and naïve mind?" The shapeshifter freezes in place at Hildingr's question, her heart skipping a beat before it thunders in her chest. She has not explained to him why they're being pursued, or what they've experienced up until this point. She has not confided in him the horror and grief that caused them to run, though she knows his eye lets him see everything, learn everything he wants. She is unsure what to say or do. Hildingr appears to understand, even though he hasn't turned back around to look at her since he asked the question and speaks up again.

"I told you, Saga. I'm old enough to remember when the Goddess and her Children walked the earth. To find a shapeshifter with a *lone* child without neither a lovemate nor a lifemate, well, I can connect the dots, even without my eye." Saga feels that familiar burn in the back of her throat, the sting in her eyes she stubbornly blinks away. Not yet, she tells herself, not yet.

"I do not wish to talk about it," she chokes out, and turns away from the cyclops, laying down and curling up around her daughter, and decides that she too needs her rest.

Hildingr spares a glance back some time later, when the sky has grown dark to ensure both his passengers are indeed sleeping, before he looks heavenwards, seeing the constellations and clusters of stars the deities supposedly live amongst now after leaving this world.

"I know there is no such thing as a fair or unfair world because we all possess free will," he begins calmly, before his lone eye narrows and a growl works its way from deep within his chest and up the back of his throat, "but if those humans get away with their brutal savagery, I will find them myself and even the scales."

It is not an empty threat; he will do it. Hildingr is all for free will. The slaughter of innocent children is something he does not condone. And he doesn't fear balancing out the scales, no matter what the verdict will be when his time comes. Hildingr is all for free will, and he is a firm believer in facing the consequences of one's actions. And he does not find it too terrifying to be the consequence the hunters may have to meet.

The next day he makes a stop by a river long enough that his passengers can wash themselves and their clothing. They hang their clothing to dry over the edge of his cart and sit wrapped in blankets as they move on. Even though the reason he has passengers is probably for an unpleasant reason, Hildingr finds it nice to have the two together with him here. It's been some time since he's had intelligent company.

He misses when he brought that young priest Sigmund along on his trips, but that was decades ago. He is no longer around to go along with him. Hildingr had been quite surprised to see what had happened to that little village the last time he passed through it. He didn't even see that young boy again, the one who had asked to come along once he was old enough to do so. Hildingr shakes that thought away and glances behind him, the corners of his lips quirking up a bit.

Especially amusing is the fact that the moment the little one had overcome her surprise of being in the presence of another sentient being, she showered him in all kinds of questions, eager to explore and learn anything new as children are prone to be when they come across something or someone they've never seen before. It is an enjoyable experience, seeing her eyes go wide, to hear her gasp in astonishment and call out to her mother, asking if she knew all of what the cyclops' is telling her.

Of course, when Saga announces a few days later that she and Runa will go on their own come morning, it comes as no surprise to him. It is a bit saddening because he has grown quite fond of them, already used to having them around.

"Alright, then," he says with an easy shrug, "but do be careful when you're on your own. We've crossed quite the distance, but still, don't let your guard down."

"I won't. Thank you for your help, Hildingr. I'll never forget what you did for us."

The next morning the two shapeshifters bid the cyclops' goodbye, one slightly more tearful than the other.

"Don't cry now, Tiny. The world isn't as big as some think, trust me, I've been all over it several times. We might meet again one day." Hildingr tries to console Runa, who sniffs and wipes at her eyes.

"I'll be bigger by then, promise you'll recognize me," Hildingr just chuckles warmly, and points to his eye.

"I am a cyclops, Tiny. The moment I see you, I'll recognize you, even if you should miraculously grow to be as big as me."

"I'll hold you to that!" With those last parting words, they wave and go on their way. Hildingr watches them for many moments more before he cracks the reins, and his Sleipr begins pulling the cart along the road again. The days following pass by peacefully, but the silence is heavy. He supposes that is just a consequence to being so used to the chattering that had happened the last fortnight before they had parted ways.

It was nice to have passengers-

His thoughts come to an abrupt halt when he hears yelling and the heavy stampede of hooves, and he groans. If it's bandits, his peaceful afternoon will be ruined. He is doubly sure of this when the new arrivals urge their mounts to continue beside him.

"You there, creature!" Hildingr feels the urge to roll his eye. Humans are ever so articulate. Brave of them to speak like this to him though, considering the obvious size difference, though perhaps that is a mix between an unhealthy dose of confidence and superiority.

"Do yourself a favour and try to fall into the grace of our Goddess' light. Tell us if you've seen a tall woman with a beak-like nose and red hair, and her devil spawn!" Hildingr doesn't even need to pull the reins for his beast to stop, stamping her six hooves into the dirt road furiously as she tosses her head. Hildingr is completely still, a shadow passing over his face.

"Why are you looking for a woman and her child, boy?" Though he can easily guess why, he wants to hear them say it. He wants them to confirm it, admit it. He wants them to hang themselves on the noose he's dangling in front of them.

"They're shapeshifters! Even a non-intelligent creature like you understands that such evil being destroyed and wiped from the face of this earth is the will of the Goddess!" Hildingr can't quite help the grotesque grin spreading across his face at the bravado and holier-than-thou attitude of the human. Unhealthy dose of confidence, indeed.

"For someone who has never met the Goddess or even heard her voice, you *do* sound very certain of yourself, don't you? What will you do, when you meet your maker, and she scolds you for your impertinence?" The human bristles as the giant turns leisurely in his seat, one arm resting on the wooden edge of his cart, taking in the group that has surrounded him.

"There's only five of you?" They grow wary at his darkly cheerful tone. "Oh, you're simple scouts," he laughs sinisterly.

"I do believe it is time for me to even out the scales some." With speed no one would associate with his hulking mass, the cyclops reaches out and encloses the man's head within his fist. He squeezes, and the head pops in his hand before the man has the chance to scream.

"*Bjorn!*"

"Well, would you look at that." Hildingr turns towards the rest of the group as he slides off his cart, his Sleipr stamping her hooves again, whinnying loudly. "He popped like a grape."

CHAPTER FIFTEEN

Bragi jolts to life by the, frankly, inhuman sound Aske emits in his sleep. He scrambles to his feet just as the redhead turns onto his side, gasping for breath, fingers fisting into the long grass by his bedroll, tearing fistfuls of green up from the ground.

"What was that?" Bragi sputters, eyes looking around wildly until he notices the wooden cup by the fire. Full of the potion he's been making for a while now, a potion that helps Aske rest without being plagued by nightmares.

"You didn't drink the potion?"

"Didn't-"

"If I had wanted to hurt you, I would have done so a long time ago! I would have gotten rid of you out in the tundra!" Bragi is irritable, he had been enjoying his rest, and to be pulled out of it as rudely as he was, by the screaming of his companion suffering nightmares, well, he isn't in the mood for it. Not with the way Aske has been acting rather difficult lately. It's just another thing to put on his ever-growing list of things that Aske does to annoy or anger him. It is shaping up to be a rather long list, and despite Bragi's usually strong patience, he just isn't in an agreeable enough mood this morning to accommodate his travelling companions stubbornness.

"I forgot, alright?!" Aske snaps as he tries to gather himself. He is pale and shaking, he looks a right mess as he tries to gather himself, pressing his forehead into his arm, teeth digging viciously into his lower lip as he tries to keep any sound from escaping him. The way his whole body shudders and jerks betrays him though. He speaks again, all fight leaving him, voice so low and weak Bragi barely hears him.

"I just forgot, I'm sorry, alright?" Bragi's anger melts away, and he looks to the sky. Dawn isn't too far away, he notices, and hoists himself up with a sigh. He is too tired to start the day with another argument.

"Come on. We'll just get an early start today." He tries to not watch how Aske wipes away the sweat on his forehead, the gaunt look in his eyes, nor the exhausted slump of his shoulders. If he does, the indignation will give way for pity instead, and Bragi is not in the mood for it now after this rude awakening. He will reserve his right to be annoyed for the rest of the morning, thank you very much.

When they are on the road again, the human glances at Aske and sighs. Aske doesn't enjoy these nightmares he keeps suffering. They leave him exhausted and jittery, so the healer concludes that it truly had been an honest mistake.

Not much is said during the next few days, but Bragi notices that the nights have become much cooler, and that even when Aske consumes the potion dutifully, under Bragi's constant vigilance, he sometimes appears to have slept terribly.

"Would you mind telling me what the nightmares are about?" He asks one evening. Aske grimaces and looks to the side, uncomfortable, but he doesn't immediately shut Bragi down, and that, well, it is progress. It is not so long ago that Aske would have glared at him, even snarled at him, for such a question. Now, he just looks uncomfortable, which isn't great either, but at the very least they are now much more amicable towards each other. Or rather, Aske is not as aggressive towards Bragi anymore.

"I had siblings-"

"You have siblings?" Aske glares for being cut off and Bragi raises his hands apologetically. He has a habit of interrupting Aske whenever he is surprised. He's never been like this with others, only Aske. That's, well, he should investigate that. At a later time.

"Shapeshifters, when we're born, we're linked together, in some way. Long story short, siblings are always aware of each other. It's like a beacon, of sorts. Anyways, our minds are connected on some level."

"So, you know where each of your siblings are, in a way? Isn't it difficult to keep track?"

"It's not that hard with mine."

"Oh?"

"Only one is alive. The other three are dead." It feels like someone has tossed freezing water over his head, Bragi thinks. Aske says it with practiced ease, like it is just a fact, and not something to be grieving. Bragi wonders if he had seemed just as nonchalant when he told Aske about his own brother being long gone. Considering Aske's awkward reaction and the even clumsier and awkward way he tried cheering him up, Bragi can safely assume he was not as successful as Aske is here.

"The nightmares aren't just nightmares. They're a mesh of a memory belonging to my last remaining sibling, and my own, old ones. They're horrible, and they'll last a while, they always do. At the very least until I find her, I imagine."

"Is that where you're going then?" Even as he voices the question, Bragi expects to be shut out, for the simple reason that if there is one thing Aske has been very clear on, is that he will not entertain any questions about his destination, but he's shared this much, he's practically admitted to it now. Aske doesn't look angry, or even all that wary of him anymore, but he does hesitate in answering.

"Yeah," he nods, "that's where I'm heading. She needs help, so I'm going."

"Quite admirable."

"Yeah, well." Aske squirms, avoiding Bragi's gaze. "We're the only ones left, we're all we've got. Can't leave her to fend for herself when she needs me." He seems uncomfortable with admitting that he cares for his last living relative, cares enough to leave the safety and comforts of his home to brave the roads filled with humans that he cannot trust won't attack him on sight if they realize what he is.

It *is* admirable, truly.

"She's quite lucky to have a brother like you," Bragi comments, voice filled with sincerity, and it must catch Aske off-guard, if the way he startles is any indication. His mouth opens, his jaw works around a series of vowels, before he sputters and gives up, turning his head away. It's almost endearing to watch him grow so embarrassed. Almost. He is still the most annoying person Bragi has ever met. And, well, if Bragi can get a little amusement out of teasing the other man as payback, no one can begrudge the healer for it. Also, it isn't as if his words, while also yielding the result of the redhead becoming embarrassed, isn't what Bragi thinks is the truth.

"I mean it, Aske. You're a good brother." Aske is apparently not used to compliments and doesn't know how to respond to it all. Bragi lets the shapeshifter stew in it for a couple of minutes with more glee than is strictly necessary before he takes pity on his squirming.

"Would you mind telling me a bit about a family of shapeshifters? How are you linked after birth? Is it a connection the parents make by using magic to connect you?" When Aske doesn't say anything at first, Bragi wonders if he pushed too much at once, that he's put his foot in his mouth again, but considering that the shapeshifter is neither glaring nor scooting away with clear distrust as he has in the past, Bragi dares to hope his request will only be rejected in a nonchalant way.

"It happens in the womb." But Bragi is pleasantly surprised when Aske actually does answer his question on this.

"We're born in litters, so to speak, never less than three. I know of someone who had seven siblings, but they didn't last long." And the answer is so intriguing as well.

"In the womb, you say. Is it something that happens because you're very in tune with magic, and because children in the womb are close?" Aske shrugs, scratching at his throat. Bragi tries to avoid looking at the marks left by old wounds there. He can't see them too clearly, but he can see the scarred tissue beneath Aske's fingertips.

"I've never wondered why. It's always been a fact, a normal thing for me, just like changing my shape is. I've always just assumed that is how the Goddess made us." That is a fair assumption. The Goddess, upon her creation of the world and all those who live in it, had made sure to give every species something others didn't have. The diversity of abilities is endless.

"Can you shift into another person?"

"If we could, we wouldn't be living in hiding now, would we?" Aske snarks, and Bragi raises his hands in apology once again.

"Fair point. Is the animal form set from birth?"

"What's got you so curious all of a sudden?" Aske narrows his eyes, that familiar spark of suspicion in his eyes once again, but Bragi rolls his eyes.

"It's not 'all of a sudden'. You know I enjoy knowledge. If you're willing to share, I'd love to learn. People are less afraid of what they know. Knowledge and understanding brings peace and makes it easier to avoid conflict." So, Aske explains it, curtly and snidely, how shapeshifters experiment as children, and as they grow older, they find a shape they are the most comfortable with, and at a certain point in time, they stop changing into more than just the one animal, because it just feels so wrong. Like a limiter. It is quite fascinating to learn all of this, and Bragi laments that he doesn't have any parchment and ink on him. Then again, Aske might not have taken well to seeing Bragi writing down everything he tells him now. He will just have to do his best to remember until he does have some paper and ink on hand.

"I've never quite understood why some groups of humans suddenly began attacking you. It's not written down anywhere, and you're as much children of the Goddess as the rest of us are." Aske stares at him. Each and every creature in this world exists because the Goddess willed them into being, that is indeed true, but that's never stopped anyone from committing atrocities towards others in her name before, either.

"The last one who got me told me it was the will of the Goddess for us beasts to die."

"Now that is just preposterous!" Bragi exclaims. "Absolute bullshit, really! Never once has it been recorded in any temple or scripture that the Goddess would want that!"

"How would you know?" Aske challenges, but Bragi is undeterred.

"Aske, my friend, I've travelled for over two decades, reading every little tome I could get my hands on, and I've found no such intention anywhere. Even priests haven't! No, this was no order from the Goddess, it's just pure audacity by a group who've decided that what they say goes! They use her as a convenient excuse, and that is all there is to it!" It is oddly nice to have another human grow so incensed with the notion that the Goddess would wish for her creations to hunt down and hurt each other in her name. He is much too used to seeing people turn away from those in danger, muttering excuses so as not to be dragged into trouble and keeping their conscience clean while not *'taking sides'*. It is refreshing to see Bragi condemn such a notion so vehemently.

"Goodness, it would be the same as if cyclopes, shapeshifters, fairies, trolls and magical beasts all banded together to erase all of humanity from the face of the earth and claim it to be the Goddess' will."

"If such a thing were to happen, all of humanity would band together and decide that all non-humans must be exterminated." Aske mutters.

"Quite!" Bragi exclaims, before deflating. "Oh, we would, wouldn't we? We have a nasty habit of thinking we're superior, and therefore favourites of the Goddess."

"Oh yes, it truly is a nasty habit of your kind." Aske throws out nonchalantly. He tries to ignore the way Bragi has deflated beside him, but it's hard to do so. He looks crestfallen at the thought, and much older than he truly is, as if the cruelty some humans show others, the pain they inflict deliberately with savage glee is his responsibility. It's ridiculous, because the responsibility isn't on some lone human out here travelling the world and doing some good. Bragi isn't like the ones who hunt non-humans. He seems to truly care less about someone's species and more of what he can learn about them. And an eagerness to learn, that's not so bad. Because Bragi is right, it is easier to not fear what one knows.

Aske has slowly come to realize that he's been letting his guard down more and more lately. It is no surprise he has slowly begun to trust the man, or at least his intentions. It is a scary thought, terrifying even, but not surprising. Even so, he trusts the man's intentions, but not the man himself, not fully at least.

Yet he can't help but feel a slight nugget of guilt about the gloom they're surrounded by now, because he hasn't treated Bragi *well*, exactly. And Bragi has done nothing to deserve being mistreated, besides being a bastard at times, so with the most dramatic groan he can muster to lighten the mood, as if his next actions will be a considerable hardship, Aske makes an effort at being somewhat kind.

"Relax, it's not like *all* of humanity is nasty, just like not all of us other species are inherently good either." He throws his hands in the air again.

"You just have a tendency to, you know, all too quickly believe that if one of us do something inconvenient for you, we're all bad." There's the slightest tug upwards of Bragi's lips, and Aske, for some reason, counts that as a victory. At the very least the brunet no longer appears so melancholy or sad. Sad just doesn't suit this human. He has laugh lines across his face, crow's feet crinkling the corner of his eyes, and it's more attractive when he smiles, even though his beard is more of a bird's nest now than a proper beard. He really should trim it.

"We do have a terrible habit of doing that, yes. No wonder you don't trust me."

"No, I trust you." The words are out before Aske can stop them. Rather, they escape before he even realizes himself what he said. Having the words articulated out loud solidifies the truth of them though, makes it real, now that both he and Bragi has heard it. He stops short, staring down at his feet. Hadn't he just thought that he *didn't* trust Bragi, only his intentions? But now that the words are out there, it's hard to take them back. Of course, he can make a fuss and claim that he was just joking, just pulling the human's leg, so to speak, and he contemplates it as he looks up again. The sheer unbridled joy on Bragi's face makes those words die on the shapeshifter's tongue. The words are out, they are real.

There is no taking them back.

CHAPTER SIXTEEN

The marketplace is bustling. It is so lively and there are so many people Aske feels like he is suffocating. He's let his hair down, like a curtain around his head, and the coloured lenses Gunvald gave him upon his departure are firmly planted on his face, hiding his odd eyes. He feels antsy, even as they move through the market rather quickly, picking up supplies as they go. It's been quite some time since they've passed through a settlement instead of around one, and while they've managed well until now, the weather has grown colder the further north they go. There is less to hunt, Aske just wishes this hadn't been a purely human settlement.

He is anxious that someone will knock his lenses away and reveal his eyes. He feels like the world is shrinking, as if he's unable to breathe, people flocking closer, faceless, and ominous and dangerous-

"Aske?" He jolts when Bragi pats his shoulder gently, so startled he nearly loses the glasses he's trying so hard to keep on. He scrambles to keep them in place, breathing erratically as he turns to look down at Bragi who appear worried. The redhead snaps at him, asks what he wants, but Bragi only motions for him to follow him. The human is a few steps ahead of Aske, and while the road they're taking now is less populated than the market, there are still too many people around them for Aske's comfort. It is terrifying, and before the shapeshifter is even aware of his own actions, his right hand reaches out for Bragi's cloak. If he grabs hold of it, they won't get separated, he'd feel safer, is what his subconscious tells him. He recoils when he realizes what he's doing. He's not a bloody child, he can walk on his own. He feels stupid, and disgusted by his own fear, and he grits his teeth so hard his jaw aches and throbs. Then they're at the stables, and Bragi has him readying their lone horse for the next leg of their journey while the human speaks with the stable master.

Aske leads the horse out of the gates when Bragi motions for him to move on without him, but he waits just a few steps outside. When Bragi comes out with a second horse's reins in his hands, he frowns.

"What's that?"

"This, my friend, is a horse." Aske grimaces, not amused at all as he crosses his arms, tilting his head backwards a bit, glaring down his nose at the other.

"I can see that. I'm wondering what you're doing with it when you already have Gerd here." He pats the large horse's long neck as she whinnies, seemingly agreeing with the shapeshifter.

"I bought a second one." Bragi just smiles, appearing very pleased with himself.

"Why?" The redhead sputters. He may not have travelled for a long time, but he's well aware that horses are still very much beasts of burden that human put a high value on. They aren't cheap, and while Aske doesn't understand the new currencies or how much of value Bragi carries with him, a second horse is just a waste at this point.

"Why not? Our journey will progress much faster like this."

"It's a waste of coins, Bragi!" Aske finally exclaims, not believing that he must explain this to the human who's so far not appeared to be a person to do wasteful things.

"We're parting ways soon! What's the point of a second horse?" The brunet's smile drops a little bit before he recovers by clearing his throat.

"Well, when we part ways, you can keep her. She's been a good horse, I'm sure you'll find her useful, and you wouldn't look like a grown man riding a pony with her. I'll keep this one." That strikes Aske speechless. This human is good. To the very core of him, honest to the Goddess, good. He should be used to this now, shouldn't he? At this point, for the short time they've been travelling together, Bragi's been nothing but kind and good. Why is Aske still finding himself surprised of this by now?

"Besides, I got her for a very low price because of her limp."

"Limp?" Aske exclaims. "You bought a horse with a limp when you're journeying great and uneven distances?" Aske takes back every kind thing he's ever entertained about the human, that is just cruel. To use this poor creature as a beast of burden when she has an injured leg, he wants to punch the other in the face for it. It must show too, because Bragi waves a hand at him.

"Hush now, there's a reason for it. You'll see when we've left the town." Bragi winks at him, but the shapeshifter doesn't join the cheer, he just scowls at the other. He follows without a complaint though he watches the horse carefully. True, she has a limp, and she appears to be in quite a lot of pain too. The kind thing to do here would be to put her out of her misery, but here they are, with Bragi forcing the poor thing to follow him on an aimless journey.

"Ah, this should be far enough," Bragi says as he stops the horse from moving any further. He offers apologies the beast probably doesn't understand much of as he pats her flank and hands the reins over to Aske, whose scowl has darkened considerably during the short distance they walked.

"Keep the poor lass still for me."

"Still? Poor lass? You're the one forcing her to walk on a hurt leg!"

"And now I'm going to heal that hurt leg," he tells the redhead with a wide grin and Aske just stares as he takes the reins into his own hands. Bragi kneels onto the ground and carefully palms the wounded leg. The mare jerks, as if anticipating more pain, but the human shushes her gently. Aske watches in fascination as Bragi's hands glow faintly, and the horse seems to relax her stance after some time. It takes quite some time, more than Aske thought it would since it's magic, but the glow fades, and Bragi smiles again, even as he's slow to get back up on his feet. He winces as his body protests the treatment it was subjected to.

"There, now she's all fine. Just need some nourishing, tasty food, and exercise, and she'll get plenty of both while she's with me," he says, to assure both the animal and shapeshifter. Aske just stares, dumbfounded, before he bursts out laughing. Bragi is surprised. He's never heard Aske laugh like this before. He's quite sure he hasn't heard Aske laugh at all, now that he thinks about it.

"You're a real bastard!" The shapeshifter exclaims while holding his sides, nearly falling over with the force of his laughter, only keeping on his feet by leaning on Gerd. "You cheated the stablemaster!"

"*I did no such thing!*" Bragi huffs, offended. "I paid what she was worth! She had a *limp*!"

"Which you now have healed! You bought her because you knew you could heal her!" He's still laughing, it's just too funny. This person whom he had almost started to believe was a saint, is turning out to be as shrewd and devious as any other, though in the best kind of way. Bragi appears both greatly flustered and embarrassed, which just enforces Aske's view that he is a bastard. He knows exactly what he did. Bragi huffs loudly though, trying to do so much louder than the redhead's laughter, straightening his back the best he can to look stern, despite his apple-red cheeks rimming his beard.

"Was I supposed to let her suffer?" This does nothing to stop Aske's laughter, he actually devolves into snorts and gasps as he tries to speak.

"No one said you had to buy her." And that is fair, Bragi could have healed her back at the stables out of the goodness of his heart before following Aske.

"And why did you feel like you had to move us away before healing the poor girl?" Aske throws out accusingly, though in a most amused manner, waiting for Bragi to explain himself for his secrecy.

"Oh, w-well, I…" Bragi begins valiantly, but quickly trails off, words failing him because he has no excuse. He has no explanation at all, and it makes Aske, who had managed to calm down a little, burst into a new fit of snickers as he begins leading Gerd down the path. The horse whinnies again, seemingly just as amused as the shapeshifter. Bragi feels quite outnumbered. By a horse and a serpent, no less.

"You are a bastard."

"That is *quite* enough!" Bragi attempts to go for stern, but the pink in his cheeks and ears do nothing to help him salvage his dignity. Aske just shakes his head at him, the smirk so wide on his cheeks Bragi nearly hopes his face splits with it.

"An absolute bastard!"

CHAPTER SEVENTEEN

It is a cold and dreary evening, the heavy rainfall outside the cave they were lucky to find before the sky opened up on them trapping them both physically and emotionally. The heavy rain mirrors the mood the two are in too. Aske tries to ignore it, tries to focus on that heartbeat in the back of his mind, the presence that keeps him aware that his last living sibling is still alive, still moving, coming closer each passing day. That's the important bit, that is why he's out here in the middle of nowhere. But the continued badly supressed sniffling from Bragi's bedroll combined with the too cold air makes it impossible for the shapeshifter to fall asleep. Despite the calming draught the healer made for him, even, which makes him drowsy. It's just not enough right now. It leaves him in a terrible mood because he is tired, he is exhausted, he wants to *sleep*.

"Bragi." He pushes himself up on his elbows, and the human stills, holding his breath. From the remaining light of their dying fire Aske can see the tremors possessing the other man.

"*Bragi*," he repeats with more force, his voice carrying a purpose. "There was nothing you could do." A hiccup tears through the air and Aske runs a hand over his face, cursing quietly to himself. That was the wrong thing to say, apparently. Even though it is a fact.

"She was just too hurt, her wounds were too great. Magic isn't a miracle cure for dea-" another whimper escapes Bragi, and Aske gnashes his teeth together, reminding himself to keep calm. The healer is upset, reasonably so, too. He is a sympathetic and empathic man, and he is a healer who wants to do what he can for others. It is just the very core of his personality.

"Are you- you're not blaming yourself, are you?" The shapeshifter asks incredulously. Bragi shakes his head.

"No, but-but…"

"But what?" The redhead snaps, just a little bit too harsh, enough that he can see the human flinch, hears another hiccup, and he bites his tongue to keep from saying anything more, anything worse, because that is kind of his thing, isn't it? Around Bragi, at the very least. He always says the wrong thing around Bragi. Always uses words which *cut*, words which end up hurting the other, even when he doesn't mean to.

"She was so *young!*" The healer practically wails, voice cracking. It's been building up for this since this morning, Aske shouldn't be surprised over the cry that escapes Bragi at this point, but it is still harrowing. And he can understand it, because he is upset too.

When travelling that morning, they had come upon a child on the road, all alone, abandoned and in a terrible condition, to the point they didn't see that it was in fact a human girl at first. Aske had known immediately that there was nothing they could do, had expected Bragi to realize it too, but the man had vaulted off his horse and hastened over, his powers coming to life immediately, however… it hadn't helped.

Aske had helped dig her grave, Bragi had offered a silent prayer, and then they had continued their journey. It had been obvious that Bragi had taken the little girl's death hard. Aske can't say he is completely unaffected either, but he's not going to cry or lose sleep over it. Yes, a little girl had died, yes, it is horrible that someone would do such a thing to her and leave her on the road like that for the vultures to pick at her once she succumbed, but still… He dug her a grave, whispered an apology for not having the ability to help, and that was that. It's not the first child he's buried. There is simply no avoiding it sometimes, the bad things in the world, but agonizing over it won't change anything. Accepting it and moving on is the best solution. Sometimes bad things happen, and you can't stop it.

But Bragi is losing sleep over it, and as much as Aske just wants to turn back around and sleep, it is not going to happen while the healer is sobbing his pretty little heart out. Thus, he gets up, grabs his bedroll and shuffles over to lie down beside Bragi, who is so surprised that his tears stop for a moment.

"Stop crying," Aske tells him as he lays down and pulls Bragi with him, awkwardly holding him as a means of comfort, like he remembers doing for his siblings as a child. The angle is a bit awkward, considering he's so tall compared to Bragi and the brunet's smaller bedroll, but he's not interested in shifting about.

"Bad and sad things happen, not everyone gets their happy ending, not everyone can be saved, it's not your responsibility, now shut up and *sleep*." It is not the kindest way to phrase things, it is probably not the proper way to phrase it either, but Bragi doesn't object. He just turns away, and after a few more sniffles, he stills. Aske very nearly sighs in relief. He's not good at comforting others. Even if he chooses the right words, he usually muck things up because he relays them in the wrong way. He had just now too. He hadn't been wrong, though. The girl had been viciously hurt, it was a wonder she had been conscious when they came upon her, and yes, she was young, too young. But she wasn't Bragi's responsibility, nor his burden to bear. The world is unfair, it's cruel, there's no changing that.

But Aske hadn't been very careful in his delivery of the message. And he knows he could have put in a bit more effort, because Bragi is someone who's genuinely good down to his core. It's just that even though Aske knows that the brunet is good at heart, he is out of practice showing gentleness himself. He grunts, tries to roll his shoulder, but it only serves to make him more uncomfortable in his position. At the very least Bragi is warm, which helps to make the shapeshifter drowsy again.

The human is *warm,* and the part of Aske that is reptilian now, after having been part serpent for centuries, basks in it.

'Well,' Aske thinks as he sinks into sleep, '*that's a thing.*'

The next morning isn't a chipper one, but at the very least Bragi seem to no longer be in any danger of breaking into tears again. He's not very talkative either. He has no questions, and he's not attempting to start up any conversations. His gloominess is almost as annoying as his overly cheerful self is. It annoys Aske that he finds it annoying, for it is proof that he cares. Cares about a human.

True, the human has helped him out a lot for quite some time now, and apparently, Aske has grown to trust him, but still.

"Aske?" He blinks, Bragi's quiet voice snapping him out of his thoughts.

"What?" And he grinds his teeth, jaw very nearly locking, because he did it again. Snapping harshly, when he could have just asked what the human wants in a normal manner, like a civilized being.

"Thank you." Bragi seem unbothered though. "For last night. I needed that."

"What? For me stating a fact?" He sneers, and great, buggering bollocks, can he just for once be able to control his own damn tongue? He's not even aware that his own shoulders have risen to his ears, body tense and a grimace marring his face as he waits for the scolding he knows he deserves, when Bragi just stares straightforward as he answers.

"Yes." Aske is caught off guard, and his mouth works at forming words without any connection to his mind, so all that comes out is stuttered garble.

"Ngk, well, I, uh, you're welcome? I guess?" This is awkward, he doesn't quite know what to reply, he's not used to this, emotions and feelings and sincerity and all that-

"It must have been incredibly difficult for you, trying to be nice." Bragi is still sad, he's still mourning the death of a life he couldn't save. The tired lines across his face and the pronounced crow's feet make him appear so old, but the slight upwards quirk of his lips visible beneath the beard, that barely-there hint of humour, makes Aske pause.

"You're such a dick." He doesn't mean it in a bad way, there is no bite to his words, but he still wonders if he overstepped. Then the quirk blossoms into a small smile, and Aske can't help but grin a bit toothily himself.

"Takes one to know one."

"Bastard!"

"One would think that someone who is positively *ancient*-" Aske sputters indignantly at the insult, "might have a more extensive vocabulary." The shapeshifter glowers, before he straightens in his seat on his horse, nose high in the air as he retorts.

"When speaking with someone who is no older than a foal, one must use simple language that is easy to understand, even that of a baby." Now it is Bragi who gasps offended.

"*I beg your bloody pardon?*"

"Don't worry, it is quite understandable that it's hard for you to keep up, but I suggest you stop throwing tantrums if you want a good-night hug tonight."

"Oh, *bite me!*"

"Gladly." Bragi flushes an adorable pink, sputtering himself, before he bursts out laughing, Aske joining him. By the time they've both managed to calm down, they've moved quite the distance. The girl is not forgotten, her painful end even less so, but there's a slight brightness between them now, a sort of normalcy that is quite welcome. Bragi feels better, and Aske feels less awkward. Somehow, poking fun at each other like this has changed something, and despite the fact that Aske is no fan of humans, and that three centuries of pain, fear and grief caused by one single species won't be erased by such easy banter with just one person, he doesn't mind this at all.

CHAPTER EIGHTEEN

"Mam! Look!" Saga has allowed the both of them a short time of reprieve, and Runa is prancing about in a calm river. She's cleaned herself, and her clothes lay sprawled on the riverbank, and now she's playing in the water which reach just above her navel. There is something precious about watching her last remaining child play in the water, smile so brightly and laugh in a carefree manner.

"What are they?" The little girl points at a being that looks like nothing more than a slightly enlarged tuft of grass, floating in the water. If it weren't for its beady black eyes and grinning sharp teeth, Saga would have mistaken it for nothing more than grass taken by the river further up.

"A Vannokk," Saga tells her daughter, smiling in a carefree manner herself, but she readies herself to move swiftly if she must. Vannokk's are tricky creatures. They can either be very playful, or they can be deadly. It all depends on how the creature perceives the people who come close.

"This river is probably their home." And Runa is standing right in the middle of it.

"Oh no!" Runa exclaims and wades over to the vannokk before Saga can stop her.

"I'm so sorry! I dirtied your home!" Saga gets up on her feet, ready to leap forward and yank her daughter out of the water if need be, just as the girl continues.

"Runa!"

"But Mam! I peed in the water," Runa says, cheeks colouring with shame and embarrassment. Saga feels a moment of panic. The vannokk must already know, they must be so offended, angry, but bubbles break the surface of the small stream, and laughter follows. It sounds like gargling, like someone is drowning, but the vannokk appear joyful, even splashing the young shapeshifter, causing her to shriek with laughter.

Saga relaxes back in her seat. The vannokk is not offended. This could have ended very differently, but all's well that ends well, and her shoulders sag as she exhales in relief. For now, Runa can continue to play, and be a child. Saga will allow it for a little while longer. She deserves some fun, after how strong she's been this entire time.

And some food as well.

"Runa, be courteous to the vannokk while I go find us something to eat," she tells the little girl. There are fish in the river, but Saga has no interest in making the wrong move and angering the water creature. She doesn't manage to take more than a few steps before a fish is tossed out onto the muddy riverbank. Runa shrieks in delight, clapping her hands together as the vannokk toss out a couple more. Saga just stares, not quite believing what she's seeing. First Hildingr, now this little creature, offering their aid without being prompted, without any demands in return.

"Mam, you're crying?" The older shapeshifter startles, hand nearly striking her own face as she makes to check if her daughter's words are true. She is indeed crying. The vannokk has moved closer to the bank, tilting their head at her when they break the surface. Before the creature can think that she is refusing their offer, she bows her head reverently.

"Thank you." Her voice cracks. Such small acts of kindness are enough to break her composure now. After all the hardships, grief and pain, just a small act of kindness causes cracks in her armor.

"You're really kind, vannok! Thank you." Runa has trudged up from the water now and is grinning widely, as if believing that as long as she smiles, everything will turn out alright. Saga musters up a smile of her own as she swipes at the tears.

"Yes, indeed, you're being very kind. We owe you, thank you so much." The vannokk just makes that gurgling laugh again before disappearing down the stream. That is the last they see of the creature before they get dressed again, eat, and move on. The small break they've allowed themselves was very much needed to raise their spirits, and the journey continues at a quicker pace now.

Five days after they've left, a group of humans come upon the stream. The vannokk watches them trample the soft earth and kicking dirt into their home, making the once clear water turn into a dark, muddy, and dirty colour. The vannokk doesn't appreciate it. The little shapeshifter had been clueless, but innocent, good at heart. The older shapeshifter had been wary at first, but respectful at the same time. It had all been in good fun, but these people, these human men and women, they're not showing any respect or consideration. The vannokk is not pleased with this.

"This is definitively the tracks of those shape changing beasts," one of the beasts say as they examine the bank. "They crossed this stream only a few days ago. We're gaining on them."

"We're not letting them get away. For making us track them all this way, I'll skin the brat alive in front of its mother!" A man with shaved head and a scar across his forehead snarls, clearly agitated by the entire situation.

The vannokk doesn't like what they're hearing. They can also better understand the wistfulness and wariness of the older shapeshifter as the child played in the river. They are being hunted, they are scared, they have suffered. And these humans plan on causing more suffering. To do that, they must cross the stream, and the vannokk has no intention of making that easy for them.

The humans begin to wade into the water, and the vannokk moves closer, it's algae-like arms reaching out and ensnaring two pairs of feet, then it yanks. Startled yells are cut short as the water levels of the stream rises just enough for the humans to be unable to fight their way back up to the surface and to discourage the other humans still on land from getting in. The vannokk pulls them flat to the bottom of the stream, watching them fight to break free. There are yells from the humans on land as well, and swords are being drawn as they see the creature in the water. The vannokk cleverly hides beneath the body of one of its victims, grinning viciously as they fight and fight, only to quickly weaken. The group out of the water quickly realize that the only way to reach the river-dweller is to cut into their own comrades, or to brave the water themselves.

Two make an attempt only to end up in the same situation as the two they wanted to save. Four of the group drown in the little stream, and the vannokk hurries to follow the current of the stream to escape, its gurgling laughter following.

That is what the humans get for trampling all over their home and dragging mud into it.

"Fuck, it got our tracker," one of the human's snarls angrily as he glares down at the bodies bobbing in the stream.

"She managed to give us a general direction before the beast took her. Let's hurry, and we'll catch up," another chimes in, sounding far too calm for someone who watched members of his group drown so brutally. Cautiously they cross the stream, leaving their dead behind.

"Still no word from Bjorn?"

"No. The owl was a useless lead, we shouldn't have followed it, and the other tracks were fake too."

"I don't like this. It's like there's a force keeping the wretches out of our grasp. We'll keep on going, assuming Bjorn and the others will catch up later, if they haven't got themselves killed for nothing."

"What about-"

"Leave them in the fucking stream. We've got bigger fish to catch. I'll rid this world of that last piece of shape changing freak family even if it is the last thing I'll ever do." Nobody argues because they know exactly what kind of life they chose by following this man. And he is right, ridding the world of the scourge the Goddess regretted creating is more important than burying the bodies of fallen comrades while on a hunt.

It's all for the sake of correcting the world the way the Goddess truly wishes for it to be.

CHAPTER NINETEEN

Their moods have been brighter since meeting the vannokk, and Runa, in the shape of a squirrel on her mother's shoulder is playing with the other shapeshifter's hair.

"The vannokk was really cute."

"It was, because it was in a good mood," Saga replies. It could have been a less pleasant meeting if the vannokk had been in a terrible mood. Saga isn't sure she would have been able to save Runa if the river-dweller had decided to attack. It is a terrifying and chilling thought, to know that her abilities are out of her reach when they are in such a vulnerable situation.

"Mam?"

"What?"

"You disappeared." Saga blinks. The quiet, worried tone of voice Runa used is unsettling. She must have become worried when her mother stopped responding. Saga musters up a reassuring smile.

"I just got a little bit lost in thought, sweetling. What did you say?"

"Is it still a long time until we're safe?"

"Safe, yes, safer, no. Look, in this direction we're heading now, straight forward, my brother is heading towards us now. He is moving very quickly; we'll meet in a few days, at the longest. Don't worry, Runa, we won't be alone for much longer." Runa nods her head along, chirping.

"I'm excited to see him! What's he like?" Saga welcomes the new subject wholeheartedly. She tells Runa about her brother, what kind of magic he prefers, or what she knew he preferred back in the past before they parted ways, what his animal form is like, and all the things she remembers, the traits of him that she so valued, all that which makes him the brother she cares so much about. But when every little trait, every little piece of information she tells her daughter causes the girl to connect him to each and every last one of her lost siblings, she feels her steps falter a bit, her smile waver. Her heart hadn't been prepared for that, but now that it has been brought out in the open, she cannot help but admit that it is true. A reptile like Ebba, good with plants like Halle, kind but clumsy like Alv, always looking out for his family like Ana. Curious like Runa. Copper hair like herself and all five of them.

"He's also tall, taller than *me*, even, and strong. He was once called a fire serpent, when he went around as a serpent with fire breath. We'll be safe with him."

"I hope you're right, Mam. I'm really, really tired." Tired of running, tired of being scared, tired of not having a safe space, tired of not being able to play and be happy and just be a child. Saga feels horrible about it, she has from the very beginning, but they can't put down any roots on their own. They need safety, something Saga is unable to secure on her own now that she can't change her shape. Oh, if only she could, she would have been able to carry Runa and fly, fly to Sanctuary. Their journey would have been less perilous, and they would have already found her brother.

They could be heading somewhere safe already, they wouldn't have left a trail for the hunters to follow. Their situation would just generally have been better. But there's no use crying over their situation right now. She can cry when there is no one at their heels.

'Soon,' she thinks. It's not much of a journey left now, but she still wishes that they could be much closer to their goal. She is exhausted from being constantly afraid and feeling inadequate too.

"Mam?"

"Hmm?"

"I hear footsteps." Saga's heart stutters in her chest, and she tries to keep calm as she tries to rationalize the situation they are now in. It can be anyone, lots of people journey around in the world, it is quite normal, but just to be on the safe side, she'll quicken their pace. Better be safe than sorrier than she already is.

"Tell me if they get any closer." There's a city up front, Saga can see the tops of the spires. She had no intention of passing through any settlements, but maybe she'll have to anyways, to lose any kind of pursuers. It might be the only way.

"They're getting closer! Quickly!" Runa exclaims, trembling all over and losing control of her shifting, turning back into herself and tumbling off of her mother's shoulder. Saga manages to wrangle a hold of her before she crashes onto the ground.

"Runa?"

"It's them, Mam!" The little girl whimpers, clutching to her mother's worn cloak. Saga hurriedly wraps Runa in it and looks around. She can't see anyone yet, so she dashes off the road and deep into the woods and away from the city. She finds a hollowed tree by chance just as she too begins to pick up on the sound of heavy steps and raised voices. Thankfully the hollow is just big enough for Runa to climb in and hide, and she tells the girl to climb in.

"Hide here, and don't come out until it's safe!" She hisses and forces the tree bark to bend without breaking it and cover just enough that Runa can't be easily seen. It is a crudely done job, Saga has never been good at manipulating nature in this way, but it will have to do. As long as Runa stays still and quiet, it will work.

"But Mam-"

"Listen to me, Runa! You're all I have left! If I don't come back, keep heading past that human city, same direction we walked. You'll find him, you'll find Aske, and he'll protect you, I promise!"

"Mam-" Runa begins to argue, but Saga shuts her down.

"Don't argue but listen! You're not allowed to get hurt! Hide, and then keep moving so Aske finds you! He will protect you." Without giving her daughter another chance at arguing any further, Saga leaves. She is grateful that Runa makes no sound that she can hear as she sprints away, steeling herself and getting ready for a chase. No matter what, she needs to get them away from her last child.

"There!" She nearly trips as she hears the shout and chances a look over her shoulder. It *is* them. It's them. The memories of that horrible day return with a vengeance, and she stops short, legs refusing to carry her any further, her body refusing to create any more distance between them.

These people killed her children and their sire. In front of her, in front of Runa. They cheered about it, as if it had been a great feat, a great battle worthy of ballads around a campfire. Four innocent eight year old children who had done nothing, caused no harm. Four innocent children who had merely been playing together not too far from their home. Four innocent children who had been experimenting with their powers, learning and playing.

Her children!

She must have blacked out for a moment because the next thing she is aware of is throwing the one who had managed to close in on her first to the ground, flopping down onto his chest, knees pinning his arms.

"Get off of me, vile-" he manages to roar before she digs her thumbs into his eye sockets, turning his rage into pain and fear. He wails, trashing about, body trying to buck her off, but she's got a tight grip on his head, her long fingers wrapping around his skull and quickly applying pressure. She had spoken the truth to Hildingr when she had boasted her strength. Yes, she looks tall and gangly and more like awkwardly spindly and long limbs than anything else, but she's strong, strong enough to have this man's skull cracking beneath the force she's applying to it, to feel the dense bone give as her thumbs flick about erratically and cause him more pain and damage.

"I will crush your skull, human," she sneers, "like your companions did to my daughter." Before he can catch his breath to shout for help, his skull caves in, and Saga lurches forward, hands sliding through bone and brain mass as she pushes herself to her feet, hurling herself towards the next human in the party. He raises his weapon, a club. She remembers the sound such a weapon had made as it broke the leg of her second oldest, the scream she had made as she fell over with no support still haunts Saga. She dodges the swing, rolls across the ground under it before scrambling back up on her feet, turning her back to the others running towards her.

It is reckless and stupid to turn her back on her enemies, but Saga is so enraged, so overcome with all the emotions she has bottled up over such a long period of time, the overwhelming raw emotions stripping her of her reasoning. She launches herself forward, grabs hold of the club and wrenches it out of his grip. Then she attacks. She hits at his chest, the blow so powerful there is a loud crack as he falls over, gasping. She stands tall above him, raising the club and bludgeoning him until his face is unrecognizable.

There's a yell, and she instinctively swings around, the club hitting an oncoming sword with such force her new attacker loses their grip on it, and she rears back.

There are only two left. If she gets rid of these two, she can buy herself and Runa some time, just enough to get to her brother, enough to get to relative safety. She swings, intent on sending the third person to the ground, when something coarse hits her face, and some sort of powder flutters about her, fogging her sight.

"We got her!" She hears distant shouting, and just as the world starts spinning does she realize what is happening. She had seen her children's father be surrounded by similar powder and dropping like a sack of stones. She swings widely as she covers her nose, but it is already too late. Her body moves sluggishly, and her mind feels drowsy, her sight fuzzy at the corners.

"No!" she slurs as she stumbles. 'No!' She is succumbing to the powder, whatever it is, and finds herself suddenly falling over, even as her limbs swing wildly to keep the last of the hunters at bay. It is a futile act of self-preservation, and she knows it. The world is spinning as she falls, and just for a second, just before she loses consciousness, she thinks she sees Runa standing out in the open.

But that is impossible, right? After all, Runa is still hiding in the tree. Isn't she?

CHAPTER TWENTY

Bragi is aware that he is staring, but what else can he do? Aske has, quite literally, coiled himself around him like the serpent he is, and the human doesn't quite have it in him to wake the shapeshifter. He's finally sleeping well, after several nights of restless sleep because of the cold weather which his anatomy was in no way, shape or form prepared for.

To think that choosing a form makes shapeshifters not only take on an animal's strength, but also weaknesses.

But it's not only the fact that Aske is finally asleep that stops Bragi from waking him up. Aske looks remarkable, really. Such a deep, rich copper colour to his long hair, a smattering of freckles over his high cheekbones, and when asleep like this, when his brow isn't forced into a near constant furrow, he looks rather peaceful. He hadn't appeared like this at the mountain village, even while resting, never truly allowing himself to relax with Bragi around even once the pain and discomfort receded.

So, yes, Bragi is staring, but he can't find the will to stop. Doesn't make much of an effort to do so, in truth. They have a peaceful morning, the sun is just dawning, they have time. Now that they are so close, with Aske suddenly curling forward and his hair parting over the back of his neck, Bragi sees something there, branded into the thin skin, marks he has seen before but kept from looking properly at. Carefully he reaches out, fingertips brushing over the scar tissue before yanking his hand back as if burned.

He knows what those marks are, and he feels sick down to his stomach. The morning no longer feels all that pleasant.

"Whazzat?" Aske jerks away and Bragi pulls back, slipping out of the sleeping mat as casually as he is capable of.

"I'm about to make us breakfast. Feel free to doze a bit longer," he tells the shapeshifter, who does a full body stretch as he yawns.

"Is too cold for that," Aske mutters, starting to roll the mat together. Bragi offers a fond smile as he begins searching a satchel for food.

"Did you sleep well?" he asks, just to keep his mind on other things than those scars.

"Yes." The brunet's smile widens just a bit. It is not so long ago that Aske would narrow his eyes at him in suspicion whenever Bragi would ask questions as mundane as these. Now he just answers, and that's very nice, makes the entire journey less awkward. Not that it doesn't still have its awkward moments.

Such as that morning where Aske woke up first, and Bragi had been drooling all over his tunic. Aske still laughs at him for that now and again. Well, it is not awkward as much as it was embarrassing, really, and that isn't so bad. It lightens the mood sometimes, makes the journey easier. And what a pleasant journey this has turned out to become. Bragi admits that he had forgotten how nice it is to not be alone all the time while on the road.

"We'll be parting ways soon," Aske suddenly speaks up and Bragi stops short, a sinking feeling in his stomach. Ah. He turns, sees Aske rubbing the back of his neck in a manner that suggests he is highly uncomfortable with the subject, and that just won't do. Aske has been clear on it since the very beginning that he will never allow Bragi to follow him all the way to the end. That Bragi feels disappointment over that fact, that they will be parting ways soon is neither the redheads' fault nor responsibility. He shouldn't feel uncomfortable with voicing a boundary he so vehemently set from the beginning. Bragi knew it would come sooner or later.

"I understand, my dear." And he does, he truly does. It doesn't make the twinge in his chest hurt any less, but he understands. But it is not Aske's fault that Bragi's heart is a disobedient thing, it is not Aske's fault that Bragi has come to find him endearing and lovely. That the brunet has grown fond of him is no one's fault but the human himself, and he won't burden his companion with any thought of responsibility or guilt. It is why he has kept those thoughts to himself, ever since he realized they were fluttering about in the back of his head.

"I'm glad we managed to stay together for as long as we did. Truly, it has been a pleasure." Aske seems even more uncomfortable now, which truly isn't Bragi's intention. He bites his tongue in an effort to not make this worse, even more awkward and uncomfortable than it already is.

"Yeah," Aske agrees, "it wasn't half-bad." The way he avoids eye contact is rather painful too. Up until just now, Bragi had the impression that Aske had gotten comfortable around him. Had he been wrong? Is there no friendship? At the very least?

'No,' he thinks later on as they've begun moving again and Aske is in the middle of telling a tale that sounds so incredibly farfetched the healer can hardly believe him when Aske claims that it is true. No, Aske is comfortable with his presence, doesn't mind having him around. Aske doesn't mind his presence anymore, not in the way he did when they first met. They do have a friendship, tentative and frail it might be, but it is there.

Which makes a tiny flicker of hope grow in his Bragi's heart. Aske may not want to part ways either. He may not actually *want* to part ways, but that is a traitorous thought the human squashes immediately. When one thinks like this, one quickly grows to wish and crave it to be the truth. He cannot allow himself to fall into that rabbit-hole. He cannot allow himself to be expecting something that will never happen. It will only lead to disappointment, in the end. An unnecessary hurt he does not need to carry with him.

Even when evening comes, and they huddle together under the same blanket and Aske curls a bit closer to him, Bragi resolutely tries to think of everything else. But it is so difficult when he sleeps so close, so trusting, looking so lovely, when he is so completely relaxed against Bragi, whom he had distrusted so much only a few months prior. It is a precious, but also fragile thing, and Bragi finds himself selfishly wanting to hold onto it, sink his fingers in and grab an unyielding hold of it, never letting go. He's never felt as strongly as this before, and he shakes his head. It is not as if he could have known the close proximity and camaraderie would cause such emotions to spring forth and fester in his chest, but he should have. He should have known, should have fought to keep a certain distance, as he keeps with patients. It would have made things much easier.

Nothing good will come out of these thoughts, he knows it. And if he is to act on it, he runs the risk of ruining this tentative friendship of theirs. No, calling it tentative is no longer correct, is it? It has a fragile foundation, but their friendship is sturdy now, which makes it all the more important to protect it from a selfish and one-sided desire to acquire all that he can. He closes his eyes, forces himself to follow Aske into sleep before he can overthink on the matter.

It is Aske who wakes first, the next morning, and he's loath to move. Bragi is warm, and the shapeshifter feels no shame at all that he has wrapped all four of his limbs around the human. His body is just seeking warmth, and Bragi is holding him pretty tightly too. Even if it is just in his sleep. Aske shifts slightly, tilts his head to look up at the human. His hair is an ashen brown, there's nothing eye-catching about it, and his beard is a bit of a mess from their travels, but the grey streaks bring some character out. It is a becoming sight, really. Bragi has very visible crow's feet at the corner of his eyes, and laugh lines now very much hidden beneath his overgrown beard, plump cheeks and a button nose. He appears both very young and old at the same time, which is an amusing paradox and strangely attractive. And he's strong. Aske already knew that from when Bragi treated the shapeshifter in his cave, wrestling him down onto his furs to stop the redhead from hurting himself anymore with his struggles, but it is after they began sharing a blanket for warmth the further north they went that he became acutely aware of it.

And it is terrible. Bragi is a human, a fragile little thing, and Aske finds himself fonder of him than he should be. Much too fond.

'Human, human, he is a human!' He keeps telling himself. 'You treacherous thing, he's human, he can turn on us at any moment.' He cusses at his own heart, but he knows that it is a lie. Bragi has not a single treasonous bone in his body. He is a bastard, that much is true, but in all the best ways, *good ways*, and it endears him to the shapeshifter. And isn't that a dangerous thought?

Today, he realizes. They have to part ways today, before this feeling goes any further, digs its claws into his chest to the point it will be far too painful to pull them out. Before they gouge a hole in his heart when he inevitably must. Before their parting leaves him cracked and bleeding, more than he already is, because even now the thought makes his heart ache. And it shouldn't. Not after such a short time of knowing another, it shouldn't. Such feelings, they shouldn't grow roots during such a short time, when Aske has had difficulty trusting the man for half of their journey together. It cannot be.

He attempts to extract himself from the embrace, albeit reluctantly, without waking the human. Despite his best efforts, Bragi startles, his grip tightening on the shapeshifter as bleary eyes open, attempting at orienting himself. Aske freezes. It is not that he is unable to break free from the hold, it is just that he doesn't want to. It would probably startle Bragi to have the shapeshifter shove him away so suddenly when he is still waking up.

Also, Aske doesn't… dislike it.

So, when Bragi jolts and releases him with a startled *"oh,"*, he can't help but feel a twinge of disappointment, and he is unable to completely squash it before it takes root. It must show on his face, because Bragi looks apologetic, and he can't handle that, not now. He wants to say, wants to- wants to tell him it's okay to hold him, to please not let go.

He rolls away.

"Today is the last day. We'll go our separate ways after today." It feels like the words tear at his throat as he forces them out, but he manages.

"Ah, yes." The quiet of Bragi's response makes him grind his teeth.

'Don't turn around, don't you fucking turn around,' he tells himself. *'You won't be able to go through with it if you turn around.'*

"After today, we go our separate ways," Bragi repeats, and it shouldn't hurt as much as it does right now, because Aske had decided just minutes earlier to nip this in the bud before it became something meaningful. He clenches his jaw so hard his teeth throb.

It is going to hurt the next day when he leaves, when he'll be travelling without Bragi. He knows it will, but… *but*, it'll be for the best. It'll hurt for a while, then the pain will dull, until it is nothing, until it is unnoticeable. He breathes in quickly, and plasters on the sincerest smile he can manage as he turns around. He *turns around, the fool.*

"You're not so bad, Bragi, for a human." He feels like hitting himself. That is not even remotely close to what he wants to say, but it is the closest he is able to go, the most he can admit without laying himself completely bare, flayed open and raw. Bragi smiles back, smaller, dimmer, but no less sincere than Aske.

"You as well, though I imagine I'll be getting more rest once I won't subjected to your atrocious snoring." He attempts a joke, startling a baffled guffaw out of the other man.

"*Bastard!*" Aske narrows his eyes in mirth.

CHAPTER TWENTY-ONE

If they're quieter during this last day, neither really comment on it. The air feels a slight bit heavy, even if they had engaged in light-hearted banter during their final breakfast. Maybe it is because every second is just another step closer to the very end of their journey together. Another step to never seeing each other again.

Perhaps that is the most painful part of the whole thing, not seeing each other again, having conversations and throwing some jabs here and there. Aske rolls the thought around in his head for a few moments. What would the harm be? It is just an offer, after all. They've already travelled over half the day in tense, heavy silence, what's the harm of lightening it by tossing out a boon his companion is free to either accept or decline?

"You know," he begins, tongue feeling heavy in his mouth, "whenever you feel like it, you can go back to the mountain." Bragi blinks, surprised by this sudden turn of events.

"You'd be okay with that?" Aske stutters, vowels and consonants tripping over his tongue before he finally manages to articulate himself properly.

"Well, yes? You seemed to like their library, and they seemed to like you." Bragi is quiet for a few moments, seemingly contemplating something before glancing towards Aske, chin dipped low.

"Will you be there?" Oh, don't ask that, Aske thinks. Bragi isn't supposed to ask him that, but he clears his throat and nods.

"Well, it's my home. I did… I did plan on returning at some point." He just hasn't thought of exactly *when* he'll be making his way back. If Bragi will even be there when Aske returns. If *anyone* he knew will still be there when he returns.

"Ah, well, then," Bragi says, beaming like the sun. "You're right, I did enjoy myself there, and their library. I would very much like to return." Aske nods. At least it is out there. It is an option, it's all up to Bragi where he ends up now.

If they'll meet again after this.

Well, if it happens, it happens. If not, then- Aske purses his lips. If it doesn't, then that is that. Though, of course, at that point, he expects that he'll have gotten over this. This infatuation.

Because that is what this is. Infatuation. Nothing more. Aske is nipping it in the bud before it grows into anything stronger, *he really is,* because he just can't. He can't let himself want more, something real and tangible, he can't, not with a human. A human whose lifespan is used up in the blink of an eye, especially not a human who has probably lived over half of his already. It can't be anything else than infatuation, he can't allow it to become anything else.

The sun is high in the sky when they find themselves on the outskirts of a town.

"Why don't we stay there for the night?" Bragi asks his companion. "Stay at an inn, have a lovely meal, sleep in a proper bed for once?" Aske isn't quite so sure of this idea. They've mostly avoided staying in human settlements, focused on passing through only to resupply whenever they absolutely had to. Yet he can't do anything but admit that the prospect does sound rather inviting. As long as he wears the spectacles, he feels safe, and no one actually asks about them anyway. Humans now a days, he has learned, usually don't look twice at anyone despite them appearing odd. Also, his size is more odd than the spectacles, truth be told.

And they'll be parting ways soon. It'll be a nice memory, a definite goodbye. If there are physical walls between them, it will be easier to part ways, probably. No chatter that will drag out into awkwardness, that will make it any more difficult than it already is. No slow mornings where all they might want to do is to just hold on just a few minutes more, making it more painful than it already is. Yes, a wall should be better, make it easier.

"Alright." The way Bragi lights up makes it even more worth it. So, they steer their mounts towards the gates, Aske putting his spectacles on before they reach the guards. They leave their mounts at the stables and heads for the first inn they can find to drop off their baggage. Then they explore the town, wanders about the marketplace, and talk to the vendors. Or, rather, Bragi exchanges small pleasantries and talks with the vendors, Aske just watches. Neither of them wants or need anything here, but it is too early to eat supper yet. The sun is still out, it is still some time until it is supposed to descend, and even though neither of them has said it out loud, they want to use their last day properly. Aske finds nothing that interests him in the stalls, not enough to acquire at the very least, so he mostly follows Bragi around, but that is not so bad either. It is amusing, actually, the way he grows so excited over every little thing.

'Ingrain this into your memory,' Aske thinks to himself. *'It's all you'll ever get."* And then, when their stomachs start protesting, they head back to the inn for a good meal and drinks, while the workers drag up tubs and make ready for a bath in both their rooms once they are done. During supper, Aske regales Bragi with a tale of one of his siblings from their early years, just to keep the conversation flowing. At least, that is his excuse to himself.

"They sound remarkably amusing, my dear," Bragi says over a roasted chicken.

"They were. Inge was creative, and were any of us in trouble, we could all always count on them to get us all *out* of trouble safely," Aske says, tilting his head back wistfully.

"They were a treasure."

"Sounds like it," Bragi agrees as he finishes off the rest of his plate. Aske is a quick eater, appearing to swallow without chewing much, as a true serpent, and is merely nursing a cup of water now. Now that they are done eating, there is no reason to drag this out any longer, so Aske prepares himself to speak the words. Bragi beats him to it.

"After refreshing ourselves, would you mind if I came over with a jug of wine? A toast, of a sort, for our time together?" Bragi rubs the tips of his fingers together, a nervous habit of his, but he looks the shapeshifter in the eye. Aske should refuse. How long haven't they already stretched out this final day? The separate rooms, the *wall* is supposed to make this easier. He must say no.

"Of course. Come by once you're done." Alright, treacherous, weak little heart of his, one final drink, then he'll tell him to leave. What's the harm in that?

They climb the stairs together, Aske passes by Bragi's door to open his own and enters without even glancing in the human's direction. Best to be quick about it. The wooden tub is rather big, which considering his size is good. The tub occupies a good portion of the room, but the water is steamy and inviting, so he undresses quickly. He drapes his worn clothes over the lone chair before he sinks into the tub with a loud sigh of pleasure, and begins working on undoing all the braids.

It soothes aches he had not even been aware he had, and he sinks further into the water, his long ginger hair drifting about around him. Aske admits begrudgingly to himself that this idea of Bragi's had been splendid. He should probably tell him so when he comes over with that wine, give credit where it is due.

When the water begins to cool down, he swipes a hand gently over the surface with a muttered spell. He hisses when the water heats up a notch more than is strictly comfortable but makes no move to get out. It is just too comfortable to soak. He only realizes he's been drifting in and out of light sleep when there's a knock on the door.

"Aske, may I come in? I brought the wine." Bragi's voice is muffled by the thick, sturdy wood the door is made of, but Aske hears him clearly enough, nonetheless.

"Come in," he calls, stifling a yawn behind his hand, forcing himself to sit up properly in the tub. Bragi shoulders his way into the room. He has shaved his beard away completely, and he's holding two jugs and goblets in his arms, a small smile on his face. It quickly disappears as his eyes widen at the sight of Aske still in the tub.

"Oh, I am so sorry!" He exclaims, casting his eyes about, trying to find something to focus on that is *not* his naked companion in the bathing tub.

"What for?" Aske tilts his head curiously as he leans forward to cross his arms over the side of the tub. His hair sticks to his skin, and water drips to the floor. He knows damn well the sight he makes right now, and it is rather amusing to see Bragi flounder about like this, considering he's seen him rather undressed before.

"I, well, you're not clothed," Bragi says, eyes still darting about, having yet to find something he can focus on. Ah, a chair, he thinks, only to realize that all of Aske's clothing is draped over it. Not that chair then.

"Is that a problem for you?" Aske raises a brow, because he is far too comfortable to be bothered to move, to bow to a human's wish for him to be dressed because nakedness might offend the brunet. Aske never quite understood why humans thinks that nakedness and skin is "inappropriate" or "embarrassing". A body is a body, and they all come in a different sizes and shapes and what not. It is not a new phenomenon.

"Well, no, if it doesn't bother you?" Bragi is no stranger to skin. Many of his patients have been stripped bare in front of him, but that was by necessity. There no necessity here, and by the Goddess and her creations… Bragi shakes his head and closes the door behind him before any curious passer-by's decides to look inside. He's seen Aske's upper body undressed before when he treated him in his cave. It's not exactly new to him. But this is a vastly different situation. He is completely naked, and the shapeshifter has never been this unguarded around him. It is the final eve, perhaps Aske is so comfortable because Bragi has proven true to his word the entire time they've spent together? It would be nice if that is true.

"Wine?" His voice pitches higher, but Aske doesn't comment on it, thankfully. Instead, he just holds his hand out, waiting for the goblet. The human hands it over, fingers brushing over warm, wet skin. He swallows his words alongside the wine.

I want to stay with you.

But the words cannot be uttered. They're selfish and childish, and it would ruin everything they've built together up until this point. He swallows another mouthful. Nothing changes, the aftertaste is still bitter. No amount of sweet wine can change that, apparently, so he slows down, tries to enjoy himself. Even if the words nag at the back of his mind, ever present and ever hurting, he relaxes. He enjoys the conversation, the atmosphere, the warmth, and the steam from the bath water that heats the air in the room and the wine warming his belly. It is in a way more intimate than anything else he's experienced so far in his life.

Perhaps it is because they are both so relaxed and comfortable right now. Perhaps it is because Aske's smiles and quiet laughter comes so easily now, without him analysing every little word or action of the human, and just lets himself be? Perhaps it is the way his eyes nearly glow in the dark lit room now that the sun has descended and there are only a few candles lighting up the room. Is it because they are in a safe space? Who's to say? Bragi is just sad that such an event could only happen when they are about to part ways. He wishes they'd been able to do this more. He wishes they had been comfortable and amicable like this before tonight.

Aske is thinking along the same lines. Bragi's voice, usually higher in pitch, takes on a huskier tone here in the room. Perhaps it is because it is so quiet that there's no use raising the volume? Perhaps he's more receptive to it now that he is so relaxed after a good, long soak? The warmth of the water soothing his weary body, relieving the aches and stress he has accumulated over this journey? The way his skin is pruning? The wine warming his belly and helping make him more doozy with every sip?

Perhaps it is all these combined? He feels so relaxed, so at peace, and he can't remember the last time he did so. He can't recall ever having been so at ease around a human being before. It is… it is nice, though he's bitter that he's only achieving this now that they are about to part ways. He's come to like Bragi, he wishes more humans were like him, infatuation aside.

But there are though, aren't there? The humans in the village, they'd known all along, but pretended not to for his sake. So there, it is as safe as his home. He can return there, he can, he can take his sister there too, should she wish to follow him. He glances at Bragi, the human deep in a tale of his journey before he came upon Aske, his cheeks now clear from the scraggly beard, and rose red from the wine and warmth. He is handsome, broad and strong. It is speaking to Aske on a level, and the warmth he has stored in him, both physically and emotionally is attractive to the redhead. The physical warmth was especially attractive to the reptile part of Aske when they were outside in the cold. How long since he's been hugged or held? With care and affection instead of violence? Held willingly, and not shackled down to keep him from wiggling away from the monsters with sharp tools like a worm in the dirt?

Not since before he came to the mountain, not since he last saw his sister.

And he craves it more now that he's had a taste of it, having experienced waking up in the mornings being held firmly but comfortably, knowing that he is safe. He has forgotten what it feels like, but now that he has experienced it again, he is overcome with the need for closeness. He craves it much like he craves food and drink. A hundred years to ween himself off the need for anyone, and now he is addicted all over again.

Realizing that he won't wake to that tomorrow morning is nearly unbearable, but he can't bring Bragi along. No matter how much he wishes to do so, it will be far too selfish, and Bragi has his own goals. And his sister has suffered as much as Aske, she trusts the humans no more than him. It'll be hard enough to convince her to follow him to the mountain, that she'll be safe there, that the humans there do not care about them being shapeshifters.

But it will be, because the people knew all the time that he is a shapeshifter, and they kept that secret. For a century. They can keep her secret too. It will be a safe space, and there are many secret pathways in the mountain, should the worst come to pass. It will take time though, for her to feel safe so close to a human settlement. It will take time; therefore, he cannot show up before her with a human. She will be so frightened, probably react in a violent and unpredictable way. Someone will end up hurt, there is no doubt about that. He shifts in the tub, looks at Bragi over the rim of his goblet.

But oh, how he *wants*. How he wants to bring Bragi along, to enjoy sleep filled nights in the comforts of a warm embrace, to know he is safe and cared for, that he has the opportunity to be on the receiving end of affection as well. Aske wants it, he wants it, craves it, needs it like his flowers needs rain- *oh*. He pulls his goblet back, sees it is empty. He looks to Bragi, who is holding the second jug, mere droplets falling from it into his goblet.

"It's empty." And he sounds and appears nearly as crestfallen by the fact as Aske feels. He wants to reach out, to thread his slim fingers through Bragi's stockier ones, to tell him it is alright, he can stay, at least for the night. But if he does that, allows himself that indulgence, the temptation, he will falter, he will lose that battle with himself and give in to all his desires and wants. He will never be able to let go.

So instead, he forces himself to hand over his empty goblet, and speak these words;

"Would you hand me a towel?" Bragi hastens to listen, and as he climbs to his feet, Aske stands up and wrings his hair before he clambers over the edge. Bragi is waiting for him, towel open for him to walk into. So, he steps closer, allows the brunet to wrap him and pat him dry, and Aske immediately regrets it. It is too intimate, he should have just taken the towel himself, he should have-

"It is not so long ago that you'd never trust me with something like this," Bragi speaks, breath ghosting over Aske's back. It takes all his willpower not to shudder.

"Didn't know you back then," the redhead mutters, moving the towel to wrap around his waist. He should find his tunic, at the very least. His own nakedness, or others for that matter, has never bothered him before. It is not really a bother now, either, but Bragi's touch is too real, too gentle. It feels like his touch brands itself into his skin, searing, leaving marks no one can see, but marks which Aske knows are there. Indents that will haunt him for as long as he'll live. It makes him feel uncomfortable and frustrated to feel this way. He needs to find his clothes, in a hurry, he must be quick, so he moves forward exactly one step before stopping short, standing ramrod straight. Bragi's fingertips are ghosting over his back in a touch so featherlight it nearly tickles.

They catch on the scar tissue and welts, some deep and jagged, and the human feels sick as he remembers one of Aske's tales about his captivity in the hands of a proclaimed healer. He's seen them before, he did so when he was taking care of the shapeshifter, but to know the context to some of them when he sees them anew… The words tumble out of his mouth before he can stop them, tongue loose from all the wine and the safe bubble they have ensconced themselves in.

"What caused this?" He trails a finger lightly across the redhead's back, from hip and nearly up to his shoulder, mixing grotesquely with the ones running up his spine.

"A whip," Aske replies quietly, not daring to move. He remembers it, all leather with steel braided into the tips. It had quite literally shredded the skin over his hip, up his back.

"And this?" Bragi's voice trembles, much in the way Aske is aware his own body is doing as well, with each new touch. Bragi's fingers press lightly at an indent in his side. Aske wants to flinch away but finds that he can't.

"A spear." He manages to sound calm, even as he remembers how he had thought he would die back then, the expression on his attacker's face as he speared him through. The delight on his face, that he thought he was victorious. Aske had thought that too, for a moment.

"A-and this?" The way the brunet's voice cracks as he traces the jagged marks over his shoulder and down his back, so dangerously close to that slim throat, makes Aske turn around.

"A bear." They'd still been so young back then, barely a century old. Their youngest had been tossed into a walled bearpit with a broken arm. Aske had nearly been mauled as he had pushed her up to Inge, who had miraculously managed to pull the both of them out. The details are still hazy, it all happened in such a rush.

"And- "This time Bragi is unable to voice his question as his eyes land on Aske's chest.

"A lot of things. I mostly remember screaming a lot." It is like a dam breaks, and Bragi sniffles as tears escape him.

"Oh Aske, I'm sorry, I'm so sorry."

"What for? That my body is like this, riddled in scars? I may not be a great beauty with these- "Aske begins jokingly, trying to lighten the tense and dark atmosphere, stop the tears running down the human's cheeks, but Bragi won't have it.

"But you are!" He bursts out. "You *are* beautiful, Aske! Every part, every aspect of you, from your hair, your eyes, your human, *and* snake form, to your kind but battered heart! Every part of you is beautiful, and the only ugly thing here are the *reasons* for these wounds, the people and creatures who had the audacity to hurt you, only *they* are ugly!" It all comes out in a rushed breath, the words pouring out without much thought, and it catches Aske unawares. The reasons are ugly, and Aske can agree to that, even though a few of those reasons are his own fault, the consequences to his own actions. They were still ugly reasons, but there is something much more important.

Bragi thinks he is beautiful. His soul, his *eyes*, which are so unnatural? Bragi manages to calm down enough to realize what he's been saying out loud, and pales when he sees the expression on Aske's face. The flush on his cheeks disappears so quickly he feels faint, and he stammers as he stumbles back, rushing to apologize for his outburst, for his unwanted words of comfort. Aske had neither asked nor wanted them, Bragi is sure of that, and he has made a terrible blunder, on this final eve. What had been a lovely evening has ended rather tensely because of him putting his foot in his mouth. They were supposed to have a nice night and say good bye, not for him to toss out all these unwanted words as proof of his affections.

"I'm sorry, I shouldn't have, I forgot myself-" He moves to turn, but Aske yanks him back, wraps his arms around him tightly, like a snake coiling around its prey, and refuses to let go. He's still trembling, he can't quite shake it yet, because his mind is reeling, still trying to catch up, but there is one thing he is certain of.

"Don't say sorry," Aske says, no, nearly *pleads*, eyes fixed on the closed door, abhorring the sight of it, what it means when Bragi passes through it.

"Don't, please, *please*, don't say sorry." His voice cracks, his grip tightens to the point Bragi finds it hard to breathe, as he begs Bragi to not apologize, to not apologize for reassuring him, caring for him, for thinking he's beautiful, a person *worth* something-

"Oh my dear boy," Bragi says as he hugs Aske back, holds him nearly just as tightly, and suddenly the shapeshifter is aware that they've sunk to the floor, and that he is crying, scrabbling to keep a secure hold whenever the human shifts just the slightest bit on his knees, fingers digging into rough fabric.

"Don't go, please don't go, Bragi-" the words tear out of him in sobs, and the human soothes him the best he can. The shapeshifter can't help it, something has broken free, he can't hold whatever emotions these are back anymore. The overwhelming relief of having someone there, of having the loneliness he's been trapped in for a hundred years chased away, and now he risks being caught by it again. If Bragi walks through that door, if he leaves through that door, then-

"I'm not going anywhere, Aske, I'm right here, I'm right here, hush now, I've got you."

"No, *no*, I'm-" Aske pulls back, pupils wet and blown wide, as he swallows after several failed attempts at finding the words.

"Come with me," he finally manages. "Don't go where I can't follow, please- no, what I mean is, come with me." Aske doesn't care that it is a selfish request, he wants it so bad, but all he can do is ask, beg, plead for Bragi to say yes. He needs it, he needs it so much. Right now, it feels like it is as important as breathing. Aske hasn't asked for much this last period of his life, he's been trying his best to keep from asking for too much, being too greedy, coveting what he shouldn't, all to ensure the well-being and comfort of those around him, the person he seeks, but right now, right now he wants to be selfish, he *wants* to reach out and take what he can. He doesn't want scraps, he doesn't want crumbs that falls his way, he wants all that he can have. He wants, he wants, he *wants!*

"Of course I will." It takes a few moments for Bragi to overcome the shock of what Aske just asked of him, but once the words sink in, he can't think of any reasons why he should reject the request. His eyes brim with happy tears as he clasps the shapeshifter's face in his hands, thumbs valiantly rubbing the tears away.

"I'll go wherever you lead me." Aske stares, before crumpling into Bragi's embrace again, sobbing in relief.

Bragi doesn't head back to his rented room that night. He stays with Aske, holding him as close as he has for some part of their journey now, and presses soft kisses to his knuckles every now and then until they both fall asleep.

CHAPTER TWENTY-TWO

Just because they've agreed on some kind of relationship now, it doesn't mean their pace has slowed any. They move at the same speed as before, but Aske seem more excited yet also apprehensive now than before their night at the inn. It warms Bragi's heart to see him like this, unburdened with heavy thoughts of scenarios he doesn't want to see played out. Maybe it is because they got that night at the inn, but everything feels so much better, even after Aske had explained that his sibling might not take well to the sight of the human.

"She'll be as friendly as you were, I imagine." Aske grimaced, quite sure that she might be even more hostile than he was. Still, they are so close now, soon they'll meet for the first time in over a century. He can explain everything then.

He leans back in the saddle, exhaling.

A whole century, it's been so long, and it's only now that he realizes just how much he's missed her. He has always been aware that he's missed her, but now that she is just within reach, it hits just how *much*. He looks forward to seeing her again, even if he must explain Bragi's presence. She'll hear him out, she'll let him explain. She might not be willing or emotionally capable of understanding at first, but he hopes she'll come around.

It's all he'll ask for, no more. But for now, he should push those worries aside. Nothing can be done before they meet up with her anyways.

Something feels off though. For the past few days, it's as if she hasn't moved at all. After being constantly on the move for months, it is quite suspicious.

"Bragi, let's up the pace today." He doesn't give the human a chance to respond before he urges his horse on into a trot. It is not far now, they're close, he can feel it, they're almost-

Something runs out on the road in front of him, and Gerd rears back so suddenly he very nearly falls off. He curses as he holds on tightly to the reins, knees digging into his mount's sides in an effort to not be thrown off as he tries to calm the poor creature down. He is forced to slide off in the end to be able to properly calm the horse, but once the deed is done, once she is no longer whinnying or struggling, Aske turns to see what it is that scared his mount so, only to stop short.

A child, a small child, crouched on the ground, eyes wide and fearful, face gaunt and cheeks hollower than they should be. Her expression isn't what confounds him, it is the fact that a small child is all on her own like this.

"Aske, are you alright?" Bragi exclaims as he stops his own horse. The child scurries back on the ground, so Aske holds his hand up to stop the human before he hands over the reins.

"Hold her for me," he tells the brunet, never once looking away from the child. It is suspicious enough that a child is all on their own in the wilderness, it is even more so considering the child's hair and eye colour, her near on identical appearance to his sister when she was that age. The child is slowly climbing up to her feet, her eyes roaming over him, a spark of recognition flashing through her eyes, but her body screams her wariness of him.

"Did I scare you?" he asks. She doesn't respond. It might be that she is terrified of him, considering how he is towering over her even from a distance. He can see her bend her knees; the way she shifts that tells him she's going to flee. But first, she speaks, voice uncertain, yet carrying a trace of courage he admires.

"Can I see your eyes?" He doesn't expect the question, and he hesitates for a moment before pulling the spectacles off, spectacles he put on because there had been people along the road. Her eyes widen, and she straightens up just a bit. Her next question is hushed, yet still her voice holds firm.

"Are you a big black snake?" He hesitates, before he nods, because this is no human child. She bolts, but not away. She runs straightforward and he's the one startled when she fists her hands into his pant leg.

"They took mam, Aske, they took mam!" Bragi said his name loudly earlier, it shouldn't surprise Aske that she used it, it is the familiarity she infuses into the syllables that catch him off-guard. Aske kneels hurriedly, frowning as a thousand questions whirl through his mind. The child resembles his sister so much, she knows he is a serpent, and she acts as if he is someone she knows she needs, but while this is a lot to process, he focuses on the more pressing matters.

"Who took Saga?" The child whimpers, and that is answer enough. He dreads the answer to his next question, but he must ask, has to be *sure*.

"Where are the rest of you?" The way she pales and begins sobbing uncontrollably is yet another answer. He lifts her up, to her surprise, and heads back to the horses and Bragi. She scrambles to get out of his hold when she sees Bragi, but the redhead shushes her.

"It's alright, it's safe, I promise. He won't hurt you." She doesn't appear to believe him, if the way she shies far away from Bragi is any indication, but at the very least she sits still when they're on the saddle.

"What's your name?" Aske asks as they move on.

"Runa," the child answers. "Mam said we would be safe with you."

"You are, and she will be," he promises her. But first, they need to find a safe place to stay, to learn the entire truth of what has happened. They give her some food and water, because it is obvious that the girl is starved at this point. The sun has shifted quite the distance across the sky when they come to a stop atop a hill overlooking a town. Aske's face is expressionless, but he turns the horse around.

"Aske?" Bragi questions, but the redhead just shakes his head.

"We need a place where we can hide." Which is fair enough. There are many questions about the girl they've picked up, and Aske understands much more of what is happening than Bragi does. But one thing the human does know; Aske had not been expecting to come across a child in his search.

It's already starting to turn dark when they find a cave big enough for both them and their mounts, and both Bragi and Runa witness Aske manipulate the plant life with his magic to cover the entrance once they're inside. Bragi sets about removing the saddles and packs from the horses. He finds himself bringing out what little wood they had left and stack them together. A flick of the wrist from Aske ignites them, and soon the dark and dreary cave is filled with cosy light and the crackle from the fire. As Bragi continues to make this place ready for their continued stay, Aske kneels on one knee before Runa, resting his elbow on his bent knee.

"Saga is in that town, and I'm going to get her out. You'll have your mother back soon," he assures Runa, who nods hopefully, teeth digging into her lower lip in an attempt to stop the wobbling of her chin.

"I'll wait until it's completely dark, so you just get some rest."

"Don't leave me alone with the human!" She bursts out, then clamps her hands over her mouth, eyes wide with fright. Aske just smiles, patting her shoulder.

"I swear, you're as safe with Bragi as you are with me. But I cannot bring you with me, it's too dangerous. You understand, right?" She nods reluctantly, glancing up at him before suddenly hugging him. The action catches him off guard, and he gives an awkward pat on her back.

"Please come back. It's scary," she pleads. He promises he will. He tugs the worn cloak around the girl and tells her to wait. Bragi follows Aske to the mouth of the cave, wringing his hands nervously.

"Do be careful, Aske," he pleads as well, watching as his companion nods curtly, but not quite looking at him.

"May I ask, before you go… why did you think Runa was with others?" It had been obvious that Aske had been surprised to learn of Runa's existence, so why did he think there would be more of her?

"I told you before." Aske turns to look at him, steel and fire in his eyes. "We're born in litters," the redhead grits out before leaving with no more words shared. Bragi is left behind, the implications leaving him shaken. He turns to look at the girl who sits there, all bundled up in a dirty, worn-down cloak, staring resolutely at the ground. One, sole little child.

If Aske doesn't return with his sister, if neither of them return, this little girl will be all alone. No, Bragi shakes his head. It won't happen, he believes that Aske will return safely, along with his sister. His sister who apparently is the one he has been searching for this entire time, since the day he marched out of the mountain village.

He walks back inside, hears the plants move to cover the entrance back up now that he has passed their barrier, and offers the child a reassuring smile. She doesn't return it. She actually appears terrified, and he can hardly blame her.

"Do you want any food or water?" She shakes her head.

"Is there anything you'd like? Something I could do to make you more comfortable? Less afraid?"

"Mam says feeling fear makes you smarter," the girl retorts, and Bragi chuckles.

"Yes, it can give you the chance for sound reason and good judgement, though only if in healthy doses. Your mother sound like quite a wise woman," he offers kindly.

"How do you know Aske?" Runa demands, and Bragi tells the tale of when he arrived by a mountain village, and the little girl grows curious to learn that her uncle has lived peacefully so close to humans.

"Why did you help him?"

"Well, he needed help, and I had the means to help him. It is as simple as that."

"Just like that?" she wonders.

"Just like that." He nods. She appears to find it hard to believe, so he waits for her to wrap her mind around it.

"Why are you travelling together?" By being allowed to ask all these questions, Runa seem to be more at ease, to momentarily forget her situation, so he indulges her.

"We met again as we were journeying. He was again in need of some assistance, and I was happy to help."

"But…" She's moved closer during the tale. Not much, but a little, and he's not sure she's even aware that she's moved closer at all.

"But humans hate us," she says, obviously confused, not sure what to believe. Because she's been on the run for some time now, and what she's experienced and what she's learning of here are very contradictive.

"Not all of us," Bragi says quietly, "not all of us enjoy causing others pain, my dear," he tells her with a small smile, and Runa looks up, eyes widening as she finally realizes that she's moved closer to the human. She freezes, tiny frame trembling terribly beneath the worn cloak. Bragi keeps up his smile, but shuffles away from her, shows that he respects her boundaries, even though it is she who forgot herself.

"I-I-"she begins, but the brunet shakes his head.

"Don't fret, my dear girl. Do get some rest, I'm sure Aske will return soon with your mother."

Despite her very best efforts to stay awake, Runa falls asleep not long after. She's curled up in that cloak, and while she doesn't wake, it is undeniable that she isn't experiencing a restful sleep. She's tossing and turning, whimpering, and Bragi just can't stand to watch it. If she wakes, she'll probably recoil in terror, but he chances it anyways. He moves over and properly tucks her cloak around her. Then he carefully pats her head, running is fingers through her filthy and matted hair, avoiding snagging his fingers in her tousled curls. It's caked with dirt, stiff and clumped together, yet it is the same colours as Aske's. And to be perfectly honest, she smells. She is in dire need of a wash.

"Poor thing," he mutters. She is too young, too innocent, underserving of the harsh reality she's been forced to experience. She should not have to be so terrified, restless, to feel so unsafe and alone. She should never have had to experience such a terrible loss. Bragi prays for Aske to find his sibling quickly, and for the both of them to return safely.

And just before the break of dawn, Aske returns with a body draped across his back and a grim expression on his face.

CHAPTER TWENTY-THREE

Aske watches intently as Bragi's faintly glowing hands hover over his sister's body, the most serious injuries slow to mend even with the gentle force of insistent healing magic. The redhead dares a quick glance up from the bloody and bruised body on the ground and to the healer. The furrowed brows, the tightly clenched jaw, the concentration, the beads of sweat trailing down his face scares the shapeshifter enough to look down again.

Watching Bragi struggle is terrifying. Aske knows that Saga's injuries are severe, that is undeniable from just looking at her, it was obvious from the moment he saw her strung up in that cellar. However, he has hope, because Bragi is here, Bragi with his healing magic, Bragi with all his medical knowledge and experience. Someone who can help. Someone who wouldn't fumble about in the dark.

Aske is feeling incredibly relieved that he had let Bragi come along, that they had grown close enough that he dared to be selfish, that he had managed to learn to trust this human, because if he was alone with Runa and Saga right now, he isn't sure he would know what to do. He'd be panicking inwardly as he'd futilely try and help her, even though he wouldn't rightly know how to.

At least with Bragi here, he knows the chances of her survival is higher. Moreover, the quicker she heals, the sooner they can be on their way. By now, the hunters must have realized that their captive is gone. As such, even though he has manipulated the plant life to properly hide the entrance and most of the area around them naturally, he feels far from comfortable being in such close proximity with the city in which they held her.

There is only so much foliage can do, and the horses must be let out sometimes too. And the smoke from the fires they will need at some point…

Suddenly, Bragi's hands stop glowing, and he slowly pulls his hands back to lay in his lap. The sigh he releases is so heavy, and Aske for some reason feels dread knot in the pit of his stomach. Why is Bragi stopping? Saga is still seriously injured; she *needs* his help! The healer *cannot* stop now! As if sensing the inner turmoil of his companion, Bragi speaks up.

"There is a limit to how much I can do with my magic."

"What do you mean?" Aske hisses, trying to keep the panic out of his voice, to keep quiet so he won't wake Runa and alarm her.

"My magic can only hasten her recovery if she possesses the strength. She needs rest, food, and water," Bragi assures him. "Magic isn't a cure-all; it is a tool. You know this." Aske lowers his shoulders, understanding that nothing is as terrible as he first thought it was. Saga's condition is horrible, but she will be fine, as long as they give her a chance at recovering, bit by bit.

He'll have to see if he needs to cause or play bait to lead the hunters on the wrong trail.

"For now, watch over her for me while I prepare something to sustain her." So Aske does just that, and when Runa awakens, he does his best to comfort her when she sees her mother lay so frail on a sleeping mat, wrapped up in bandages, some of which are stained red. It must be such a horrifying sight to the girl.

But recovery is happening, and they manage to coax her awake long enough to sip broth and drink water, though Aske isn't sure she's truly conscious during these times. She would have reacted to Bragi's presence differently if she was, he's sure of it.

And he is right.

Though he's outside when she does wake, Runa comes running out of the cave calling for him, and he follows inside, sees Saga lie there beneath Bragi's magic, shaking in terror and unable to move due to her injuries. Aske is by her side in an instant, filling her sight and murmuring reassurances that she's got nothing to fear, that she is safe, *Runa* is safe, and that Bragi is there to help. It assures her somewhat, having her focus on him, and not on Bragi. It allows the healer to completely focus on his task of mending wounds and lessen the pain.

It is a great relief when Saga has recovered enough to move her hand without causing too much agony to herself, enough movement to grab Aske's hand in hers. The grip is tight, despite the obvious discomfort she feels by doing it.

"You're here." She sounds like she's eaten sand for weeks, and like it takes all her strength to just whisper the words.

"I am."

"You're really here." A sob escapes her, and the other shapeshifter starts crying himself, brushing a hand over the top of her head, pulling her torn and jaggedly cut hair back in the process, wiping the sweat gathered at her brow, resolutely avoiding looking at the left side of her head, where bandages are wrapped rightly, the lack of a lump alerting him to her missing ear. Cutting pieces off of her had been a pastime of her captors when the normal torture did not yield the results they wanted. At least, that is what Aske believes.

"I am. You're going to be fine, we're all going to be fine. I'll take you somewhere safe, I swear." She nods, trying to rein in her own emotions, but it's all coming out now, because Aske is here now, they are much safer than they were days prior, and she is not alone anymore.

She lays there crying for quite a while, even after Bragi has deemed that her body needs more rest and nutrients for his magic to have any effect on her. Of course, when she's calmed down and he's making a type of soup for her, she asks her brother why he's travelling with a human.

"I wouldn't have found you so quickly if it wasn't for him. He's trustworthy, I promise." She seems doubtful, and who can blame her? For nearly three centuries they've been hounded and hurt by the humans, it is hard to drop painful memories and a deep-rooted grudge, but Aske has not dropped any of his memories himself, he has forgotten nothing, and he never will, nor will he forgive what he's experienced.

However, he has accepted that not all humans are the same, and he has had a lot of time to think during this journey. He's had a lot of time to grow fond of Bragi. Of course, he cannot tell her that, not now, not when she's as vulnerable as she is right at this moment. She won't accept it. Instead, he reassures her, and decides that as soon as she's able, as soon as she is strong enough, he'll ask what happened, and *their* names as well. He wants to help her properly mourn.

And if she wants revenge, well, he'll help her achieve it, even if… he glances up as Bragi returns, handing him a bowl with soup for her to drink. He watches the man walk some ways away for the sake of his patient's well-being, smiling brightly.

Aske swallows the lump forming in his throat. He'll help her get her revenge, even if it means he might lose Bragi. Even if it means that the healer might never want to see him again, even if it means he can't stomach the sight of Aske, think of him as a murderer and monster…

Even that, he will endure, because it is his choice. And Saga, Saga deserves closure. If revenge is what she needs, he'll help her.

"How's Runa? Truly?" she asks, throat dry and hurting still.

"Strong," Aske replies, smiling. "Curious, joyous little thing. Once you're all better, she'll be much better too." Saga nods, exhaling and slumping onto the bedroll. Knowing that her daughter is safe is all she needs to know right now. She is grateful that he doesn't ask, about *them*, of what happened, of where she's been all these years. Why she never told him about the litter, even through their shared Dreams. She feels bad that she has hid this for years and is suddenly depending on him for aid. Right now, compared to him, she is powerless. Saga has no choice but to ask him for help, and she feels wretched for doing so after having been apart for so long. For her cruel parting words that she said to him before they went different ways.

"Aske." She watches as he puts the bowl down, helps her rest up against his bent knee so she can eat without choking on the hot liquid.

"Hm?" The words are difficult to find, because not even one of them feels adequate enough. She's seen his way of living through their Dreams. It is a lonely one. She, on the other hand, has lived a much better one since they parted ways, and kept a huge part of it hidden from him mostly out of an unnecessary long bout of resentment. A resentment she now knows is ridiculous. She wonders if he would have come the moment she learned she was carrying if she had told him.

Even as she swallows mouthful after mouthful of food, she knows the answer. He would have, because he abandoned everything to reach them now when she called out for help. He came running as fast as he could and risked a lot by sneaking into a hunter infested compound to save her. As he has always done.

"I'm sorry," she finally says, her lower lip trembling. She's remorseful for a lot of things. She feels immense regret for what she said during their argument, she's sorry for hiding her new family from him, she's regretful for only seeking him out now, when she's in desperate need of help. She feels wretched that she is taking advantage of his kindness and selflessness when she knows he would never turn his back on her, no matter what.

"Saga." She can't bring herself to raise her eyes to his, so instead she casts them to the side, visibly ashamed. Sadness swells in Aske at the sight, so he carefully guides her to look at him, fingers clasping her chin. She's hesitant to follow, yet she does not possess the strength to deny him. What she sees makes her heart twist in her chest, because the emotions on his face, in his eyes, mirror her own.

"I'm sorry too." Because Aske also said words he wished he could take back. At any point in his life after their parting, he could have reached out to her himself, but he'd been too much of a coward about it. Neither is to blame, or perhaps it is more correct to say they are both to blame? Either way, none of it matters, because they are both here now, and honest with each other this time.

Saga finishes eating, rests for a little bit, and then she calls Aske over when Runa falls asleep as night rolls in. He changes his shape halfway, every part of him until just under his chest shifting from skin to glimmering, hard scales as he coils around the two securely. It's the safest Saga has felt in months.

"Aina, Alv, Ebba, Halle and Runa," Saga says, her voice cracking as she looks down at her daughter curled up in dark coils of muscle and scales.

"That's what I named them." And with that admission, the words fall from her not easily or painlessly, but she finds little strength to care. She said their names, out loud, and the horror that happened months ago spill from her too.

CHAPTER TWENTY-FOUR

The fire Bragi had been tending to before he retired for the evening has mostly died out into smouldering embers. It is late, so late that it will soon be early. Aske is tired, but not interested in sleeping, something he knows Bragi will hound him for in the morning, since the healer often claims that rest is important for one's health.

Which is why Aske finds it odd that Bragi himself is not sleeping. He is resting on his bedroll, with his back to them, but he is not sleeping. It is odd. Aske would have found it highly suspicious when he didn't know him as well as he does now. Still, if it isn't for the fact that he is worried he'll wake the two he's holding, he would have slithered over to ask his companion what's keeping him up. He decides not to, until he hears sniffling. He raises his head, brows furrowing.

"Bragi?" He speaks quietly to avoid waking the other two, but loud enough for Bragi to hear him. And he does, if the way his shoulders rise nearly up to his ears is any indication.

"Bragi, what is it?" The human is silent for a few moments, shoulders shifting as he rubs at his face, and throws over his shoulder a simple;

"It's nothing." It is undeniably not true with the way his voice cracks. Something is terribly wrong, and Aske chances uncoiling himself from his sister and sister-daughter, thankfully waking neither of them, and changes his tail back into legs as he moves over. Bragi tenses up at the feel of the redhead's hand on his shoulder but doesn't much fight it when he's pulled around. Yellow eyes widen at the sight of the man's tearstained face.

"Bragi?" What caused this, Aske wonders. He doesn't believe it to be Saga's cold and avoidant behaviour towards him, Aske was just as bad back at the mountain, if not even worse. Bragi knew to expect this, this kind of behaviour from someone who has lost a lot to his kind, recently so too. Therefore, it must be something else that has gotten into him.

"What's wrong?" The brunet averts his eyes, unable to meet Aske's gaze for some reason, and it is like a punch to the gut. Bragi has never avoided eye-contact with Aske since they met, not like this. He seems just as terrified as he appears grief-stricken, and Aske cannot understand why, if not for Saga's story. Saga hadn't spoken too loudly, and Bragi had busied himself as she told her tale, so Aske had thought he hadn't been listening.

"Saga's story," he hiccups, eyes pinching together. Aske relaxes somewhat. Saga's story had been horrendous to listen to, it had dug its claws into his own trauma and nightmarish memories and pulled it to the surface of his mind, it had picked and reopened old, scabbed over wounds, made them bleed again. Even so, he had put all his focus on listening to and comforting his sister and making sure her daughter slept peacefully on.

Bragi's had no such distractions, and it must have been harrowing to hear that his own kind are capable of such horrible actions. It is bad enough that they had attacked unprovoked, but to hear that they had killed innocent and defenceless children…

"It was horrible to listen to, yes," the redhead agrees.

"Absolutely horrendous!" Bragi chokes back a sob as he sits up. Aske keeps his hand firmly planted on his shoulder, because Bragi appears to be ready to shake apart at the seams. The human is truly empathic, to feel for another's loss so vividly. Aske was so focused on the other two, he barely spared the human a thought.

"And it's my fault they experienced it." If there has been a moment in his life where Aske feels like the ground crumples beneath his feet and his tattered heart breaks, it might be right now.

CHAPTER TWENTY-FIVE

Bragi is but a youth when it happens. His brother, Sigmund, is a priest in a small village by a lake. Everyone knows everyone, and they're welcoming to travellers. Bragi wants to become a traveller too, when he grows up, like his brother, who sometimes goes on short journeys. He's never gone for long though, but Bragi wants to explore the world created by the Goddess and her Children. The travellers come with the most fantastic tales, and he wishes to experience some of his own.

His village being open to all kinds of travellers also means that it is open to all kinds of creatures and beings that pass through as well. Bragi is fascinated by them, especially the cyclops that passes by on his cart pulled by a six-legged giant of a horse he learns is called a Sleipr. These giant horses were apparently created by the Goddess to help the cyclops' farm and the like.

He's sad to learn that there aren't many Sleiprs left in the world, but he asks the cyclops if he can come with when he's older. The cyclops nods and tells the boy that he'll pass by every year, so when he is old enough, he can come along. Of course, he also needs to be able to fend for himself, the cyclops warns him, and Bragi nods eagerly. His brother is already teaching him how to use a sword, so that is alright. Of course, it is under the rule that he only uses the skill to protect himself. The cyclops leaves, as he always does after a few days of rest and trade, continuing his route, and everything is rather uneventful for a time.

Until a wounded livwyrm rushes into the village, pleading for sanctuary. Sigmund allows it, swiftly carrying the creature to a safe place in their little temple. Not long after, a group of men and women, both young and old, come through.

"Have you seen a wicked beast nearby?" The perceived leader of the group demands, and Sigmund, having returned after hiding the livwyrm before their arrival, shakes his head.

"No wicked beast has come through here. No one and nothing have passed through for quite some time. What is this about?"

"We move on!" They don't answer Sigmund, they just shoulder past him and move out of the village in a hurry.

The livwyrm, a small serpent-like creature who glow faintly when the rays of the sun hits them just right, is quite grateful for the rescue. In exchange, they offer to teach a select few their art of healing magic. Bragi is one of the six chosen, and he possesses and affinity for the magic which frankly surprises him. Yet it brings him unlimited joy to know he can help people in need with his abilities. Especially for when he will begin travelling himself.

Two years pass before the group returns. Most of those who could have been called the elders of the group are gone, and it is quite clear that they have a new leader. A younger man who has shaved his hair off and sports a nasty scar across his forehead stands at the forefront of the group. When they see the livwyrm, their gazes grow dark. The creature in question tenses, ready to flee should they chose to hunt it again, but to everyone's surprise and horror, the group deems the lives of every villager forfeit for their earlier deception two years prior.

The livwyrm doesn't flee, despite their lack of power to fight back in this horrible situation. They perish alongside Sigmund who tries his best to fend off the attackers.

Bragi, overcome with grief and a burning fury he never thought himself capable of feeling, grabs his sword. He doesn't quite know how, doesn't quite remember how he does it, but he manages to catch the leader unawares. There are screams all around him, there are still villagers alive, and if he can just end the leader of the group, the rest of them might just turn tail and flee.

He knocks his opponent to the ground, raises his sword, and victory is at hand.

Yet, he hesitates.

'Only to defend yourself, Bragi.' Sigmund always told him, a mantra the younger brother had to learn and understand before the other even deigned the thought of teaching him how to wield a sword.

Killing this man is murder, Sigmund would have strived for a different method. This is what causes Bragi to hesitate, and that's why he loses the battle. Someone approaches from behind and something solid connects with the back of his head. He crumples to the ground like a ragdoll. He can hear them talking, though he expects he won't wake up again.

'So this is where I die,' he thinks.

But it is not. He gains consciousness later, much later. The sun is shining, still brightly, when he comes back to life. His head hurts, the bright light blinds him at first as he struggles to get up. He's disoriented, his mind a jumble of images and sounds out of chronological order, and he groans as his entire body protests his movements. His sudden movements and groans of discomfort cause a flurry of flapping wings and he looks up startled.

His breath catches in his throat as he takes in the scene in front of him, his mind suddenly understanding the horrible smell now that he is witnessing the aftermath. His stomach rebels, and he throws up what meagre content is there, dry heaves and clutches his chest as his throat constricts. It is terrible, straight out horrible, he can't wrap his mind around it, it is too gruesome, and all that he manages to do when he finally regains his breath is emit choked off screams, fat tears wetting his cheeks.

He passes out again, not from any outside physical violence this time, but out of a need to protect himself from the sight of his ruined home, and all of its people slaughtered like animals, left out to rot.

CHAPTER TWENTY-SIX

Bragi isn't trembling as he tells Aske his tale. He just has this lost, empty look in his eyes, like he has fallen deep in some kind of memory, not aware of what is going on in the present. Aske himself is quiet, waiting for Bragi to continue, to finish. Any thought of sleep has long since taken its departure from his mind. This is more important.

When Bragi had admitted to a responsibility for Saga and Runa's loss, Aske had been stunned, at a loss for words. He'd felt hurt, betrayed, but most of all, he had felt like a fool. A fool for trusting this human, for letting his pretty words breach through his defences, making him vulnerable, for falling for said pretty words, the endearing touches he'd often gift the shapeshifter with. Then he'd felt anger, and the only reason he hadn't yelled or screamed or even physically attacked him was because of the last remains of his family resting very close by.

And because… all these feelings, they are real to Aske. And his most precious possession.

This is also what gave Bragi the chance at explaining why he is the one at fault.

"When I woke again… I dug graves, packed what belongings I had, and left." Bragi's perceived responsibility makes no sense, it doesn't correlate at all with what he just told Aske. The way he had said it made it sound like he had once been part of the group of hunters, but that's the furthest from the truth. He's another victim to the group. His home, friends, teacher and family became victims of these men and women.

Bragi is not responsible for anything.

Aske is caught in a wave of relief so strong it nearly drowns out the sounds of the world around him. The anger and hurt he had felt his heart aim at Bragi changes, morphs into sympathy instead. Aske knows loss well, he also knows what it is like to live on thinking that the loss of loved ones hangs over his shoulder, as his burden and responsibility and *fault*, but this…

Bragi is still crying, avoiding looking at Aske, so ashamed, wretched, grieving. He's taking responsibility for the actions of a group he is not a part of, and he shouldn't.

"Do you possess the gift of foresight?" The question catches the human off-guard.

"What?" Bragi is confused, doesn't quite understand why Aske is so calm when he should be cursing him and tell him to leave and never come back ever again.

"Do you possess the gift of foresight?" He repeats his question.

"Well, no, but-"

"Then why are you saying it is your fault?" This seem to baffle the human. By all means, he appears to be expecting Aske to cast him aside, and Aske would have, at the beginning of this journey. However, right now, with how close they have become, after hearing this horrible truth, how could he? Aske is many things, but he is not a malicious piece of trash. He won't hold Bragi responsible for something that was out of his control, he won't hold Bragi responsible for a crime he did not commit, especially not when he himself has been a victim of the exact same group.

"Bragi, what happened to Saga and Runa, it is not your fault. How can it be your fault? You're not part of them, you weren't part of the attack, you were in the mountain village with me. You're a victim too." Bragi just stares at him, uncomprehending, and Aske wonders what kind of burden the human has carried for all these years. How long has it haunted him, to the point that he thinks that it is his responsibility how it all ended up?

"Bragi, why… why do you think it's your fault?" Bragi looks down, brows furrowing, so confused, so bewildered as he tries to make sense of things. His fingers flex where they grip his tunic, as if he is not sure whether he wants to have something to hold onto or not.

"But... I... if I had, I had him, and if I'd just- people were screaming, if I'd just-"And it is so clear then, why Bragi takes on the responsibility for something out of his control. It relates to the guilt of not being able to save his own people. By Bragi's logic, if he had managed to take out the leader of the group when they attacked his home, he might have been able to save his own people, his own home, and in the long run prevent the tragedy that befell Saga and Runa. If he had just been able to bring his sword down, if he had managed to kill the leader, a lot of people would have been saved, they would have survived.

Perhaps even Saga and her flock could have avoided such a fate. That is Bragi's logic, and the reason he blames himself for the horrible tale they've just heard the tale of hours earlier. Aske, however, is quite sure that even if Bragi had managed to kill the man, it wouldn't have stopped the carnage from happening. It would have just ended up with him being killed off too. His village would still have been left in ruins, and the group would have continued with their savagery.

Which they have, repeatedly. It is not just one man or woman leading a group that is responsible for the savagery they commit. Someone who joins a hunting group like that will not stop simply because their leader has been taken out.

And if it wasn't this group, another one would have gone for Saga. There's no shortage of hunters in the world, there's no safe place in the world, not truly.

Except for maybe one.

But Saga had not been there, and therefore her and her family had been at risk. And she knew it, the risks, the dangers of having a litter out here in the world, she's lived through the tragedy before. She knew, and Bragi carries no responsibility for it.

Furthermore, Bragi needs to understand this. Still kneeling on the ground in front of Bragi, who's looking down in his lap, confused, Aske reaches out, slowly, as to not startle the other man, and brings his hands into his own, turning his palms up.

"Bragi, you are not responsible for the actions of others. And these hands, they're not meant for killing. These hands offer warmth, comfort, and healing. They're not meant to cause an end to life, not in such a brutal manner. Use your sword to protect yourself and those you care for, but don't force yourself to use it to end someone's life if it causes you such misery. Not being able to end a life out of anger and desperation isn't a weakness, Bragi, it is *strength*."

"But…"

"I want you to continue on as you are, don't change this part of you," Aske tells him earnestly, because it is true. The Bragi in front of him now, the one moulded from all his years of living and his experiences, the person he's right now, that is the Bragi Aske knows and wants.

"But-but if they've followed Saga and Runa this far, they'll continue to do so until they are dead. What should I do if they catch up? Just watch?" The brunet is anxious, desperate for an answer, but all he does end up is being contradictive. Aske shakes his head, understanding Bragi's outrage, but also feeling how he's trembling more than just a little bit in his hold. He carefully drops the man's hands and move his own to clasp Bragi's cheeks.

"If it comes to that, and it probably will," Aske agrees, there is no use denying something that is more likely to come true than not, and it is best if they are all prepared for such an event happening. Optimism should not be the cause for them letting down their guards in front of their pursuers.

"I'll fight, and you will heal. I'll be the fangs that bite and crush, I'll shed blood. You be the shield that protects and heals. Can you do this for me, Bragi?"

"I- but you can't fight alone! What if you get hurt, what if they outnumber you?" He argues, shaking his head, trying to pull back, but Aske holds him still, gently but firmly, and leans forward to avoid losing eye-contact. It seems to be the only way that Bragi might truly *hear* what Aske is saying.

"I do have a plan. I need you to trust me, can you do that, Bragi? Can you trust me?"

"Aske, I don't want to see you hurt again. What will happen to Saga and Runa if-"

"Can you trust me to not get myself killed? I'm not bad at fighting, you know, especially groups. Did it several times back home. Practiced the art my whole life, really." Bragi hesitates before swallowing.

"You have a plan?" Aske nods. Bragi traps his lower lip between his teeth, mind whirling with questions, but then he nods.

"Alright," he whispers, chin wobbling just a little bit.

"Good." Aske moves his hands up and back a bit, long fingers delving into brown curls and rubbing tenderly into his scalp. It makes the brunet slump forward, forehead pressing heavily into Aske's chest. He is so tired, from the use of his magic to the emotional turmoil he's put himself through the last few hours. He has been downright terrified, and the weight of the burden he's carried almost his entire life has been crushing him, grinding his weary bones into dust. He's been afraid, so scared of Aske turning him away, of looking at him like he looks at nearly every human. Bragi doesn't want Aske to look at him with those eyes, he's not sure he would be able to take it.

No, the truth is that he would certainly not be able to take that kind of heartbreak. And perhaps he should be more honest about that to the man who has shown him so much trust, when every instinct he has probably screams at him not to.

"I... selfish as it is to say, I was afraid you'd leave me here." There are more words clamouring to escape, but he bites them back. He shouldn't push his luck too much.

"I don't think I'm capable of that, not anymore," Aske replies just as earnestly and Bragi's eyes widen before they well up with tears yet again which he stubbornly tries to keep from soaking the other's tunic. His hands move to grip the shapeshifter's sides, as if afraid the other might disappear if he doesn't, and then...

Then he lets the tears fall, and weeps, taking comfort in Aske's presence. By the fire, on the other hand, curled up around her daughter, Saga trembles with rage.

CHAPTER TWENTY-SEVEN

Bragi isn't completely fine. The cry was cathartic, he cannot deny that. He truly needed it. Having Aske hold him and comfort him had been nice. Having the redhead tell him that it isn't his fault that his failure of killing a man ended up in a tragedy twenty odd years later helped relieve some of the burden. Aske's words make sense, of course. Saga and Runa aren't the only ones who have faced a tremendous loss at the hands of these people. Two decades have passed, they must have committed countless atrocities during this stretch of time.

Taking the blame for all of them, it truly does not make sense, he understands that, but he's carried this thought and belief for so long... it is hard to think that he is not somehow responsible for the whole mess. Because the fact is that if he had just managed to kill that man... his hands start shaking at the very thought. Using his sword to protect others doesn't bother him, but the thought of causing the light to leave the eyes of another person... he can't, he just can't, the very thought robs him of all strength, makes him sick to his stomach.

He knows that makes him a coward, walking about with a sword, yet not having the courage to use it. How much pain could have been avoided if he'd been able to-

No.

He cannot think like this. No matter how many *'what ifs'* he comes up with, it won't change what has already happened. Knowing the truth of

what happened to Saga and Runa, well, it makes it hard to look at them. When he works on healing Saga, he finds himself unable to keep eye-contact for long. She never speaks to him, so that does gives him an excuse, and he is frankly relieved by her ignoring his presence as much as she can.

Runa, on the other hand, questions everything, and she actively seeks out proper eye-contact when she speaks with him.

It helps though, when Aske reaches out, offers him a comforting touch; a clap on his shoulder, a squeeze of his hand, a nudge of his elbow. It helps alleviate the guilt he feels, because if Aske doesn't blame him, then… it can't be his fault. If it is, Aske would have chased him away. If it truly was his fault, Aske wouldn't have held him close that night, he wouldn't have comforted him, or even smile at him now. He certainly wouldn't help him as he is now.

So that alone is reassuring.

Yet it is hard still. Especially when he's healing Saga, whenever she deigns to look at him. There's something in her eyes, a look he can't quite discern what is, but it makes him uncomfortable, it makes a chill settle in his bones, the way she looks at him. It is like she is seeing through his physical body and surveying him from the inside, sees through to his very soul, as if she is trying to uncover something, anything, and it frightens him.

And he knows why it scares him. It is because Aske is wrong, isn't it? Bragi is terrified she will see the truth, learn the truth, because he can see it on her; the distrust, the cold anger, as if his very existence is a plague on her life.

And it is. Because, truly, his failure that day led to her losing nearly everything. Saga won't see what Aske does, she'll see the truth and then… No matter how happy he is at the thought of Aske defending him, he can't-no, he *won't* allow for himself to come between the siblings.

He will never forgive himself it that happens.

Bragi finds himself searching for that fragile resolve he had at the inn where so much changed in such a short time. He hopes to find it, for he might have need of it soon. The thought makes his heart twist painfully in his chest.

But… Bragi prides himself on being selfless. As selfless as it is possible to be, at the very least. How many times has he not sacrificed feelings for others? There are a few to count, as he has always done his best to keep from getting too close to people. Even so, after a certain period of time, he would crack beneath the need for company, friends, like any other person.

But he's always managed to say goodbye whenever there was a need. So, if the unthinkable should happen, he knows he'll be able to do the right thing here too. Though he should tell Aske beforehand. It is only right, after all, and Bragi would rather not that Aske believes the human doesn't care, or Goddess forbid, that he is abandoning him.

Now that he simply cannot let happen.

He is running out of time, however. True to Aske's claim back at the mountain, a shapeshifter heals at a much quicker rate than humans. While Saga will become bedridden if she exhausts herself, so to speak, and is still very much hurt, her most serious injured have mended quite nicely, cleanly, and if it continues like this, well, then she can soon begin travelling short distances.

Just a few days shy of a fortnight, and she has healed to the point she can sit up and eat on her own, even move about on her own as long as she's careful. If he wishes to speak with Aske, or at least have an informed conversation, it must happen soon.

The main obstacle is that Aske has been gone for days now. He had said something about ensuring their pursuers wouldn't find them, but it sounded so dangerous, and he's not back. Bragi is worried. The other two shapeshifters don't appear worried though, and that helps his frayed nerves some.

But as Saga grows ever stronger, Bragi grows ever more stressed. He is happy she is recovering well, of course he is; however it is a universal truth that for each day she improves, his chances of speaking with Aske grows slimmer. Once she has recovered enough, they will move again to wherever Aske thinks is the safest location for them. While technically they *can* speak during the next part of their journey, he prefers the thought of doing it here, where they can more easily have some privacy.

That evening, by what Bragi thinks is a stroke of luck, Aske returns. He's sweaty, his clothes are filthy, and his hair is a mess, but other than that there is nary a scratch on him. He also appears very smug and proud of himself, so his plan for the hunters must have worked. For now.

"That'll buy us some time. If we're lucky they won't catch our scent again at all."

"Crossing my fingers," Bragi says, smiling wanly. Aske grins boyishly back before he heads over to his sister who is sitting up on her own, with her daughter by her side. He appears ecstatic over Saga's recovery and Bragi wonders how to ask his companion if they can talk.

As evening draws near, however, Aske must have noticed that something is off about Bragi. As they're cleaning up after supper, with Saga and Runa already in deep sleep, Aske gently nudges the other with his shoulder.

"Is something wrong?" Bragi shakes his head, trying to assure Aske that everything is alright. Even so, his attempt must be rather unconvincing if the worried furrow of brows Aske is sporting right then is any indication.

"Don't lie to me." There's no edge, judgement or anger in his voice, he's not accusing Bragi of anything bad. The human still flinches, as if he had.

"I'm not, I just… I wish to talk to you, privately, if you'll allow it." Aske swallows, and he's not sure he's ready for whatever it is that Bragi wants to say.

CHAPTER TWENTY-EIGHT

They've wandered some ways from the cave. There's still some light out, casting the forested area in a warm, orange hue. It reminds Aske of a cosy hearth, yet the situation he is in makes him think of anything but a cosy, warm place to curl up in front of. Despite the warmth of the light, Aske feels a chill settle in his bones as Bragi stands with his back turned towards him for longer than is natural after coming to a stop like this. It is not like the other man to do something like this at all, and Aske's mind is already conjuring up with the worst possible scenarios he can imagine shaking his heart.

After all, since Saga woke up again, since they learned her story, Bragi has been… different. Not as cheery, not as bright, not… him. He's not been acting like the Bragi who Aske's gotten to know these last few months. The man who's managed to see the bright side of nearly everything they've faced up until now, the man who wears his emotions on his *every* sleeve, the man who is mischievous when the situation suits it and a bastard in all the best ways, *that* man has given way for someone who appears to have lost that spark.

It is terrifying because it feels like he is losing Bragi. He can't, just doesn't want to lose him, not now, not ever.

And then the brunet turns around, and the look in his eyes, the resignation, is enough.

"No." Bragi furrows his brows. He hasn't even said anything yet, and Aske is already denying him, but then again, it must show on him how he feels, that something is wrong. Aske is perceptive, after all.

"Aske-"he begins, hoping to be able to get the words out before his courage fails him, before he breaks and falls for the easy temptation of not bringing up the subject at all. Aske, however, seems adamant in not letting him.

"No." Aske has this feeling that Bragi's next words will hurt. As in, it will cause him enough heartache that it will cause physical pain. It is the way he acts and the way he speaks the shapeshifter's name, it is wrong. It is wrong, it is not how he usually says it. Bragi is lacking the fondness he usually projects when saying his name, the fondness he has laced Aske's name with for months now, and it is worrisome. It is like he's given up on this fragile thing they've built together, yet Aske is far from ready for that. Not now, probably not ever.

He has allowed Bragi in now. After being alone for so long, he's finally allowed someone close, finally allowed someone into his heart again. Add that to the fact that Bragi is a human and Aske is aware that it makes him look like a madman to his family, and every friend he has if they were to ever find out, it doesn't change this irrevocable fact; Aske doesn't *care* about their opinion, not if he has Bragi.

But this, to have Bragi give up now, it is unthinkable.

"Don't say it."

"Say what, Aske?" Bragi prods, daring the redhead to guess what he planned on speaking about, daring him to guess the subject that haunts him, and in turn will set its claws into Aske once it is out there. The other man's expression twists, tongue heavy and big in his mouth.

"Don't say you're leaving." Leaving *him.* The implication hangs in the air, heavy, painful. Bragi doesn't say anything at first, he just exhales, shoulders slumping for a moment, just long enough for Aske to think that he concedes defeat, before he straightens up again.

"Aske, I-"but he stops, swallowing. It is hard, so incredibly difficult, to find the strength to keep going when Aske looks at him with that expression. Staring at him as if he is wilfully going to hurt him when that isn't Bragi's intention at all. He just wants to tell Aske that he won't have to pick sides should the day come when he is faced with a situation where he has no choice but to make such a decision.

"I don't want to come between you and the last of your family. I just... I just want you to know that I'm not going to make you choose. If it comes down to it, I'll go, voluntarily," his voice is on the verge of breaking, but he swallows it back.

"You won't have to do or say a thing. I want to make it easy for you-"

"*Easy?*" Aske snarls, pupils thinning. The chill turns into a fire raging and egging him on to lash out.

"You're not making it easy for *me*, you're making it easy *for you!*" Bragi is taken aback by both the words and the way Aske fills them with fury and vitriol. Aske has shown him many emotions since their first meeting, but such outright anger directed *at him* is entirely new, and it catches him off-guard. The words as well, he finds, they're wrong! He is not so selfish that he is saying these things to save his own heart from breaking, he *is* saying it to help Aske!

"What do you mean? I *am* doing this for you!" he argues back, hoping that the other man might see the reason for why he's doing this. He is giving the man an out should it come down to it, because there is a very big chance the redhead will be forced to make a choice before the end of this. He's no fool, he sees Runa and Saga's discomfort, their fear, the pain they've felt at the hands of humans. And Bragi is human, and that alone is making them feel unsafe.

Besides, Aske himself had been hesitant in bringing him along, had outright said in the beginning that when the time comes, he should scamper off. Those were Aske's own sentiments in the beginning! Of course, many things had changed during the course of their journey. They had become friends, for one, and feelings had blossomed quietly yet quickly, ending up with that night at the inn. The night where they had silently confessed and just held each other, acknowledging the fact that the feelings they've both been trying to hold down are there to stay. Acknowledging that they both wanted them to stay together, to nurture them and bring about something even more beautiful. That they both wanted to *try*.

And they *have* tried, and Bragi can honestly say that he has never been happier in his life than when he could freely seek out Aske's hand and hold it in his, for being responsible for the smiles thrown his way and the way the other would squeeze his hand back with silent assurances.

But if there is one thing he will not be responsible for, it is getting between Aske and his family.

He cannot in good conscious allow that to happen. He won't be able to live with himself if that happens. He just can't be the reason for that, not when Aske made such an effort and sacrifice to find them, and even ran himself ragged while doing so.

"No, you're doing it to avoid taking responsibility." Aske narrows his eyes. "You're saying this so that *if* it happens, you don't *have* to fight for it. *That* is what you're doing!"

"That is not it at all-"Bragi feels like he is losing control of the situation. What should have been an easy conversation, no, not easy, it would have been emotionally heavy either way, is turning into a fight. He did not expect for it to do so. As heavy a subject this might be, and as painful as it would be for the both of them, Bragi still expected Aske to be rational about it. Instead of understanding the sacrifice Bragi is offering, Aske is arguing, turning his words against him.

"It is *exactly* that!" Aske is dangerously close to shouting now but manages to rein himself in before it escalates into a screaming match.

"You think you're making a sacrifice for me and you, but all you're doing is attempting to wrestle control from me, to take my choice away from me and running away like a *coward*." Bragi doesn't think it is like that at all, and argues back, raising his own voice a bit in a bid to be heard. Even so, no matter what he says, Aske won't listen, and it is frustrating.

"That is not it at all! I told you; I don't want to come between you and your sister!" he very nearly yells. Aske falls silent, but he is shaking in anger, hands clenched into fists at his sides.

"Keep telling yourself that, Bragi," he grits out between clenched teeth. "If this is all it meant to you, I wish that night hadn't happened at all." His words, spoken out of anger and heartache, feel like a physical punch to the gut, and Bragi staggers backwards. He can't stop the few tears from escaping, he can't stop Aske from seeing them, and the shapeshifter's yellow eyes flash with something akin to regret before they harden again.

"Feel free to leave whenever it is the most convention for you," he spits out, turns sharply on his heels and stomps away, paying no heed to the flowers he crushes beneath his boots.

A small growth of lilacs, petals scattering about from his hurried kicks. Bragi can relate to the crushed blooms. He feels like he is in a similar state. The sun is gone, and so is the warmth of the waning sunlight.

CHAPTER TWENTY-NINE

Saga watches how the human and her brother interact after that night where Aske had come stomping back in. She had managed to hear most of their conversation without having to follow too far, their raised voices had done very little to keep their secrecy. Runa had thankfully not been woken up by their quarrel. That girl has more than enough on her shoulders, she doesn't need the dramatics of Aske and the human added to it as well. This situation they are now in, however, is a gift, she thinks. Saga has long wondered how she can split the two of them up. A terrible thought, she knows it is, but she is not comfortable with having a human around herself and her daughter. Not after what happened.

She knows she should not be thinking like this. She should be happy for Aske, because the light in his eyes has filled her with a sort of envious joy. He is happy with this human, or at least he was until their argument. On another note, knowing Bragi's tale and knowing what his teacher was, Saga also knows she should be more rational about this.

Even so… to send the human away, it is just too great of an opportunity. The best part is that she didn't have to do anything to prompt him to do so, he offered it up himself. Bragi offered to leave himself, to not have Aske make a choice, because there is a choice to be made here.

Just not only by Aske, but by her as well.

Centuries long distrust fuelled by a newly returned hatred and grief is not so easily uprooted. Bragi is human, and any and all memories she has of any human only ended up in pain and grief and a hollowness in her chest.

Saga has lost her siblings to humans, she lost her lovemate and children to humans, most of the marks on her body are directly connected to the actions of humans. How can she trust Bragi to be truly safe to keep around when centuries of memories tell her otherwise?

Her brother though, he is vouching for the human. Her brother cares *deeply* for him. She might even call it love, but that is just ridiculous. Aske cannot be in love with a human, because their two species just don't mix. Saga can't do much though, she won't get between them like that, she won't be the person to crush her brother's happiness, no matter how much she wants Bragi gone. She won't say it to Aske, but she can now tell Bragi that she is not comfortable with him around.

And he'll leave on his own.

But even as she thinks this, she finds herself unable to go through with telling him. It might be because she loves her brother and want to see him happy, and she can't bear to be the one to ruin it.

Also, there are several little points which stop her from being anything but a bit cold towards the man. The first is that she most likely would not have survived her capture had it not been for Bragi, even after Aske's rescue. She had been in a terrible shape, she is still not in a good shape by any meansl, and as such, she knows she wouldn't have lasted for long.

The second point is that he is kind to Runa. Every question she asks, he answers patiently, never annoyed, never exasperated with her. It truly does appear that he finds her questions relieving.

The third point is the way he looks at Aske. The fondness in his eyes, the quirk of his lips beneath the growing beard and relaxed posture, the fact that he looks just as happy when he's close to Aske just as the shapeshifter does when near the human.

It is conflicting, these feelings. Lately though, after their last conversation, they've both been silent around each other. No upward quirks of their lips or smiles. Bragi appears as if he wishes to speak with Aske, but the redhead just turns his head away. A clear and silent demand to be left alone. And the way Bragi just deflates and turns away to hide that heartbroken expression each time, it does invoke a sense of sympathy in her.

The way Aske glances over his shoulder to see how Bragi reacts, only to take on the appearance of being regretful and angry at the same time, makes her exasperated, and she wants to shake him.

"He's a human!" She wants to yell at him, but she can't blame him, not really. One cannot control their own feeling. The heart wants what the heart wants. Bragi must have done something right to have been able to capture Aske's heart.

And Saga has no idea how long they've known each other, how long they've been while travelling together. She doesn't know what it is about Bragi that endears him to Aske, what he did to get pasts the distrust she *knows* her brother too harboured against humanity. What is so special about this human which enables him to walk straight past the walls they made before this human was even thought of? Before his parents were even born?

If she wants to know, she will have to ask one of them. And she is positively curious, so, one evening when Runa is asleep and Bragi is on the other side of the cave, as far away from the fire as it is possible to be without freezing, she questions her brother. Aske has been sitting by the entrance, the greenery pulled back a bit to allow some fresh air as they fall asleep. He looks up when she limps over to stand beside him.

"What makes him so important to you?"

"Hm?" He glances at her, arching a brow. Compared to how he was when he came back from turning the hunters around, joyful, proud, light-hearted, he is much more sombre now, with bags beneath his eyes. He looks tired and a little bit lost. Her heart hurts just from the sight of it.

"What makes him so special?" She expects him to look down and away from her, she expects his eyes to pinch in discomfort and sorrow. Saga does not expect him to narrow his eyes at her in anger. Her eyes widen as he nearly snarls back.

"What does it matter to you?" She hobbles back a step, surprised by him, and more than a little hurt by the outburst. His expression softens before he looks out into the forest, regret instantly catching him in its grip.

"I'm sorry. You didn't deserve that," he mutters, clasping his hands together and hunching forward. He looks small like this, and it is wrong. Aske has always been tall, strong, nearly unshakable. To see him curled up like this, small and vulnerable like a child, it is wrong, and she hates to admit that it is not just Bragi's fault, but hers as well.

She alienated him for nearly a hundred years, after all. Bragi isn't the one who crushed Aske's confidence. He may have caused the blow to shatter it, but Saga caused the first cracks to appear in the first place.

"I think I may have," she responds, before stepping closer again, gesturing to the space beside him.

"May I sit?" He makes a half-hearted gesture beside him, and she drops down carefully, mindful of her aches and still healing injuries. She may not be hurting as much as she used to, but there are still some residual stabs of pain if she moves too abruptly, and her body is stiff, hard to move. She gets exhausted so easily now.

Even so, they should be on the move soon. Even if Aske did manage to lead the hunters astray, they might still find them again.

"I'm sorry," she tells him. He doesn't look her way, but she continues nonetheless. It needs to be said, the air between them needs to be cleared.

"I didn't tell you about them because I thought you'd be angry, or sad. And I… I just clung to what we said to each other back then and used it as an excuse to keep my distance. It was unfair of me though, and I'm sorry." Aske doesn't say anything at first, he doesn't even look her way and she has to make a conscious effort to not squirm while she waits for him to acknowledge her, and her apology. She *hopes* he acknowledges them.

"I'm sorry too," he finally says after minutes of silence, and she bites back a sigh of relief. "For being a coward."

"You weren't a coward." She pulls her knees up to her chest, resting her chin on them. It hurts, she can't quite hide the flinch, but she refuses to move again.

"You respected my stupid decision."

"It wasn't stupid." He finally turns and there's a tiny grin on his face. "We'll go all night if we keep on countering each other like this." She grins back. She's tired, she doesn't want to argue, especially since she knows he is right.

"Can I ask?" She gestures to Bragi. The grin fades from Aske's lips and he appears thoughtful, attempting to find the right words. He struggles for a few moments.

"He's…" Aske's brows pinch together, the words eluding him before he tries again. "He's someone I trust. And even when he saw the ugliest parts of me, he found me beautiful. And when I was hostile and unkind, he was endlessly patient. And if it weren't for him, I wouldn't have found you in time. He did everything he could to help me, even when I gave nothing back. He is warm, kind, witty, clever and a bastard." It is said with such fondness and warmth it takes Saga by surprise. She's never heard Aske talk about another person like this. Not someone who isn't, *wasn't*, family anyway.

And she knows that look. Not that his slightly dilated pupils aren't a dead give-away on their own. And it hits her then. She can't request Bragi to leave. It will crush Aske if he leaves, and she won't be the reason for it. Absolutely not. Because this *isn't* just an infatuation or simple adoration. This *is* love.

And she's not sure Aske is quite aware of it himself.

Saga is quite sure that if Bragi leaves, Aske will realize just how much the human means to him. She doesn't want to see the raw heartbreak on his face should that come to pass. The Goddess and her Children be damned, she must learn to accept the human as a part of her life going forward, isn't she? She will help her brother find a way to mend this relationship, even though she almost fears that her next questions and probing will allow for him to realize just how deeply he is feeling.

"Have you told him this?" She asks. Her brother shakes his head. "Don't you think he would fight to stay if he knew?" Aske sits up straight, face twisting into a confused frown.

"If he knew how deeply you feel, maybe he wouldn't think leaving would be the best choice for you." They sit in an awkward silence for several heartbeats, Aske trying to find the words, but ultimately giving up.

"How do you feel about him staying?" And it is kind of him to ask, but Saga's feelings on the matter isn't important right now. All she's done lately is think of her own feelings. Saga, with all the information she has now, knows that right at this moment, Aske's heart is more important. She has ignored him for a century, he deserves her consideration, especially since he has saved her and her daughter's life. He came running for her even when she didn't deserve that kindness from him.

"I can tolerate him, if he makes you happy." Aske's lower lip quivers and he bows his head. She reaches out and links her fingers with his. The way he squeezes her hand, it makes her happy. Makes her happy to know he understands.

CHAPTER THIRTY

A few days later, they've taken a chance of being outside for a little bit, enjoying the good weather before they move on. Runa had been on the verge of going crazy inside the cave, and Saga admits that being able to go out and breathe fresh air does improve her mood.

And makes her feel much better too.

She sits with Aske, after he saddled the horses, keeping a watchful eye on Runa, who's hovering around Bragi, who is unearthing roots and apparent herbs which grow in the area. Runa is fascinated by whatever Bragi tells her, and she moves around the area, picking flowers and plants and greens, showing them to Bragi and learning their names and uses.

"You haven't talked to him yet?"

"What makes you think that?" She gives him a look, as if he is at all capable of fooling her at this point.

"You're still barely looking at each other." He sighs, shoulders sagging.

"No, I have not."

"You probably should."

"I should… but I want him to fight for me. After what he said, I don't want to just sweep it under the rug and act as if it didn't happen. "

"I'm not telling you to forgive him," Saga huffs, carding a hand through her short hair. She wrinkles her nose at the feel of it, greasy and tangled. She is desperately in need of a wash.

"Just tell him what he means to you, and that it hurt, and you wish that he'd understand that. He seems like a clever enough person to be able to connect the dots."

"It's a bit scary though," Aske murmurs, linking his fingers together in his lap, shoulders rising a bit.

"Of course it is," Saga says in an offhand manner. "You're quite literally telling someone just how vulnerable your heart is to them." Aske doesn't answer at first, so she turns. He looks both unimpressed and terrified at the same time, and she wonders if she should have kept her mouth shut.

"It's… not as terrifying as I made it sound."

"It absolutely fucking is!" He hisses at her in a panic, and she can't help but laugh a bit as she turns back to watch her daughter. She's still happily picking flowers, enjoying the peace and quiet, quite some distance away from them now. She's making a flower crown, all her attention on braiding the stems together as neatly as she's able.

And she doesn't see the man behind her with a raised sword.

Saga can't properly progress everything that happens after that. She knows she screams as she leaps to her feet. She can see Aske from the corner of her eyes, throwing himself forward, swiftly changing into a serpent and racing through the tall grass, but she knows he won't make it. Aske won't make it, and the humans will take away her very last child!

They've taken Aina, Alv, Ebba and Halle, and now they will take Runa too.

The girl is frozen in fear, the flowers falling from her hands as she looks wide-eyed over her shoulder.

Saga's entire body screams in agony at the sudden strenuous movements, but she doesn't care. When Runa falls, Saga's world will shatter, and nothing will hold any meaning ever again.

The sword comes down, swift, decisive, deadly, and Saga feels like her heart is about to burst in her chest, when Bragi is suddenly there, broad hands *grabbing* the blade as he slips between Runa and her assailant, using speed and strength Saga never thought he was capable of as he twists the trajectory of the weapon, forcing the man to stumble to the side.

The man falls just as the healer spins on his heels, lifts Runa up with his still bleeding hands, and runs towards them. Aske slips past him, and a painful yowl alerts them to Aske's attack. The redhead leaps out of the tall grass, human-shaped again, and follows them just as Bragi shoves Runa into her mother's arms and runs straight into the cave.

Time pauses in a confusing manner to Saga as she clings to her daughter, because suddenly Bragi is there again, with the horses, and Aske is taking Runa away from her. Saga lashes out, but Bragi is already strong-arming her onto his horse. Aske and Runa leap up on the other. They ride like a forest fire is snapping at their heels, leaving their temporary hiding place behind in the dust.

They both ignore her when she demands hysterically to have her daughter back. Bragi's arm around her is like an iron bar preventing her from leaping off the horse.

Saga is stuck.

However, with one look at Runa, a proper look where Saga *sees* her, Saga realizes slowly that while the little girl's mind is reeling from what just happened and she is obviously still scared, she is sitting completely still in front of Aske. She is not crying or fighting him, she's holding onto the front of the saddle, eyes wide, as they quickly ride away.

It feels like time passes in the blink of an eye, thankfully, even though hours have passed before they find the courage to stop. Their mounts are exhausted, their legs trembling once their riders slide off.

Runa is immediately handed off to Saga as Aske stalks past, heading straight for Bragi who is slightly leaning against his horse.

"You great bloody imbecile!" He very nearly roars as he marches over to the brunet, grabbing his hands, glaring furiously down at the bleeding palms. It registers to Saga then. The human had grabbed the sword with his bare hands, and she notices now how pale he is, the sweat trailing down from his temples to his chin, his hair plastered to his forehead. He looks horrible, swaying on his feet, brows pinching together. He is obviously in pain, and Aske isn't handling him gently enough right now. He is angry on the outside, but it is quite clear that he is more panicked than anything else.

"Why aren't you healing yourself?" Aske demands, but Bragi just shakes his head, though it seems to worsen his balance when he does it.

"I can't heal myself-"

"Mam, mam! Bragi is hurt!" Runa stutters out through chattering teeth. The haze that kept Saga from feeling fully in control of herself lifts as she hurries over to the other two. She must be out of her mind, utterly raving mad for even considering doing what she is. She does it anyways because she owes the human.

So, she shoulders Aske away as she puts Runa down, and forces Bragi to sit down on the ground before he passes out. He's breathing heavily, and she scowls. If they had treated this immediately, he wouldn't be like this. Even so, she knows that stopping and taking the time to clean and wrap the wounds was never an option. None of them were in the sound mind of doing so. All three had been panicking. She more so than the other two, even more than Runa. But Saga's mind is clearer now, and she examines the wound properly.

They're deep, the blade cut deep into the meat and muscle, and he needs stitches. The wounds are so deep Saga is astonished he managed to hold both the reins of the horse and her for as long as he did. Fortunately, his palms got the brunt of the attack, his fingers aren't as bad off and just needs to be bandaged.

"Aske, water!" she barks out as she climbs to her feet to retrieve Bragi's medical bag from his horse. From there, even though she must snap at her sibling yet again to pull him out of his stupor, everything happens methodically and quickly.

The wounds are cleaned and with groggy guidance from the healer, she patches him back up as best as she can. While she does this, Aske keeps Runa close and occupied in a way to distract her while her mother is busy. Once Saga is done though, she immediately turns to her daughter without saying a word.

"Thank you," Bragi exhales tiredly, shoulders slumping. He looks much older now than this morning, the loss of blood leaving his appearance to be, quite frankly, ghastly.

"Don't mention it," she mutters. She owes Runa's life to him after all. They had been careless, let their guard down, and it had nearly become a disaster.

"What happened to the attacker?" the healer asks Aske, who appears vaguely uncomfortable as he avoids Bragi's eyes.

"I bit him," he admits quietly, hesitantly, fidgeting as he glances up for no longer than a heartbeat before averting his gaze again.

"It's… it was slow."

'Good,' Saga thinks. The bastard deserved it. She glances over to Bragi as well, curious to what his reaction towards Aske's admission will be. Will he judge Aske for what he did? Will he be horrified or disgusted by his actions. Will he create more of a distance between them now? Will he deny Aske the opportunity to mend things between them?

"Are you alright, Aske?" Bragi asks instead, and the redhead blinks, meeting the human's tired gaze with surprise and confusion. He obviously thought the same thing as Saga, that Bragi would find his action abhorrent, horrifying, that he would create more of a distance, that he would use this as an excuse to leave.

"Yes," he finally says, meeting Bragi's gaze without even an ounce of shame or regret in his voice. Bragi nods.

"Good- oh dear." He clutches his head, swaying in his seat. "That made the world spin."

"I'll…" Aske swallows. "I'll make you some food. Replenish the blood you… the blood you lost." They risk a small fire. The warmth of it helps chase away some of the terror that had seeped into their bones, and the food, while a bit bland and boring, fills their stomachs and make them feel just a little bit better.

They don't stay where they are for long. They eat, clean up, douses the fire with dirt and covers the evidence of ever having been there as well as they can before they move on.

Bragi is helped up on his horse, while Saga and Runa are seated on Aske's. Said man takes both the horses' reins in his hands and begins to lead the mounts away. They are all exhausted, but they cannot rest just yet. What happened back by the cave is still rattling them.

They need to move on.

CHAPTER THIRTY-ONE

"Snake bite," a dark-haired woman says as she examines the dead body in front of her. The body is a disturbing sight to see, with marks around the man's neck from him most likely clawing at it. From the looks of the area they found him in, he suffered a lot, for quite some time, and had tried to get away for help.

"Imagine that. This area should be clear of any such venomous beasts, though. It's not warm enough for them," a scarred man says, grinning despite seeing one from his own group of people on the ground, dead.

"We've found the trail," he adds as he gestures for the group to continue. They've grown in size since the river incident, the survivors of the other group having joined them. Their final tracker is already checking to see if they can find any leads.

"Here!" They call out. "Heavy hoof prints. They fled on horses. There's more than just the original two now, considering how deep the hoof prints are."

"We shouldn't have followed the cyclops for as long as we did," one of the newcomer's snaps. "If we had been more alert, we would have noticed that they split from that beast long before we caught up to him. We lost several of our people and almost all our horses to him!" They're frustrated by the losses they've suffered during this hunt. What should have been an easy hunt has turned into a several months long tracking mission to avoid letting their prey get away. What upsets them all the most is that they had one of the two they were missing, but that she got away somehow too despite all they put her through, and now they are back to the starting point.

"What is done is done," their leader sighs in annoyance. "The fact that we keep finding their trail no matter their trickery is proof that the Goddess is sanctioning our hunt. She wants them gone just as much as we do. We move on!" he orders. They leave their fallen comrade on the ground, his remains a reminder of what happens when one is encountering shapeshifters. Certain, slow, and painful death. His body will return to the earth and nourish it. It is a risk they take when they go out on hunts. Out of the original number they boasted when they began this hunt, they've lost nearly half of the group, and one person here points it out.

"There's only thirteen left of us, chief," she comments, voice tight as she looks over the people trudging along behind them. He glances at her from the corner of his eyes.

"Yes, we'll have to do some recruiting once we're done," he acknowledges.

"We should have just killed the bitch when we got her. The spawn would have been easy to find afterwards." She sounds rational, but she is challenging his decision of interrogating the adult shapeshifter. Few shapeshifters disclose any lead of their spawns and nests, even during the most horrific torture. Their latest catch was no different. She had screamed, oh how she had screamed, but she had not told them anything. But he enjoys it, and he won't be dissuaded. Not now, and not in the future.

"True, it would have been easier, but it seems like we've unearthed two more shapeshifters, so I'll call it a successful endeavour." The woman scowls, so he stops and towers over her.

"Are you siding with them?" She stops short, just like the rest of the group. Cold sweat trails down her back as she struggles not to tremble and cower in front of him. The way he's staring down at her with those wide, empty eyes honestly terrifies her. She feels like prey in front of a snake just waiting to strike. She swallows and shakes her head.

"No, chief," her voice is barely above a whisper when she answers him. He doesn't respond, and she feels her hands twitch towards her knife at her hip, ready to defend herself if needed. But then he just turns and keeps on walking, and she releases a breath she didn't even know she was holding in. She's safe.

Then, in a rush of movement she isn't prepared for, a fist collides with her face, and she finds herself sprawled on the ground. Her leader is crouching over her, arm raised. Her face throbs, but she barely registers that over the paralyzing fear she feels at the sight of him above her.

"Don't *ever* question me again," he tells her as he hits her again and gain. The sound of crunching bone echoes in the forest with each hit. Everyone else shuffles back a bit, watching silently with different levels of discomfort, but no one intervenes.

She's still alive when they all move on, their leader at the front with bloodied fists. Of course, with a skull half-caved in, she won't last.

She lays there for quite some time before she succumbs, not too far from her fallen comrade.

CHAPTER THIRTY-TWO

Bragi is doing better. Physically, at least. Emotionally and mentally, well, he could do much better, if he was to answer anyone honestly, should they ask. As it is, no one asks, except for Runa, in the rare instances she finds her voice after the attack, and he doesn't want to worry the young girl. Whenever she asks, he tells her he's doing fine, and he is telling half the truth. His hands are healing nicely, much better than he could have anticipated, so yes, he is physically fine.

It is nice of her to ask. At the very least *someone* asks about how he is. Aske is no longer indifferent or angry, but he's awkward and uncertain, avoids talking to him as much as possible.

It is almost worse than when he was angry.

Saga, well, she looks over his wounds, but she doesn't say much. Her expression doesn't give much away either. All in all, the next leg of their journey is rather, well, unbearably quiet is a rather apt word.

The moment he has enough strength for it, he walks on his own, with Saga and Runa on a horse each. Runa is the one who carries the conversation when it occurs, and while her chatter, although quieter and less lively now than before, keeps the heavy silence away, it should not fall on an eight-year-old child to keep morale up.

Bragi decides that no matter what the outcome, he'll have a real proper talk with Aske, to clear up the misunderstanding. It might end up with Aske banishing him though, and, well, that thought makes Bragi's stomach turn.

But it is a very real possibility, and he cannot ignore that fact. So, he spends an entire day gathering his courage.

When they stop to rest for the night, nearly a week after the attack, the shapeshifter disappears, as if he is sensing Bragi's resolution. It discourages the healer, whose shoulders slump.

Then, something happens that catches him completely off guard. Saga speaks to him. Her speaking *to* him surprises him even more than her actual words.

"Why aren't you fighting for him?" He blinks, momentarily struck dumb before he gathers himself. Aske had become angry, but Saga, she might see reason in all this. He searches for the right words when she speaks again, deciding that he is taking far too long to gather himself and find the words he needs to explain the situation.

"Was it fun?"

"What?"

"Playing around with him?" Bragi doesn't understand what she means by this. He's quite certain that he and Aske were not playing at all up until this point. Certainly not now with their arguing.

"Was it fun leading him on?" The confusion gives way to shock, which then concedes its place to the anger Bragi feels well up in him.

"I beg your pardon?" Anger is good, Saga thinks, even if it makes her slightly uncomfortable. She hasn't witnessed him showing anything but the most amazing length of patience with her, but still, anger is good. Anger shows he cares.

"How dare you? I've never once, *never once*, I, no, how dare-" he works himself up into a state, but she doesn't have time for him to show any more outrage and throw a fit. If he wanted to be allowed to blow off the steam from her insult, then he should have done so much earlier, instead of acting like a pitiful man who lost everything he could have wanted. When it is his own damn fault.

"Then, if he's so important to you, why don't you fight for him?" And her question catches him off-guard again, but this time he just grows hopeless. He looks down in his lap, at his bandaged hands which stings badly after he had curled his fingers into tight fists, nails digging into the fabric.

"I... I don't want to get between you. You are family, and he was so desperate to find you, he ran himself ragged in his search, I can't... I *can't* bear to unravel that effort and the ties he has to you for-for-"

"But that's not your choice to make," she cuts him off. He seems both affronted and thrown for a loop. For someone so clever, he sure has a hard time following simple logic, the shapeshifter thinks.

"You're right," she forges on, "I am not the most comfortable with you being a human, something you didn't chose to be born as, but no matter. I'm not stubborn enough to not admit that I wouldn't be here right now if not for you. Runa would have died if not for you. Aske might not have found either of us if it wasn't for you." It is easier to say the words aloud than she thought it would be. Saga honestly thought she had to fight to get the words out, that she had to lean forward, shove her fingers in her mouth to throw the words up. They rather escaped her without much effort. She's not sure if she's grateful for that or not, yet she's got more to say. It is good to know that she can stay rational, even now.

"But me not being comfortable with you around shouldn't dictate my brother's happiness. I've come to realize that there isn't a bloody bad bone in your body, as infuriating as *that* is to admit. I also know now that you won't turn on us. I'll... I'm working on it, I *want* to treat you better, but it will take time. Alright? So, don't hurt my brother and put the blame on me." Bragi gestures, turns in his seat, stammering as he tries to assure her that by no means does he put any blame on her. It is almost adorable the way he panics.

"I understand that you don't *mean* to put the blame on me, but that is essentially what you are doing. Don't use me as an excuse to achieve a clean get-away, I don't appreciate it. If you want to stay, fight for it. Don't be a bloody coward who ran away and then feel sorry for yourself. You are, quite literally, the only obstacle to both of your happiness here." She's growing progressively quieter the longer she speaks, eyes narrowing as she feels both insulted and annoyed with the whole situation, because truly, that is how the situation has turned out. Bragi just stares at her, mouth flopping about with no sound escaping him, quite like a fish on land. It would have been quite amusing if it isn't for her being quite cross with him right now.

"Well?" She snaps and he startles so bad he nearly falls over. "Get going!" Bragi scrambles to his feet, and she can practically see the wheels turn in his head as he turns away and then back to her, away and back to her, blinking in rapid succession, before he appears to reach a conclusion. He squares his broad shoulders, inhales, exhales, then practically sprints after Aske.

Runa, who had been silently watching, crawls into her mother's lap, gazing up quizzically.

"What did you mean?" Saga smiles wanly, just hugging the girl close, breathing her in. She smells of sweat, dirt, and in just as much a need of a bath as Saga is. Aske and Bragi too now that she thinks about it. The next time they come across a big enough water source, they should all clean themselves properly.

"It's something that was really easy to solve that the two of them made much more complicated than they needed to," she tells the girl who appears thoughtful, nose scrunching together adorably. She rather resembles a little piglet as she does it, it causes Saga to laugh a little.

"Did you and Da do that?" It still hurts, being reminded of her former partner. There is a difference between her and her partner, and Bragi and Aske.

She didn't love her partner romantically. Not like that. He had been a friend, a close one, and she had loved him, just not in a romantic sense. They had never told their children this, however, and she's not about to tell Runa this now. Instead, she shakes her head in answer to Runa's question.

"No, nothing like this. The two of us, we talked, always. If we argued, we always tried to clear any misunderstandings quickly. We made sure to always talk, especially after you were all born." A fluke Saga doesn't regret. Her partner had been someone sturdy, a great support and a devoted parent. He had been someone anyone would wish to have by their side.

She regrets none of her choices since she and Aske parted ways all those years ago, other than the fact that she allowed her partner to talk her into staying in the area they inhabited. She should have begun the journey to a safe place the moment she learned she was carrying. If she had, she wouldn't have experienced that horrible day, and Runa would still have two parents and all four of her siblings.

That regret is gnawing at her, hurting the same way an animal gnawing through flesh and muscle to reach the bone does. This feeling will shadow her for the rest of her life. She still sees them in her dreams, mangled and beaten and rotten with empty gazes. Saga wonders if Runa suffers such horrid dreams too, but she lacks the courage to ask, afraid that if she prods, Runa will be triggered.

All she prays for, is that Runa won't grow up to resent her. She hugs the girl tighter, watches as she ponders over who knows what.

"So, talking is important?" Saga chuckles.

"Very. If we don't talk with each other, how would we know what the other thinks or feel? It is the same with questions. How would you get any answers if you don't ask questions?"

"Oh!" Runa exclaims, understanding finally dawning on her. She likes asking questions. "So, me asking questions makes me clever?" Saga nods.

"In my opinion, children who seek answers to their questions and queries might be much cleverer than any adult."

"I know I am. No one found me after all." The smile fades from Saga's face, and she brushes a hand through her daughter's short curls, pressing a kiss to her forehead as she does so.

"I'm sorry I left you in that tree. You were so brave. My clever little girl, fighting on your own, I'm so sorry I put you in that situation," she murmurs, and her heart is twisting with shame in her chest. The way Runa casts her eyes down intensifies the feeling. Of course the girl must have been terrified. Saga is an adult, and *she* is terrified of the potential the humans carry for violence upon her and hers.

"I was scared," Runa admits, "but I trusted that I'd find Aske if I kept running. You told me I would."

"Clever girl," Saga praises her again, proud of her daughter, proud of how she listened and did what she had been told.

Proud that she fended for herself and survived, even though she never should have been put in such a situation in the first place.

CHAPTER THIRTY-THREE

Bragi hurries as fast as he can after Aske. He's not sure if Aske is just going out to hunt something to eat, secure the area or going a distance to hide their tracks. Even so, he must hurry while he still possesses the courage to speak the truth. He just hopes that the other man will allow him to explain, to prove as best as he is able that he understands how much he hurt Aske. And, of course, how he had not meant for it to hurt him at all, even though he knew it would, but that it had been a misguided attempt to take any burden off Aske's shoulders.

Bragi just hopes that Aske will listen, allow him to speak, hear not just an apology for the sake of it, but a sincere heartfelt apology because he now understands just how wrong he was. That he wants to take responsibility for the grief he caused. Bragi deserves a tongue-lashing and he's bracing himself for it as he scans the area, hoping to catch sight of the shapeshifter.

He does not find even a glimpse of red hair, that unique colour he's only seen Aske, Saga and Runa adorn. The colour that stands out so vividly against the world, it is impossible to miss.

He does, however, notice the massive serpent suddenly slithering up behind him. He yelps in surprise, until the serpent lifts its head, yellow eyes staring down at him, belly red.

"Oh, Aske." Bragi lays a calming hand over his rapidly beating heart. "You surprised me," he exhales. The serpent says nothing, which unnerving since he knows that the other is fully capable of verbal speech even when in the shape of a beast. It just goes to show just how badly he has made a mess of things between them. It almost feels like they are back to how they were at the mountain. It is a saddening thought, to think he might have ruined all their combined efforts up until now, ruined the trust, ruined Aske's belief in him. After all, the shapeshifter's life has taught him to do anything but trusting a human with anything of value, especially his heart.

His fragile, tattered heart with so many scars it is amazing he still possesses any kindness and compassion. Aske had offered it so tentatively to Bragi, who has with his recent words and actions, quite literally thrown it to the ground, stomped and spit on it.

Well, now he feels even worse. Bragi may not have seen his actions this way before now, but Aske must have, considering his response. But this isn't about how wretched Bragi feels for having caused such pain, it is about apologizing, ask for forgiveness if it is possible to be granted one, and trying to make things right again. It is about making Aske feel better, for that trust Bragi shattered viciously with his ignorance to be perhaps grow into a new foundation. This is about showing Aske that he knows that he did wrong, and that the other is well within his right to be upset and that Bragi *understands* that and doesn't hold it against him.

He is well-deserving of being sent away should Aske find his apology lacking, yet Bragi hopes, he so desperately, *selfishly* hopes, that Aske will listen. He knows that Aske will let him *talk*, but the healer is worried that he might not *listen*. That he believes that whatever Bragi tells him will be meaningless.

Nothing will be resolved until he speaks, though, so he clears his throat and looks up, as the serpent has curled up in a more relaxing position which doesn't stop him from towering over the human at all. Yet even with a shape that betrays no emotion, a body with such strength and agility which could end him before Bragi would even know what hit him, and a size that makes him appear like a small child in comparison, Bragi does not feel intimidated. Aske is still here, he hasn't left, he's waiting for Bragi's next move. That is a positive thing, the brunet can't help but think. He clears his throat for a second time before he finally manages to tear himself from his spiralling thoughts to speak up.

"I want to apologize. I meant well, back then, but I know you didn't see it the same way I did. While I thought I was taking a burden off you, all I accomplished was hurting you. I made you think you didn't matter to me the way you do, that you aren't important to me when the truth is that you are the most important person in my life, for the first time ever, I believe. I just…" Bragi hesitates, his tongue heavy with regret.

"I didn't want to come between you and your family, I didn't want to have you chose if it would come down to it, however… By doing that I robbed you of having the- the opportunity to *make* a choice. And I'm sorry for that." Aske doesn't say anything, and it is hard to guess what he's thinking, but Bragi forges on. He needs to get it all out. No more misunderstandings. No more awkwardness, indifference, or anger.

"I just… I didn't want to hurt you, but I ended up doing so anyway, and I am so sorry. I care for you, greatly, and, well, what I truly wish for, is to be able to continue staying by your side, if you will allow me," he hurries to add. Still there is no response from Aske, and Bragi feels his heart sink in his chest. It is too late for apologies now. Too much time has passed since the argument, and Bragi cannot blame the other, especially not since the healer only realized while conversing with Saga what he had truly done to the other man. He looks down, partly because he is too ashamed to meet Aske's silent gaze, and partly to hide the growing wetness in his eyes. He won't let Aske see a most wretched human's appearance as a plea for something Bragi is most undeserving of.

He won't let his expression be some sort of accidental emotional manipulation.

Then, Aske moves, shrinking in size, tail splitting, head shrinking, hair growing out, scales melting into skin. And then he stands there, human-shaped again, the shape Bragi is the most familiar with, and now his expression is not so unreadable. It is obvious that he is still quite vexed, hurt and he is not letting it go so easily. He had let himself be vulnerable, and he had been burned. Bragi's heart aches at the sight, and he fists his hands in his tunic to keep himself from reaching out. He knows the gesture won't be welcome at this moment, if ever again.

"Aske-"

"No, it is my turn." Bragi snaps his mouth shut and stands so still that Aske for a moment wonder if he stopped breathing.

"What you did, no matter what your intention, was hurtful!" Bragi nods. "Yes, I'm going to forgive you, obviously I am, but what I am *not* going to do is forget it happened! Do you understand that?" Bragi nods yet again, hurriedly. Even this is much more than the brunet could ever dare hope for. He'll take whatever scraps is offered to him. Anything to be able to grab onto a lifeline where he can fix this, to ensure that Aske feels safe again, that Aske feels as if he can trust Bragi again. To ensure that Aske can truly believe that his heart is safe in Bragi's hands, to be allowed the chance to prove that he won't make the same mistake again.

"I'll never forget that you tried to take that choice away from me-"Bragi flinches, clutching the fabric in his hands harder to keep from doing something unwelcome, "I'll never forget that *you* decided that your opinion, without consulting me beforehand, was the better option. You didn't ask me what *I* wanted; you just decided *you* knew better." Bragi already felt like a wretched fool, even before he sought Aske out, but he feels much like an insect now. Yet he cannot be upset at anyone else than himself for it because Aske is right.

"All I can do is ask your forgiveness, and suffer whatever penance you believe will-"Aske throws his hands in the air, yelling so loud in frustration the human startles. The sound is raw, echoing in the air as he looks heavenwards.

"You don't *understand,* Bragi!" He exclaims, rubbing his face viciously. "It's not about you punishing yourself or having me come up with a punishment! It is about you violating the trust I put in you! I am willing to work on building that trust back up, but if you think that what you need to do in order to fix this is a punishment, then I'm- I'm not so sure there's even a point in trying." Bragi is horrified by the vulnerability he hears at the end as Aske crosses his arms in front of his chest, shoulders rising nearly to his ears.

Oh goodness, oh no! Goddess, *no!*

Being allowed to try and rebuild that trust they had between each other, that is a gift like no other, and no matter what he needs to do, he'll never think of it as a punishment. This happiness he cannot recall having ever felt after the destruction of his home, he wants it back, greedy thing that he is.

"Not at all do I think that whatever it is that I must do to regain your trust will be a punishment," Bragi says as he cautiously ventures closer.

"And I am willing to do whatever it is that you ask of me. You providing me with the chance to make up for my folly is the greatest gift I've ever been given."

"Are you telling me I am not your greatest gift?" Aske can't quite stop himself from uttering the joke even in this serious situation they are in. he wants to hit himself, shove his fist in his mouth and bite down on it, but what use is that now? Bragi grants him relief from his mortification, though, as he gathers the other man's hands in his, cradling them ever so gently as he pulls them up to his lips.

"Once I've managed to make myself worthy of you again, you truly will be the greatest gift in my life." The shapeshifter's cheeks flush nearly as red as his hair. The sight makes Bragi blush as well, surprised that he had managed to utter such words at all, yet he feels no embarrassment, only smug joy. Joy that he'd managed to put such a look on the face of the subject of his affections.

Oh, oh dear, he thinks, that it is just now that he realizes just how much he cares for Aske.

"Yes, well, we should talk about how to do that." Aske clears his throat, trying to dispel the awkwardness he now feels. He tugs on his hands, feels how Bragi is reluctant to let him go, even when he pulls with a bit more force, and averts his eyes. Only then does Bragi fully let him go.

"I need… I need you to promise me something."

"I shall do my very best," Bragi says, his focus completely on Aske, just waiting for his request. Whatever Aske asks of him, as long as it is within his power, Bragi will do whatever it is.

CHAPTER THIRTY-FOUR

Runa is a very perceptive child. She might be a young child of mere eight summers, but where her siblings had been rather gifted with magic, she is more prone to noticing the tiny details most ignore during their waking hours.

The moment she had her mother back, obviously she had paid more attention to her uncle and his companion. She'd already asked Bragi questions, and while her instincts and experience told her he was a danger to her, she had managed to stand her ground. And she also clearly saw how Aske and Bragi acts around each other.

The way they interact; speak to each other, touch each other, gestures between them whom no one would notice if they weren't watching.

She noticed the way they look at each other early on. Now, she doesn't know what all the emotions she sees are, but she knows some. Amongst them is fondness, badly concealed happiness, a certain mischievousness she often saw in her siblings faces when they came up with pranks, and a faraway look with smiles she cannot identify directed at one, when the other isn't looking. Or, when they think the other isn't looking. Or anyone, really.

But Runa is watching, and she sees it all. Her mother and father, they didn't look at each other the same way Aske and Bragi look at each other. There was fondness, of course, because they cared for each other, that was obvious, but not the same way these two do. And that does raise some questions in Runa's mind, though she pushes them away for later.

But then something happens.

One night everything appears just fine before she goes to sleep with her mother, apart from Bragi having been more fidgety than normal. The next morning, the two aren't speaking together. Aske appears constantly angry or sad, while Bragi is perpetually downcast. And so quiet. He doesn't stop answering Runa's questions, but he doesn't initiate conversations as much as he did. When it comes to Aske, he seems like he loses the courage to do so before he even opens his mouth.

As for Aske himself, well, he does his very best to *not* look at Bragi, or even just glance in his direction, during any part of the day. It is such a stark contrast to what the girl knows to be normal between the two men.

Runa finds it sad, and a slight bit frightening as well. It happened overnight, while she slept. Something happened between her falling asleep and waking up that made their happiness and closeness twist into sadness and a distance, and it happened just as quick as it did when she lost her entire family, and it nags in the back of her mind. Of course the girl wonders what has happened.

First, she wonders what made them so close in the first place, how they became friends, and what the emotions she couldn't name are. As she's never seen them before she has no name for them.

When Runa asks her mother, she almost appears sad at being asked, like it pains her for some reason.

"It's… a complicated feeling. It can be the most exhilarating feeling in the world, or the most painful one."

"Are they hurt now?" Runa asks, even though she struggles to understand how a feeling can be both good and bad at the same time. Saga appears uncomfortable as she looks at both her brother and Bragi, eyes darting away for a moment before she turns back to her daughter, mouth in a thin line as she answers.

"Maybe. Perhaps, though they caused that hurt themselves." However, her mother's answer makes no sense to Runa. Why would anyone willingly hurt someone they're close to? Only bad people hurt others. And neither Aske nor Bragi are bad people. So how have they managed to hurt each other? It is all very confusing to her, and at that point it made no sense, but the more she watches them, and the more answers she needles out of her mother, she comes to understand that it is love.

Not the kind of love she has, *had*, for her siblings, but the kind two people who aren't family have. It makes Runa wonder if her mother and father didn't have that kind of love since they are, *were*, family, a mother and father. Runa asks her mother about it, and the way her face twists at that question makes the little girl realize that she's wrong there too.

But it is love, and no one can tell her otherwise.

But if that is love, and her parents weren't looking at each other the same way, did her parents not love each other? Or did they love each other with a limited capacity so that they wouldn't hurt each other like Aske and Bragi has now? Did they decide to only love a certain amount? Is that possible? Can adults control their feelings and emotions?

Then Runa remembers how her mother can't change her shape, and how she had so violently fought, caused pain to their pursuers… no, adults can't control their feelings either, which means, maybe, her parents didn't love each other?

She asks Bragi about love while they're outside the cave one day. He says the same as her mother;

"Love can be both joyful and painful, depending on the situation yet I wouldn't wish to go one day without it for the rest of my life."

"Even if it hurts?" The way he looks at her, pondering, wondering, acknowledging, makes her squirm. It is as if he can see what she sees, understands that she notices what is happening around them. It is a bit worrisome, because Runa isn't sure she's allowed to observe and watch to the extent she has, she worries that it isn't welcome, and they'll tell her to stop. Bragi doesn't.

"Even if it hurts, because most of the time the pain might make you think about how to solve it, to make it stop hurting."

"Are you learning from your pain?" He just smiles, a wan, rueful smile as he glances towards the cave where Aske and Saga are conversing, a distant look in his eyes.

"I'm learning something, but not what I want to learn." He seems so sad, and Runa has had enough of sadness, so she asks about the herbs he pulls out of the ground, and then she asks if he wants a flower crown.

Runa thinks Bragi will look good with a flower crown. And she feels antsy and restless. She's been stuck in a cave with three adults and no one to play with because the situation is so tense, she needs something to take her mind of it. Perhaps he agrees because he realizes she needs an outlet, Runa isn't sure, but she's jumping for the opportunity to do something else than watch the world burdening everyone.

That is when it happens. That is when the unknown human who snuck up on her strikes, and all Runa can see or hear as the sword is raised is that horrible moment that turned her world inside out.

She's going to die, she's going to die, she's going to die-

"*Runa!*" Bragi jumps in between, and she sees the man fall over moments before the healer sweeps her up and runs away. Even at the end of their running, Runa trembles as her mother holds her.

The girl is so tired, tired of being afraid and hunted, tired of all the arguing.

She just wants to be safe.

CHAPTER THIRTY-FIVE

Aske has given his conditions, and Bragi is eager to do his part. Saga has, in a somewhat begrudging manner, accepted that his is happening. Bragi does find it a tad bit amusing that she appears a bit disgruntled over the fact that he and Aske is reconciling, especially since she is the one who made it possible in the first place.

Even so, he's decided, no, he has *agreed* to let Aske handle it, because that is one of the shapeshifters conditions; to let him handle his family's reaction and any eventual fallout. All Aske needs is for Bragi to be there and support him when he needs it. Advice is fine, as long as it isn't an opinion that is forced on him.

And Bragi can do that. He can absolutely do that. Especially now when he knows what it is Aske wants and needs from him. And if there is something that he is unsure about, he should just ask. It is frustrating and embarrassing to realize they could have avoided their argument if he had just asked, instead of assuming. However, what is done is done, and they're trying to move past it. They know better now.

So, Aske is doing better, and by extension, so is Bragi. Saga is still a bit shaken from that incident and doesn't let her daughter out of her sight at all.

Runa, though…

She's been rather quiet ever since the attack, not speaking a lot. None of the three adults can blame her. They understand that she is scared and suffered a big shock. She seeks constant physical contact with her mother, and her questions appear to have dried up. It is both saddening and worrying at the same time. While at first Bragi believed they should provide her with the comfort she needs and give her the space and time she needs to achieve a sense of safety again, he begins to worry when Saga tells him that when it was just the two of them, even when Runa was scared, she never pulled away like this. She had never curled back into a shell of silence.

So, they all watch the girl more intently, but there is nothing they dare prod into until Saga, during their daytime travels, assures her daughter that they're headed towards a very safe place. Words that should have brought the girl comfort instead makes her explode in a flurry of emotions. She yells, screams, calls them all liars.

"No place is safe!" she screams, startling the horses enough that Aske has to tighten his grip on the reins so they don't bolt.

"Humans killed da! Humans killed Aina, Alv, Ebba and Halle! A man nearly killed me! No place is safe!" The outburst takes them all by surprise, even though it probably shouldn't. From the moment Aske and Bragi found her, she had been as positive as she could be in the face of what she has experienced, she has done her best, been cheerful and burying all the bad things with questions and endless chatter. Now it is all coming to a head.

"Runa, sweetling, I promise, there is a place-" Saga begins but is cut off.

"Then why didn't you bring us all there before it was too late?" There are probably no words in their entire langue that can hurt Saga as much as those words. They cut into her, leaving a vicious sting, a gaping wound, and a hollow ache beneath her ribs. Saga has thought the very same thing every day since the tragedy occurred, berated herself and hated herself for her complacency and the result of it. To hear her own daughter spit the same accusations against her, it hits different.

It makes a much greater impact.

"Runa!" Aske exclaims, but he doesn't have the words to refute her, because she is right. Saga has admitted to it, Aske knows it is true as well. Bragi, on the other hand, has no preconceived notion, and jumps in.

"Runa, dear girl, all your emotions and feelings on the matter, they are valid and goodness me am I relieved you're releasing them instead of bottling them up. However, *what on earth* are you saying?"

"I'm not wrong!" Runa snaps back, with all the righteous anger an eight-year-old can fit within her tiny frame.

"Perhaps not," he concedes, moving his horse to be closer so he can lean down low enough to be on her level.

"But who could imagine such a horrible thing happen to their children?" It gives the girl a reason to pause her outrage.

"Your mother is desperate to protect you, and she's doing her best. You have a right to be sad, angry and afraid, especially after having been so brave for such a long time, but please, not like this. It resolves nothing. Yell and scream and cry, but don't aim to hurt. Please."

"*I'm* hurt!" The child retaliates. "I'm scared, I'm lost, my family is gone!" She's not saying anything that is false, and she is a young child who has experienced so much during a very short period of time. Things she shouldn't have experienced, situations she was not equipped to deal with. No one can blame her, or even be surprised when angry tears start dripping down her cheeks.

"Yes, you've experienced something horrible, and it is hard to see the positive in all this, but *you're* still alive, Runa. And we will all endeavour to make sure you reach a place that is safe, where you will have nothing to fear, I promise you that." Bragi assures her.

"How can I believe that?" How can she believe anything, at this point? Because no matter how far they've run so far, the bad people just keep on catching up to them.

"Because I swear it on my magic." The words fall from his mouth so easily, but the air grows heavy with tension.

"Bragi!" Saga gasps, outraged, just as a sigil carves itself into the back of his left hand, leaving it bleeding even as the skin knits itself together instantaneously. Aske is by their side in a heartbeat, reaching out to take hold of and wipe the blood gently away, revealing the mark left behind by the vow.

"What's that?" Runa angrily wipes at her eyes, not understanding what just happened, but knows from the adults' reactions that it is something important. Magic had shimmered in the air, a mark had appeared on the back of Bragi's hand, blood running from cuts. Magic that calls forth blood is unique, even Runa can understand that.

"Bragi vowed on his magic that he would bring you to safety," Saga tells her, eyes narrowed, an exhausted furrow between her brows.

"What does it mean?" Runa snaps impatiently, sick and tired of being given only half of the explanation to so many things now.

"It means that if he breaks that vow or doesn't manage to do what he promised he'd do, he'll lose his magic." The tears dry up and the little girl pales as she turns towards Bragi. To lose your magic, she can't imagine it. She doesn't want to imagine it, it sounds horrible, the thought scares her. To Runa, losing her magic means losing a vital part of herself.

And Bragi willingly takes the risk.

"Why would you do something like that?" She stammers, but Bragi just smiles, reaching out to pat the top of her head in a comforting manner.

"Because, my dear girl, it is worth it if I can make you feel safe again. This world belongs to you just as much as it does anyone else, and you deserve to feel safe in it." Runa have not, up until this point, been able to understand how Aske can look at Bragi the way he does, *love* him, when he is a human. Bragi is nice, but still a human.

Now she knows. Bragi isn't nice, he is *good.* And "good" is very much something she needs in her life now.

CHAPTER THIRTY-SIX

After the vow, their travels have mostly been done in silence. That is not to say that their moods have been sombre, though, the truth is quite the opposite. They are all rather relieved that the misunderstandings have been cleared up, emotions and feelings are out in the open, and they're moving at a greater speed now than before. The reason for that is that they're pacing themselves better now, instead of panicking and riding for as fast and hard as they can. With proper rest in between, their mounts have more time to recuperate when they stop for the day. As such, they are all faring better both mentally and physically.

In turn, it improves their moods drastically, and while they may not talk as much, their hearts are lighter. Of course, they are not completely without worries. They do worry over their constant pursuers who obviously has not given up on them, they worry over Bragi's wounded hands, though they are healing up nicely. They are worried over the vow he swore upon his magic.

Aske is especially aggravated over it, but the two have spoken openly about it, when Runa couldn't hear them of course. There was more than just one hissed word and more than once did they raise their voices at each other. Saga, while thankful that Bragi managed to calm Runa down when she had been unable to, had offered regrets that he had felt like he had to go to such extremes. Such a vow is not one to be made lightly, and the fallout can be disastrous.

Bragi, in turn, had simply told Saga that should he fail, he deserves to lose his magic. She did not agree on that view, but didn't argue more, respecting his decision. There is nothing she can do to change it either way now. Once a vow is made, it cannot be revoked. Bragi is only safe the moment he has fulfilled his vow.

One thing Bragi has noticed though, as they continue, is that they are most certainly not heading back towards the mountains which he and Aske left several months ago. He didn't pay it much mind in the beginning, trusting that Aske had a plan.

He still trusts the other man, but as they now know that their pursuers haven't been thrown off their trail, he very much wants to know their destination.

So, of course he asks.

"Where are we headed, Aske?" The other man glances his way from his mount, Runa in front of him playing with the horse's mane, much to the animal's apparent joy.

"A sanctuary," he answers, gaining the young girl's attention. "A long time ago, maybe nearly two centuries ago now, give or take, if I recall correctly, several of us had grown so tired of fighting for our survival. We chose to create a safe place for our kind instead."

"How did you manage such a feat?"

"Lots of physical labour, a ridiculously large amount of magic and joint efforts. Frankly, it was exhausting work, but as far as I'm aware, it still stands safely. So, we're headed there. The hunters won't be able to find us no matter how hard they search if we enter," he speaks with much confidence, chest puffing out beneath his overly large tunic. Bragi is glad to see him so confident, it is a feeling they've all severely lacked lately, Aske in particular. It is also a good look on him, it almost makes Bragi smile. But there is just one little hiccup with the shapeshifter's plan; the volatile relationship between shapeshifters and humans.

Humans have hounded, hunted and killed shapeshifters for such a horribly long time, so, at this sanctuary, while the three shapeshifters will most likely be most welcome, Bragi is a different matter all-together. He is a human, and as such, he will most likely not be allowed into such a sacred place. He voices this worry, and Runa huffs, arms crossing over her chest.

"They'll let you in, because you're a good person!" she declares, and all three adults laugh, with Aske ruffling her short hair as he agrees with her.

"Yes, they'll let him in if we vouch for him."

"Vouch?" It is a word she has not heard much before, so the girl turns to look at her uncle, curious.

"Well, it means to go good for someone, to speak on their behalf in a good way," he tells her and she nods.

"So, it is about telling the truth?"

"In a way." Aske shrugs, causing the girl to narrow her eyes at him, annoyance rolling off her in waves.

"It either is or isn't, Aske," she nearly scolds, causing them all to burst into laughter again. The simplicity of her view of the world is rather refreshing, and it brightens the mood even more. Even the horses' whinnies in amusement.

"For us, it will be the honest truth, you're right about that," Aske agrees with her again, glancing towards Bragi and grinning at the expression on the human's face. Bragi appears to be a mix of moved, flustered and happy at the same time. It causes a heat which colours his cheeks pink, makes his words devolve into an adorable sputter as he avoids eye contact.

Behind him, Saga raises a brow at her brother, lips tugging into a barely-visibly smirk, questioning. Aske just grins back, challenging. Her expression turns fond as she sighs, shaking her head. She won't start any arguments, they're long past that point, but she does find it a bit awkward to start a conversation with Bragi. Though, of course, that is of her own making. He has been nothing but accommodating since they met, and she's greeted that with hostility and suspicion. She knows very well that Bragi isn't holding it against her, considering her experiences up until now, but he didn't deserve it, and now she can see it with clear eyes. Still, even though she knows better now, sees things clearer now, it doesn't erase all that hostility up until now. So, yes, she finds it hard to speak with him. Saga thinks she should remedy that before they arrive at their destination, though according to the new terrain and her memories of the path, she doesn't have that much time left. At most, she's got a bit over a week.

They're crossing over a barren tundra, the dry ground and sparse shrubbery a muddy red colour that surrounds them. It is sparse and barren, not at all interesting, rather boring, really. Bragi has passed through more tundra's than he can count, and at this point, he's not getting much out of the scenery. He'd much rather reach this sanctuary, so they can all get some proper rest, without being ever vigilant all on their lonesome. Because it is obvious that they are outnumbered.

His hands are healing, but he is in no shape to use his sword now to protect them, and no doubt he'll have scars. It is not as if he hasn't got a few of those from before. Of course, these ones are a bit bigger and more serious than the ones he got from his little scuffles over the years and the naturally appearing scars he received from years of travelling the wilds.

He doesn't regret it. He'd readily do it again for any one of his three companions. He'll survive a beating and some scars, because, in his opinion, scars can help give someone a bit of character.

He glances at Aske, who's playing about with Runa on their horse. Scars shape a person, their believes, and can strengthen their true character. At the very least, Bragi believes that despite all his hardships, Aske is who he is today because of it all. Absolutely wonderful, strong, kind, caring, courageous, hot-tempered, impatient, defensive. Flaws and virtues blending so beautifully together into a person, a wonderful-

"You can stop brandishing poetics about my sibling now." Saga's voice rises dryly up behind him and Bragi stammers.

"What, I, you, did I speak *aloud?*" He is mortified if that is true. Of course he means every word, but he had every intention of saying them all in private, when they were on steadier ground, not *blurt it out with everyone present!* How embarrassing, humiliating, mortifying, how flustered he is right now-

"No, it was just extremely obvious."

"Oh Goddess preserve me," he groans, burying his face in his hands as Saga chuckles behind him. Despite feeling supremely flustered that Saga could see it so easily on him, *despite him sitting with his back to her,* he is relieved that Saga is apparently comfortable enough around him now that she can crack jokes. Still, he doesn't dare to throw out a few of his own just yet, so afraid to bungle up everything. Instead, he seeks the subject he is most comfortable with; healing, recovery.

"How are you feeling? Any pain or discomfort?"

"There are some aches, and my body is still stiff in some places," she admits to him, "but other than that, and being exhausted most of the time, I feel better."

"Good, good." Bragi nods. There are many things she's not mentioning, such as the state of her mind and the scars inflicted on her, both physically and mentally, but she is telling him something, and that is much more than what she did when she first became a patient of his.

"I'm not completely fine," she adds quietly, "but one day, I will be." Her words are full of conviction, even as quietly as she utter them. It makes Bragi smile. He, too, thinks she will recover nicely. With time.

"How are your hands?" she asks him, and he brings one up for her to examine. She did good work when she patched his hands up. She sees it now too, humming in contentment, allowing him to take his hand back.

"It'd be bad if you ended up being unable to draw your sword." Ah, there it is, the subtle, or not so subtle, challenge of the character he has portrayed himself as. No matter, he has been waiting for it. Rather, he is surprised that she has not mentioned it earlier.

"It would be no great loss," he replies nonchalantly, shrugging. "I'm not very good at using it anyways."

"No." He is surprised when she speaks and turns around enough in his seat to get a proper look at her. There's something strange in her gaze, and yet again he feels like she's seeing through him, unwrapping layer by layer to get to his very core.

"I don't suppose you would be."

"I'm not sure if I should be relieved or insulted by you believing me," he chuckles nervously.

"Depending on it, it can be both," she says airily, neither denying nor confirming anything. Bragi's not quite sure how he feels about her new attitude towards him. It isn't bad, per say, but it is unexpected. He is not sure how to act about it. It is a welcome change, of course it is, but at the same it feels very sudden. Perhaps it is because of what happened before, with that man.

The man Aske killed.

They haven't talked about it. Bragi, so far, hasn't really thought that they need to talk about it either, and after their last row leading to many misunderstandings and a rather miserable period, he'd very much like to avoid any further misunderstandings in the future. However, maybe he should check in with the other man?

After all, while Bragi himself has never been able to take someone's life, he does not judge Aske for what he did. On the contrary, he respects the shapeshifter for the ability to make that kind of decision in order to protect those he loves. Because of his decision, his ability to follow through, his family still lives. He managed to protect his family by being able to kill. And yes, Bragi doesn't approve of murder, what a horrible thought that is, but he doesn't look back and think that Aske murdered the man. Bragi looks at it as self-defence. The world isn't black and white, there are many nuances to it. What the man had tried to do was murder, what Aske did was an unfortunate action he felt compelled to take to protect an innocent. It is not right, not by any means, but what else could he have done at that time? Bragi has no answer to that question, and he knows that he would not have been able to do it. Bragi would have cost them everything.

Bragi has never been able to deliver a final blow, and as a result, he lost everything. His home, his family, all gone, and a burden so heavy to bear replacing them, weighing him down with a subconscious fear nipping at his heels; don't get too close to anyone, for he won't be able to protect those dear to him shoulder danger rise.

And danger is everywhere in this world.

The thought of his brother, his teacher and lost home still causes an ache to bloom beneath his ribs, but it is different than before. It still hurts, there is still an emptiness there, but it no longer feels like it is encompassing him, defining him. There is a warmth there now as well, slowly filling him, chasing that emptiness away. These people, Bragi thinks, is the source of that warmth, he is sure of it.

He hopes he can stay with them for the rest of his days. He desperately wishes and offers a prayer to the Goddess and her Children, that he will not lose these three to the same man who robbed Bragi of his home.

CHAPTER THIRTY-SEVEN

The terrain changes as they move on. The weather warms as well, which would have been another indicator that they are not moving back towards the mountains, had not Bragi inquired about it earlier on.

He thinks about this Sanctuary Aske spoke of again. A Sanctuary for shapeshifters, a place of hiding where shapeshifters can live peaceful lives, a place where humans have yet to reach them, a place humans *cannot* reach them. Bragi has no place there, it is not a place where he will be welcomed. Aske can boast however he wants about vouching for him, but Bragi doubts he will be allowed entry.

It is easier to be dictated by the bad memories and experiences than the good, and going by Aske's story, the people who had put their entire beings into creating this space and their reasonings behind it, Bragi doesn't think he will be much welcomed no matter what Aske tells them about him. Both Aske and Saga had been hostile towards him in the beginning, but they had been in desperate need of his assistance, and as such they had also been afforded the chance to get to know him after some time. The people at the Sanctuary have no reason to accept him, or even just afford him the chance to prove that he harbours no ill-will towards them, that he is no threat to their lives.

He really should speak with Aske about this, agree on what to do should it not work out. Bragi will not make any assumptions again. He'd rather avoid walking head-first into another misunderstanding. They've stopped for the day, and while Bragi is making their supper, his mind swirling with all these thoughts, Aske is sitting with Saga and Runa. Runa is changing shape left and right, from small mammals to a decent sized bird. She never keeps a shape for long, shaking her head each time, rolling her shoulders and seemingly annoyed. Aske laughs at her, patting her head and saying something Bragi cannot hear. Saga, on the other hand, is struggling. She sits on the ground, hands in front of her. She tries to shift forms, but she's not having much luck. She only manages to change parts of her body, but she unable to hold the change for longer than a few seconds at a time. And the way she reverts back, the change is forceful and nearly violent, causing her to lose her balance more than once. She appears to grow ever more frustrated with each attempt.

Aske is endlessly patient and supporting of her. Bragi hears him tell her that she will be able to shift again, that she has a barrier in her subconscious that blocks her off right now, but that he'll be there for her until she is able to use her powers again. That is what Saga needs, someone to support her when she's having a hard time. It will help her heal and overcome her struggles.

However, promising her that also means that it might be inevitable that Bragi and Aske must part ways. Not forever, but for a short while at the very least. Suddenly, to Bragi, the argument they had over Bragi taking the easy way out and just accept having to leave Aske feels foolish. Aske wanted the right to choose, and Bragi knows that of course he should have it, but the redhaired man's anger feels redundant now. He had been so angry over Bragi saying that he would leave without a fuss should that be what the others decided, needed, wanted, angry that to him it had seemed like Bragi was giving up what they have, and now he is sitting here, making promises to his sibling which might lead up to them parting ways anyways.

The healer can't help the flare of anger, sting of betrayal. What right had Aske to be angry with him back then, when this is ultimately what he would choose anyway? Bragi takes a deep breath, mentally telling himself to calm down and think rationally about this. Another argument will happen if they don't talk about this. And they should discuss it.

So, when Runa is asleep that night, he sits down with both Aske and Saga, because she is part of this too, in a way. She has a right to her opinion on this as well, because this also affects her well-being.

"This is not me coming with an idea or opinion that I deem the best cause of action in the future," he begins to clarify, smiling at Aske in a reassuring manner. "This is me asking for help coming up with a solution if it comes to the point of me not being allowed into the Sanctuary." Which he still thinks is the most plausible outcome, but he keeps that to himself for now.

"If the people there do not feel comfortable with having me around, I cannot in good conscience fight them on it." Saga nods, and so does Aske, although he does so begrudgingly.

"So, if it were to happen, I should find a place nearby, so you can reach me if you need me, yes? Or should I take the horses and lead the hunters on?"

"Absolutely not!" Aske exclaims, loud enough for Runa to shift and turn and mumble from her spot, before falling back asleep. They all release a breath they didn't know they had been holding.

"You will not lead them on, *on your own!*" The red-haired man hisses. "Do you have any idea of how dangerous that is?"

"Less so than what you'd face. I'm human, they don't know that the I've travelled with you. And Saga needs you. This isn't me using Saga as an excuse, just a few mere hours ago you promised her you'd aid her recovery." Perhaps it is a bit of a bastard move to use that one little fact against Aske right now, but it is true.

"You did," Saga reminds her brother kindly when it looks like he's about to argue again. Aske's expression pinch as he realizes he has quite literally dug himself in here with no proper argument to fight it. On one hand, he wants to be with Bragi to ensure he is safe, but on the other hand he also wishes to be there for his sister and her daughter who need stability right now. He is torn, unable to find a solution in which he can have both.

"Here is an idea," Saga offers, surprising both men. "If it comes down to it, both of you lead them off, then come back. Even if you're not allowed inside, you can rest outside, together. I'll come outside during daytime, for that aid." Bragi never anticipated that Saga would accommodate him like this, even if their relationship has improved lately. It is touching, he feels a warmth in his chest he can only think is relief of her acceptance.

"But we will get you inside, Bragi. Healing magic is something our kind has little affinity for, your skills will be a bargaining tool."

"But I'm human-" he begins, not sure where her confidence is coming from.

"And we'll gain you the right to enter," Saga cuts him of, full of conviction. "I know a way, and I will get you in, Bragi. No one will be separated." She appears so confident that Bragi finds it hard to argue with her. Even so, he steels himself for rejection upon their arrival. It is better to be pleasantly surprised than to feel like he will have his heart torn out of his chest.

So, he smiles in gratitude, relieved by having her support in this. He looks towards Aske where he spots the same confident expression as her. They truly are siblings, they look so alike sitting together like this.

"Alright," he tells them running a hand through his brown curls. "But now we have an alternative." Bragi tries to dampen the sudden hope and expectations he feels when Aske reaches out to squeeze his hand.

When they've cleaned up, with Saga curling around her daughter, Bragi feels exceptionally overjoyed when Aske lays his bedroll next to his. Bragi admits that while he understood why Aske has stayed close to his sister and niece ever since they found them, he has missed having the other man close like this at night. He's even more delighted when Aske curls around him, arms holding the healer close.

"That's the spot," Aske breathes out as he buries his face into the back of Bragi's neck. "Missed this," he mumbles and Bragi agrees.

"Yes, I have too."

"Good to know we're on the same page," Aske's voice is already slurring, the shapeshifter rapidly falling asleep. Bragi pats the hand around his middle, smiling. Bragi has missed holding and being held by Aske like this. It had begun as a necessity when they had begun moving towards the colder areas of the world, but then it had become something they enjoyed and wanted to indulge in more often. There's also the sense of safety and warmth, something both of them have craved for much longer than they want to admit.

Sleep comes easier to Bragi than normal, and cradled like this, he sleeps well too.

He is gifted with this comfort for the next three nights as well, and on the fourth morning, the morning when they reach their destination, they wake first. Aske is already awake by the time Bragi's consciousness pulls him from oblivion. It is odd, as Bragi is the one who usually greets the mornings first, having to pull Aske from his slumber.

Akse's thumbs rub absentmindedly over the back of Bragi's hands, and when the healer turns his head, Aske shifts to push himself up on his elbow, to properly get a look at the brunet.

"Morning," Bragi mutters, and Aske grins, reaching down to brush through his curls.

"Morning." This is nice, Bragi thinks as his eyes slide closed at the gesture. He can probably slip right back to sleep if Aske keeps this up. He hums in contentment, tilting his head to give the redhead more access.

"We'll arrive during midday at the latest," Aske's voice is a quiet rumble, pleasant and low. Bragi opens his eyes again, reaching out himself to move some of the other man's long hair out of the way before he cups his cheek.

"We will?" The other nods.

Four nights he has been held by Aske, and even though he kept telling himself to keep any hopeful expectations down, he has obviously failed as he feels his heart sink a bit in his chest. Aske notices, and pushes himself a bit closer, just enough to press his lips to the other's forehead.

"I promise, I won't let them send you away." Bragi musters a smile, and allows Aske to pull him up on his feet.

It is reassuring that the other man is so confident that he and Saga will be able to secure the healer access, but a thought does come to mind as they ready themselves for the final part of their journey. Aske claimed he helped build the Sanctuary. Bragi wonders why he left it, and found a home in a mountain where he never felt safe at all. He must ask him about it when they have the time. There must be a reason for it, after all.

They move on after breakfast, and while they had moved from the barren tundra's to light forest, Bragi finds it a bit surprising that before midday, he is wading through a cypress swamp. Runa is on a horse, but Saga is challenging her body, and is wading alongside with them. He hopes she will listen to her body before it gives out on her and get back on the horse should she grow too exhausted. Bragi would much rather she rode a horse too, but had given up the argument when she had glared at him.

Then suddenly, both her and Aske stop, and so does Runa's endless chattering. Bragi blinks, but waits quietly, wondering why they've stopped in the middle of a swamp. Up until now they've only stopped when they had to rest so this makes no sense to him. Especially when no one is saying anything.

"Pardon, Aske, Saga, why have we stopped?"

"Because we need permission to continue," Saga explains, eyes moving around, looking for something, or someone.

"Oh, so we can only move a certain distance before we must wait for anyone to come see us? How long will it take?"

"Bragi, we're already surrounded." The brunet blinks, and turns his head left and right, but he can't see anyone. And that's when it hits him; he can't *hear* anything either. No animals, no people, *nothing*.

"Get out here already, Agnar!" Aske suddenly bellows, causing Bragi to startle. "We don't have all day!" There's a long silence in which Bragi begins to think the other two might be wrong about already being watched when suddenly a man appears.

He's almost as tall as Aske, Bragi can see that even from a distance, and his skin is a rather ghastly pallor, his dark hair lie flat and matted to his skull. He looks exhausted too. They must have caught him at a bad time.

"Why have you brought a human here?" His voice is quite pleasant enough to listen to, but the harsh accusation in his tone just makes the situation less than ideal.

"He's a friend, a healer, and saved all three of our lives. He's trustworthy," Aske assures, but this Agnar only narrows his eyes as he glances over at Bragi.

"And what if it is all just a ploy? It is not the first time a human has tried to trick their way into our Sanctuary." Bragi should feel offended, yet at the same time, considering all kinds of hardships these people must have faced, he can't bring himself to feel any. They have no reason to bring Bragi into their home, and he won't have Aske arguing over this, risking their own entry. They have an alternative plan, after all. He reaches out, wraps his fingers around the redhead's arm to pull him back, tell him to calm down, that it is alright.

"He was taught his magic by a Livwyrm," Sag's voice might be loud enough to demand the attention of everyone gathered but hidden, to hear, but also calm. Bragi stiffens, eyes widening as his mind rattles to a halt. Aske turns too, surprised.

Bragi haven't told her who taught him his magic, he's only ever mentioned it once, to Aske, when he told him of his past. Bragi forces himself to look up at Aske, who appears just as surprised as him that Saga knows this fact, which means he has not told her.

Which means she had heard them that night.

She's known all along. Bragi quite feels like the ground has all but disappeared from beneath him, stomach sinking as he feels cold dread spread through him. Saga knows! She knows Bragi is the cause for her children's death!

CHAPTER THIRTY-EIGHT

Bragi can't stop staring at Saga, even as he hears the quiet murmur of words being exchanged around him. Saga, on the other hand, is resolutely *not* looking at him, as she engages in the discussion going on. It is only when Aske puts a hand on his shoulder that he snaps out of it. He looks up, sees Aske wear a small smile in an attempt at hiding his worry.

"Come, Bragi. They're letting us in."

"All of us?" Aske nods.

"All of us," he assures the brunet, who at first doesn't seem to completely understand he is allowed in, and only moves when Aske firmly, but kindly, leads him with a hand on his back. All that the human can think of is the fact that Saga knows! She knows his past! She knows how he has encountered the people who killed her partner and children, she knows that he is the reason she lost everything, the reason she only has Runa left.

He is the reason she lost everything she held dear, and she *knows!*

He feels like he is not in control of his own body as they're led further into the swamp, until they reach a rock formation, heavily dressed down in greenery from a few black willows who appear ancient. With a gesture and a whisper from this Agnar, they move aside to show a cave opening. They all enter, and Bragi pulls himself out of his stupor just long enough to understand that it is but a simple, small cave, not a tunnel.

Bragi bites his lip. He doesn't know what is going on, why they're really bringing him along, why Saga advocated for him when she knows the truth. Agnar glances backwards, eyes rowing over them all, before he nods.

And walks straight through the wall. Bragi's jaw drops to the ground, even when Aske urges him on. He moves but hesitates a bit when they're right in front of the wall, anticipating that just because Agnar could walk through, Bragi will end up humiliating himself by walking straight into a solid wall.

"Come on, it is safe." Aske clasps one of Bragi's hands with the one holding the reins to their horses. With the other, he touches the wall, and Bragi watches how he falls through it, pulling the human with him.

Bragi can only describe the feeling of passing through the wall as sinking through mud. He feels dirty, the air difficult to gather in his lungs, but it only lasts for a moment. He is through the wall, sees that they're still inside a cave, and that Agnar stands at the very exit, motioning for them to hurry up.

"Come on." Aske grins widely down at him, his long fingers twining with Bragi's. Gently, he pulls him along. The light is nearly blinding as they exit, and Bragi blinks several times, squinting. The vision before him is different from the swamp he has been muddling through until now.

First of all, the new area *isn't* a swamp.

It is half a forest, half plain grassland, trees unnaturally huge and wide, and magic must have been used to help cultivate the trees into *homes*. And this place is *brimming* with life! There are so many people here, children running about and playing carelessly, shifting shapes as easily and naturally as breathing. Without fear and hesitation.

Streams of water, leading to ponds and what appears to be a part-way hidden lake run like veins through the settlement, stones paved into pathways between all the homes and water-supplies and fields. There are *fields!* Fields in which they grow food.

All of this made possible with magic and hard work, and lots of it. This community has pooled together, used their resources and abilities and magic to create this haven for themselves and their kind. A Sanctuary indeed. A Sanctuary they have allowed him entry to.

"A sight, isn't it?" Saga's voice echoes from inside the cave, and the wonder and awe Bragi feels shifts away and morphs into cold dread. He can't bring himself to look her way, let alone look her in the eyes.

"Bragi." Aske leads him on, and as they enter the settlement the residents see them. It is apparent that some of them know Aske and Saga as they call out greetings, but then their eyes land on Bragi, and they grow silent, curious. Children stop and wave, and the human can't help but return small, uncertain smiles and waves of his own. He is not a savage, but he avoids looking at the adults. He is not sure he will be able to take the animosity surely thrown his way. At least not directly.

He follows Aske's lead, and soon finds himself standing in front of one of those homes made of giant trees. Agnar opens the door, and they all enter.

"Nothing's changed," Saga murmurs, looking around, a small smile on her face.

"Course not," Agnar huffs. "It was Inge's. We've only kept it neat and clean, in case any of you would return for it." There is a wistfulness to his voice, a certain amount of dimmed grief.

"There's only us left," Saga says, exchanging a look with Aske before she turns back to Agnar. "Thank you." The surly shapeshifter waves them off, turning his back to them and heading towards the door.

"Don't mention it. I'll go out and spread the word of what he," he jabs a thumb at Bragi, "is, so that they'll know why we let him in." Bragi flinches, despite there being no hostility in Agnar's voice anymore. The door shuts quietly behind him, and they're all left in silence, the buzz of the settlement muffled behind the door.

"Off you go, sweetling," Saga tells her daughter who is nearly vibrating out of her skin with excitement and curiosity.

"Explore our home, then tomorrow, once we're all rested, we can go outside and explore, find you some playmates, hm?" The girl nods enthusiastically, and races off. Saga turns to Bragi and Aske. The former is still not looking at her, the latter having a grip on his partner's hand. She gives Aske a look, a silent conversation passes between them before she speaks again.

"Bragi, there is one thing you must do for me. If you fail to do so, I will execute severe bodily harm upon you." The healer flinches, shoulders hunching forward as he unconsciously tries to make himself smaller. This is it. This is when she will tell him to leave, and this is when he will become the rot between her and Aske. This is the moment where his failure from decades ago will rob Aske of that little bit of happiness and peace, he has enjoyed for some time now.

"You need to stop shouldering responsibility for something you are in no way, shape or form connected to." Aske shakes his head fondly at his sister as Bragi's head snaps up in disbelief. Saga is staring directly at him, arms limp at her sides. There is no fury or disgust in her face, her entire body language looks more relaxed than he has ever seen since he met her. There's determination in her gaze, yet kindness, *sympathy* as well.

"I heard your tale. I may have been barely able to stumble along on my own two feet and would have been useless if any fight would have broken out, but I followed you two that night. I didn't trust you then. All I knew was that you were a human, and I was still… the pain was raw, it still is, but my mind is clearer now." Saga inhales, blows the air back out in a soft huff as she runs a hand through her short hair, barely flinching as she passes by her missing ear.

"The point is, Bragi, that what happened to you happened long before I met my children's sire, long before my children were even thought of. And you lost everything to these people as well, just like me. You're a victim, not a culprit. You are not part of their group; you had no direct connection with them or the atrocities they've committed against me and mine. " She walks forward, laying her hands on his shoulders in an act to express comfort and leans down as she presses a light kiss into his curls.

"It is not your responsibility to carry the burden of their sins, Bragi, and while there is nothing you need my forgiveness for, if it helps you relinquish any feelings of responsibility you feel, know this and let my words strike true in your heart; you hold no blame for my loss." Bragi stares up at her, floundering for many long moments before his eyes sting with tears.

When Aske assured him of his innocence back then, he had wanted so badly to believe him, yet no matter how much he wanted to shed the burden, he couldn't. Now, however, with Saga herself offering him absolution, grace, he feels that weight finally falling away, dropping to the ground heavily like a sack full of rocks.

"Oh my dear," he chokes out, tears escaping him as his hands fly to his face try and stem the cascade of tears.

"Thank you." His voice cracks, shoulders jerking as he heaves in a sorely needed breath of fresh air.

"Thank you so much."

CHAPTER THIRTY-NINE

"You know, it would have been nice if you had informed us that you are being hunted before we let you in." A shapeshifter named Yngvi glowers at Aske, who glares right back, yellows eyes narrowed dangerously.

"We came her seeking sanctuary with *one* child. That should have been a bloody clue!" the redhead hisses right back. "If it bothers you so much, feel free to expel us!"

"Nobody is expelling anyone!" Hildegard booms, their voice drowning out any arguing as it carries through the entire hall, a hand raised to quell any who'd like to argue. "This is not the first time someone came here while being pursued, it will not be the last. *Calm down, Yngvi!*" There is little Yngvi can do to argue against the very oldest of their kind residing in the Sanctuary, so he holds his tongue. For a moment, anyway.

"I did not say we should toss you out, only that it would be fair that you gave us a warning. We have *families here, Aske!* Young adults who grew up here and has yet to experience the uncalled-for hatred of zealots!" Aske grimaces. He can't argue with that. The Sanctuary has its defences, such as the barrier hiding them from sight, and barring entrance to anyone not invited, yet still, having hunters prowl the swamp is a risk in itself. Especially if the brutes have a powerful sorcerer in their midst. Then the risk of them finding their way in rises exponentially.

"They have no sorcerers amongst them," Saga speaks up, probably realizing the same thing as Aske, as she moves to stand in the centre of the gathering of the elders of the Sanctuary.

"I saw myself what their methods are, *felt* their chosen methods with my own body. They are brutal, they use weapons, such as swords, knives, maces, crossbows. They've caught up to us twice, and the size of their group has dwindled each time." She waits a bit, making sure she has got everyone's attention.

"I am not going to demand any help from any of you, all I can do, and all I *will* do, is ask you for help. I am powerless on my own." Saga furrows her brows as she bows her head, shoulders rising in shame as she holds her arm out. It shifts into a wing. Bragi finds it an amazing sight, but then it violently shifts back into an arm, forcefully enough that Saga stumbles. There's a chorus of loud gasps, before the people gathered starts yelling over each other.

Bragi chances a glance at Yngvi and Hildegard, who both are pale and looking horrified, Yngvi's hands clutching at Hildegard's shoulders as Aske rushes forward to hold Saga. Apparently, losing the ability to shapeshift is a terrible thing. Bragi wants to hit himself for that thought alone.

Of course it is a terrible thing, shifting their shape is a part of them, a fundamental part of their identity, and now Saga has lost that part of herself, the connection severed for who knows how long. Not only did she lose nearly all of her children and her partner, but she is also now standing without her powers and a vital part of herself.

He cannot even begin to imagine what that is like.

"Alright." Agnar steps forward without an ounce of hesitation, holding out his arm for Saga to clasp. "I will join you. This is my home, and you are my friend, Saga. When they come, I'll help you ward them off." There are tears in Saga's eyes as she reaches out to grab him, nodding in thanks. Yngvi and Hildegard joins them, followed by several others, until everyone gathered stands in a ring around them.

It is beautiful to watch, seeing a group of people come together to help another in dire need. Then, as that matter has been settled, quickly and rather anti-climatically, they all turn towards Bragi. A few awkwardly silent moments pass before he starts fidgeting.

Well, it is rather intimidating as everyone in the room, even those with crooked backs, stands at the very least a head taller than him. It truly must be a trait of being a shapeshifter, being tall. Goodness, he feels like a child when he stands amongst them.

"I've been informed that you've been taught your magic by a Livwyrm, is that correct?" Hildegard moves to stand in front of him, flanked by Agnar and Yngvi. Bragi nods.

"Yes, and while I realize that I was allowed entrance based on that fact, I am not quite sure why. Can I- am I allowed to ask?" Hildegard shoots an unimpressed look over his head just as Bragi feels Aske's hands on his shoulders, steadying him.

"He doesn't know the significance, really?" Bragi understands that apparently it is something important, but he doesn't appreciate them talking over his head like this. He is shorter than them, but really, it is just *rude*.

"Up until this point I thought he knew." Aske defends himself and Bragi reaches a hand up, waving it in front of their faces to gather their attention back to him.

"Would anyone mind telling me what significance me being taught my magic by a Livwyrm is? Please?" Both shapeshifters look at him for a moment before Hildegard huffs, and begins to explain.

"Livwyrms are gentle beings of healing. Purely healing magic. They are unable to harm another being even to save themselves, even though overusing their magic on a being is dangerous for the recipient. As such, their magic could be used to cause harm, but they don't."

"Yes, I witnessed that first-hand when I was young." Bragi furrows his brows as he recalls how his teacher fell, never once protecting themselves as they tried to save Sigmund. They just… accepted their end. Or so it had seemed.

"Livwyrms also only ever choose disciples with that same quality." Bragi blinks, looks up as his jaw drops.

"I beg your pardon?"

"We allowed you inside because we know you aren't capable of hurting anyone here."

"Oh." Bragi considers it. While he is relieved that he has been granted entry, he is not sure how he feels about gaining such a privilege based upon what his teacher was, and not upon his own merit.

It… stings, he must admit. It makes him wonder if Aske grew to trust him based on that fact, if he cares for him only because of that…

"Bragi wouldn't have hurt anyone here regardless." Aske is firm in his belief, meets Hildegard's raised brow without flinching. A warmth spreads in Bragi's chest at the other man's conviction. It does strengthen the belief that Aske's affections are because of him as a person. After all this arguing, all this stress and worry and self-loathing, he truly needed that.

"Now that we've established that I am no threat to anyone, what is our plans moving forward? These people have managed to catch up even when Aske made false tracks and led them on wild goose chases." There's a hushed tense murmur passing through the crowd. Bragi almost feels bad for worrying them, but holding back any information is much more dangerous, when all is said and done.

They need to know that these people are very capable, that they will not stop. They cannot be underestimated.

If he is to gather anything from their expressions alone, however, it seems that no one has been much surprised by this news. And why would they be? This entire settlement was built because of the brutality which have been executed upon them, simply because of their natural born abilities.

"As I said," Hildegard appears very calm as they sigh, leaning into the touch of Yngvi on their shoulder, "this is not the first time we've had hunters at our doorstep. Here is where we have the edge; we know this area better than anyone. They come here, and the swamp will swallow them whole."

CHAPTER FORTY

Agnar is a friendly man, underneath all of his surly attitude and hunched shoulders, Bragi is sure. He has just yet to see any trace of it. Such as the time where Bragi had cheerfully said that he found it fascinating how tall all of the shapeshifters were at the time when Agnar was showing him where their house of healing was, and Agnar had just looked at him and supplied;

"No, you humans are just incredibly tiny."

"I beg your pardon?" The man had laughed at him, and Bragi had been more than just a little bit miffed, but he had let it go.

However, their time spent there is not all pleasantries and teasing remarks. Aske and Saga explain all that they can to Hildegard and Yngvi and a collection of other shapeshifters who'll plan their counter-attack should the hunters show up. This is what Aske and Saga spend their days doing, Bragi spends most of his time in the house of healing. There are many in the Sanctuary who are in need of medical aid. Nothing life-threatening, but Bragi is more than happy to help. And, well, it does help make the inhabitants open up to him, be more comfortable with the fact that a human is among them. While they appear friendly, on the outside at the least, Bragi is worried they won't accept him.

"Oh, don't you worry a lick, friend," a shapeshifter named Ylva tells him, smiling brightly. She is a lovely person, wide eyes with an equal wide smile, dressing herself in colourful skirts. Ylva is the only one who's been welcoming from the beginning, neither once showing that she has been suspicious of his intentions. It is nice, having someone on his side from the settlement.

"They'll get over it quickly, I promise you."

"That is very nice of you to say," he tells her, offering a small smile in thanks, "but they mustn't force themselves for my sake. I'll be able to handle a little bit of suspicion. I am a stranger and an outsider, after all." Ylva just scoffs, waving her hand in the air as if to dispel any negativity around them.

"I'm not saying it to be kind. See that boy over there?" She points to a tall man appearing no younger than Bragi himself. Standing tall, like all the others, broad-shouldered but kind-faced he hardly appears a boy to Bragi, but then again, shapeshifters perceive time differently than humans on account of their longer lifespan.

"That boy is my son, Balder."

"A handsome lad," Bragi admits.

"His father was human." It takes a moment for the words to sink in, but when they do, his jaw drops and he stares at Ylva, who is now smiling kindly at him, taking one of his hands in hers.

"Aske isn't the first to give his heart to a human," Bragi's cheeks flush a warm red, "and he won't be the last. If the people here could accept my Balder, they will accept you as well. When I tell you not to worry, it is because there is nothing to worry about." Bragi's lower lip quiver a bit, admittedly feeling more than a bit relieved now. He has tried to not think about it much, him being human and therefore not the most welcome being here. Yet to hear this, to be on the receiving end of such comforting words… Ylva pats him on the shoulder before launching into questions about all sorts of things. How did he meet Aske? For how long did he train under the guidance of a livwyrm? For how long has he travelled across their world? What curious and great things has he witnessed? What knowledge can he share?

He takes the opportunity to take his mind of their situation and pours all his focus into answering these questions as best he can, gathering and grounding herbs, making potions and healing the ailing. It helps make the daytime hours pass by quickly.

And he does feel useful like this, like he is pulling his weight and being a part of their community. As a result of his hard work, the shapeshifters begin to feel more comfortable with his presence, and they engage him in conversations and the like.

Runa, sweet little girl, has managed to carve a place for herself amongst the other children. Finally, she is allowed to be just a normal child again. She is no longer running, she is no longer looking over her shoulder, she is no longer trembling in fear.

It is heartening to watch her run around, playing with other children, and shedding tears only because of a scratched knee or a play-fight gone too far. He can see that Saga feels that way too. She appears to find great comfort in the fact that her child crying is because of normal child-like behaviour, that she is fully capable of playing with others despite everything.

That she is laughing again. More than once, Bragi has caught Saga crying because of it, being so incredibly relieved that her daughter is finally safe. And allowed to be a child again.

Of course, it doesn't last long. Few good things have lasted, lately.

Aske is outside the Sanctuary every other day with a scouting party, and while for a fortnight everything is quiet, suddenly, one night, he returns with grim news.

Just outside the swamp, a large group of people have made camp.

Runa is thankfully asleep when he returns with the news, exhausted from a day filled with playing, laughter and new friends. She is having a good time here, she feels safe and happy here. Able to set aside the horrible memories that has haunted her every waking hour for such a long time.

Saga, however, feels a chill settle deep in her bones at the news. It feels like her stomach is rebelling and bile rises in her throat. Her heart beats so furiously in her chest she fears it will burst through her ribs at this rate. She knew, of course she knew they would be able to track them down, find their new hiding place. Even with their efforts to confuse their pursuers and actions to lead them completely astray, the hunters continued to find them. She was never under any illusion that they wouldn't come here as well.

She knew, she had done everything she possibly could to brace herself, prepare herself for the inevitable clash that would happen. She thought she was ready.

Considering that she is doing everything she can to keep the contents of her stomach *in* her stomach, she is far from ready. The very thought of them so close is enough to have her bones rattle in terror beneath her skin. Despite all the different types of spells keeping this Sanctuary hidden, despite the fact that she knows there is no easy way in, that the magic protecting the community here is certainly old, has grown roots in the land and bends itself to no one but those that have added to it as time goes by, yet still, still the terror takes her, shakes her, rattles her to her very core.

Aske's hands on her shoulders yank her out of her frozen state, his yellow eyes hard, filled with determination and a promise.

"This ends here," he vows, pressing his forehead to hers. "We've prepared for this. The moment they enter the swamp is the moment they forfeit their lives," he growls from deep within his chest. Saga's fingers wrap around his wrists as she takes deep breaths in an attempt at calming herself, to stop herself from shaking. Aske's touch grounds her, helps her find focus and her centre.

Bragi watches them, admires the strength Saga shows as she straightens her shoulders and pushes all of her fear and terror into a box, an issue to be dealt with later, once the immediate threat is gone. Then, and only then, will she open that box again, go through every little thing she has bottled up, the emotions, the memories, the pain. She will sort through them all and put them to rest once this is all over. Right now, she needs to focus on the situation at hand, what is happening in front of her right now.

"After tomorrow, there will be no trace left of them, and your lovemate and your children will find their peace, and you and Runa can finally begin to truly heal. I will make sure of it," he assures her darkly, voice gravelly with emotion. Saga just nods, breath hitching as she tries not to cry.

Every day that group was out there, searching, the shapeshifters have been plotting, preparing for their eventual arrival.

They are ready to end this.

CHAPTER FORTY-ONE

Aske is up by dawn, already on his way out the door when Bragi stops him.

"Do wait for me, darling boy." His lips quirk upwards, if only slightly, in fondness. Being called "boy" by someone who is two and a half centuries younger than him is a funny thing. His words though, is what causes the shapeshifter to halt his steps. He turns back around to face Bragi, plastering on a small smile, strained though it is and hopes that the other man just wants to wish him good luck. To see him off.

"It's early, Bragi, go back to bed." However, based on the other man's attire, it is inherently clear that Bragi has every intention of coming along. And that is not at all part of Aske's plan for the day.

They have miscommunicated. Again. He doesn't want an argument, not now, not before he is going out to kill the hunters, not so early in the morning at risk of awakening both Saga and Runa.

Runa should only be aware when it is all over, so she can spend the day not worrying. She should be allowed to have another normal day. She should be done with fearing for her life.

"You must be joking." Bragi crosses his arms. "I'm coming with you, of course." Aske purses his lips, readying an argument, Bragi can spot it. He straightens his back, ready to fight for his spot in the plan. The plan he doesn't have all the details to. Truthfully, he has little to no details about it.

"Bragi, this is not going to be a discussion between us and the hunters. I'm going out there to *kill them*." Bragi doesn't flinch, to his credit. Aske isn't loud, his voice a mere murmur in truth, but his words are harsh. This is a serious situation they can't discuss their way out of. This will end with bloodshed, and Aske does not want Bragi out there with him when it all goes down. Bragi knowing that Aske is very much capable of killing people is one thing, witnessing it is quite another. And Bragi, he's quite unable to kill anybody. Out there, he will be a liability, and Aske isn't quite sure how to tell him that in a manner that won't hurt him.

"I can help."

"How?" The delivery is far from gentle, and Aske bites his tongue, afraid he has hurt the other man with the question. Bragi, however, squares his shoulders, a stubborn set in his jaw as he glares defiantly back at Aske.

"I can heal any injury you sustain and defend the wounded. I am not *useless*, Aske."

"I have never once believed you were useless." Aske rubs the bridge of his nose. He can feel the beginnings of a headache sneak up on him. "But you're not coming with, and that is final."

"Do not make decisions for me, Aske!" Bragi's voice raises slightly. That is rich, Aske thinks, considering that it isn't that long ago since Bragi did the very same thing by telling him that he would leave if that were what Saga had wanted at the time. He made a decision without asking his partner what he thought of it, didn't even stop to consider whether or not that would hurt Aske, cause cracks in their relationship. Bragi just thought he knew better. Right here though, Aske *does* know better, and he is not making this decision to hurt Bragi or exclude him, he is making it because this concerns the safety of the entire Sanctuary, of his family, of his friends. Aske isn't making this decision alone, either. They are guests at the Sanctuary, and as such, he is more beholden than most to follow their rules. They are receiving aid they desperately need, and in return they must follow the rules that the council has put upon them.

"It doesn't feel good, does it?" the shapeshifter snaps back petulantly, causing Bragi to roll his eyes.

"That is childish."

"Don't scold me like I am some child!" He throws his hands up dramatically, and prim and proper as always, Bragi replies.

"If you don't want me to scold you like a child, then don't act like one, you ancient, shrivelled up, *legless lizard*!" There's not bite to Bragi's words, and it is not the first time he has called Aske old either, though all the other times it had been in clear jest. Legless lizard though? That one is new. Would even have been funny if not for the situation they are in.

"Oh, that is funny," Aske hisses, marching up to Bragi, crowding his space and glaring down at him. "Coming from a bearded infant!"

"Ancient man-child!" Bragi spits back.

"You little bastard!" The other man's shoulders slump, all fight leaving him in a rush of exhaled air. It honestly worries the taller man.

"I'm your bastard." Bragi's voice is quiet again, looking up at Aske, brows furrowed. There's no anger there, only worry. Aske blinks several times, mouth opening and closing with no sound escaping him before he exhales heavily. His shoulders slump as all fight leaves him too. He cradles Bragi's face in his broad palms and leans down to press a kiss to his forehead.

"Mine," he agrees, pulling back just far enough to look him in the eyes. "I'm not going out there alone, Bragi. We're going as a group, and we are not going to fight them head on. We will be picking them off, one by one, and the others, they know this place like the back of their hand. You don't. Don't ask me to risk you against these monsters. Stay here with Saga and Runa, and prepare for us to come back, alright? We are likely to need you upon our return."

It is not a particularly happy thought that Bragi will be needed after this is over. The human never thought that they would come back unscathed from all of this, though that does not mean he is looking forward to it. While it is nice to be useful, and this is a necessary evil forced upon them, it is not what Bragi wants to see, this is not how he wants to be of use to others. He knows when he has lost, however. He can argue all he wants, but Aske presents a more than solid point. He does not know the area, and he doesn't have it in him to harm others. He is a liability.

"Be careful, won't you? Don't come back to us in tatters." Bragi's eyes are wide, a slight tremor to his lower lip, and Aske swallows reflexively.

"I promise I will come back safe and sound." He can't promise that he won't get hurt, but he will promise that he will return. He is not going to fight alone. They are a group of fourteen shapeshifters going out there, after all, alongside a few scouts to keep a look-out from above.

It is as safe they can make it, and it must be done. This is about protecting themselves from someone who wants to cause them pain for no reason other than that they can. This is not him picking an unnecessary fight. Bragi knows this, Aske knows this.

Finally, Bragi lets out an exhausted sigh, shoulders slumping. He looks as exhausted as Aske feels in his acceptance that this promise is the best he will receive.

"Why did you leave this place?" Bragi asks, and Aske's lips purse, lashes lowering as he looks down, before plastering on a small smile in an attempt at lifting the mood a slight bit, even if it falls kind of flat.

"I'll tell you when I come back." Bragi stares, hazel eyes searching for some sort of hint, before he nods, accepting that he is staying behind.

"Just… keep that promise, Aske. Come back." The redhaired man nods, and for a moment he appears to want to step even closer, meld into Bragi, to stay there and ignore the threat closing in on them for the chance to spend a few more moments with the other man, but then he sets his jaw, draws himself up to his full height and leaves the home with long, sure strides.

Bragi stays, feet rooted to the spot.

Saga finds him still there, quite some time later, long after Aske has grouped up with the others and left the Sanctuary, but the redhaired man doesn't know this. The moment he turned away from Bragi in the hall, he had pushed all other thoughts out of his head and set his focus on settling this fight once and for all.

Alongside the others, he leaves the Sanctuary and sheds his human form, searching. Once they come upon the intruders, they make absolutely sure that this is indeed a group of hunters, and not just some poor lost souls. Their armour, weapons and foul disposition quickly ascertains just who they are though.

For the first few hours, they just watch the group, waiting, biding their time for the opportunity to start picking them off. It finally comes when the group starts splitting up, in groups of five, four and four. The shapeshifters split up as well, and Aske finds himself with Hildegard and Agnar. Even as they slowly pick off their assigned group, with Agnar in his poisonous frog shape, jumping about making considerable contact with exposed skin, and Aske and Hildegard finishing the weakened humans off quickly with bone breaking crushes in long coils of muscle and flesh-tearing with rows of sharp teeth, Aske feels that something is off.

"What's the matter?" Agnar mutters as he shifts back.

"Something doesn't add up," Aske answers as he drops his latest victim, shifting back as well. "Amongst them all, I never once saw anyone fitting the description of the man Saga and Bragi told me about. Something's not right."

"Let's regroup with the others, then we'll figure out where their leader is." Right now, it seems like everything is falling into place too easily, and Aske can't quite shake that something is wrong.

"This might also just be half of the group," Hildegard adds, brows furrowed as they heave a sigh at the complications this might cause. "Moving ahead of the rest." They look to Agnar, reaching out to squeeze his hand in comfort. The other's lips quirk up in a half-smile as he squeezes back.

"It might be." And somehow, that possibility eases up some of his worries. If that is the case, they might just be able to issue enough of a warning to get the rest to give up their hunt, to take their losses and go bother someone else.

CHAPTER FORTY-TWO

Bragi can't deny that he is anxiously waiting for Aske to return. Runa is still unaware, playing with the other children who also seem to be unaware of what is going on, not noticing that several adults are gone, and Saga, Saga is focusing all her nervous energy on her powers. She attempts to shift parts of her body and hold the transformation for as long as she can.

While she is not able to hold the shift for too long, the rebound is no longer so forceful she stumbles back and loosing her footing upon turning back. She looks pleased with these results, and so does the shapeshifter who is helping her regain control of this magic that is such a vital part of her.

Bragi is happy for her. In his opinion, he sees it as the beginning of her healing, the mending of her heart. She smiles more too. Just being here, surrounded by her own kind is a great remedy for her.

He wonders, when this is all over, will she and Runa stay here? Will Aske? His stomach feels like it is filled with cold hard lead at the mere thought. If Aske stays… won't he and Bragi be separated? The inhabitants of the Sanctuary are allowing him to stay for now, most likely because of the threat, but will they allow him to stay long-term? It is hard to believe.

If such a thing were to pass, Bragi won't be able to fault him for it. A Sanctuary where Aske don't have to hide, where he can thrive, a place he helped create... Bragi shakes his head. Aske won't stay in a place where Bragi cannot follow, not anymore, not with the way he reacted when Bragi offered to leave back then. And even so, maybe Bragi will be allowed to stay, considering they let him in now, and he has proven useful. No one is avoiding him, no one is looking upon him with disdain. Bragi likes to think that he has made a few friends here, Ylva in particular.

At the very least they will talk about it first. No more sudden actions and foolish decisions without discussing it first.

Besides, there are two options outside of the Sanctuary as well. There is the mountain, where Aske left his garden and little spirits, his home for a century. Bragi knows that they are both welcome there. The issue is that it is very far away from Aske's remaining family.

The second option is that they settle down somewhere close to the area. That way they benefit of both the safety and protection of the area, and they will be close to the others. He will present these options to Aske when he returns, ask him what he thinks they should do.

Because Aske will return. He promised he would. Perhaps it is more than just a little childish to cling to this promise, but it is all he has to reassure himself at this point. Bragi believes in him, Saga believes in him. Aske has survived for over three centuries, surviving countless horrors and fights. His body is a canvas filled with marks, each telling a story of its own, each a mark from a horrible moment in his life in which Aske emerged victorious.

He will emerge victorious this time too.

This belief doesn't stop Bragi from offering a few prayers to the Goddess and her Children for the safe return of Aske. And the others, of course. But mostly Aske.

Bragi is grinding herbs and mixing potions later in the day when a series of loud commotions grab his attention from outside the house of healing. He has barely gotten up on his feet when people burst through the doors, carrying a person. Ylva is being carried in, a crossbow bolt in the back of her right shoulder, rivulets of blood running down her arm and sides.

Bragi's blood freeze to ice in his veins. To see Ylva like this, in such a horrible state, in pain, when she was only supposed to support the group outside, scouting from the sky. The smell of copper fills the room, but Bragi shakes his head, pulling himself out of his thoughts. He cannot fall into a pit of despair and worry now that there is someone in need of his aid here. He rolls up the sleeves of his tunic as the shapeshifters carrying her carefully deposit her down on a make-shift bunk, and Bragi begins the process of cutting away the fabric around the bolt. He barks orders for water and cloth to clean the wound and rolls of bandages to be brought to him, and for the rest to get ready for more wounded to arrive before the day is over.

As he manages to remove the clothing and clean the wound enough to get a proper look at it, he notices that it sits deep. It is going to be painful to remove. A thought occurs to him then, as he ponders on how to best remove the bolt, that the tip might be barbed, constructed to keep from being removed easily. If he is being careless, he might cause more damage if that turns out to be the case. He crouches down to be on eye-level with Ylva.

"Ylva, can you hear me?" He notes the beads of sweat trailing down her face. He worries about poison next, recalling Aske's prone form back at the mountain. He swallows, only slightly relieved when the woman pries her eyes open.

"The bolt, how was the tip? A triangle or a barb?" Around him people are nearly shouting, wondering what the hell he is doing. The bolt is in her back, they yell behind him, how can she possibly know? Yet Ylva might know either way, the human thinks, hoping that the shapeshifter had seen the shape of the tip before being hit by a bolt.

"Normal," she grinds out through gritted teeth, and Bragi nods, leaping back up on his feet as he readies himself to remove the bolt. He has four others hold her down and steady, holds out a leather band for her to bite into, before he proceeds to remove the bolt as quickly and cleanly as possible.

This is the worst part of treating wounded patients. Their muffled screams of pain, the sounds lancing through him as they instinctively struggle in an effort to get away as he does his level best to aid them. They know he is helping; he knows that they know this, yet the pain they face during such moments makes them think that he is not. When they look at him with an expression that pleads with him to tell them why he's hurting them... The sick is one thing, but those injured by another person on purpose...

"It'll be over soon, Ylva," he assures her, magic rushing to his fingertips as he grabs a wet cloth and begins to dab at the area around the wound.

Clean, heal, ointment, dress. He works methodically, pushing all other thoughts away. His patient comes first, everything else is second. He manages well enough, until, when the wound is half-way closed, Runa comes running inside.

"Runa, this is no place for a child right now!" He only looks away for long enough to bark and give the girl a stern stare. Bragi notices the fear and surprise on her face from his brief glimpse her way, but he must focus on Ylva. She still possesses enough strength in her that the wound is healing quickly, thankfully, he notes with relief. It will scar, and she will feel sore and beat up for some time, but she will be fine. He just has to finish properly first.

"Where's mam?" Runa cries. "Mam is gone!" Bragi's concentration falters and he looks up again. People are looking around, and the person who was with Saga just moments prior is rapidly paling when they realize that the other shapeshifter is gone.

"Oh no."

CHAPTER FORTY-THREE

"Fuck, fuck, *fuck!*" Aske drags Hildegard with him, the latter wheezing from the two bolts in their arm and side.

"Where's Agnar?" The wounded shapeshifter demands, voice nearly shrill with worry.

"Don't know, lost him back there," Aske hisses, pulling Hildegard behind a tree, not that hiding will do much considering they're in the waters, betraying their location with the ripples their movements cause. He'd been right, but he's got no reason or time to gloat about it. Everything has fallen apart, and the people they have gotten rid off so far were nothing like this group.

"They were just bait, damn it!" He runs a hand through his hair, mind running a mile a minute. Hildegard can't fight anymore, they're in need of urgent medial care.

His traitorous mind supplies him with the memory of that morning, of Bragi saying he could aid the wounded. They could really have needed him now, and the very thought makes him scowl darkly. No matter what, Bragi being out here with them now in this situation would not have been ideal either way. He would have just been another target. The wounded will just have to hang on until they can return to the Sanctuary.

"Hildegard, I'll leave you here for now, alright? I'll draw them away, either take them out if I can, or lead them away, then come back for you, okay?" Hildegard wheezes out a bitter laugh, looking down at themselves.

They're pale, breath heavy. They are in a terrible shape. Leaving them behind is-

There's a rustle, Aske immediately on alert until he barely catches Agnar who trips out.

"Bloody- Agnar!" Aske very nearly falls over with the sudden weight thrown at him, but he manages to deposit the other near Hildegard. Agnar grunts in discomfort, but relaxes against the other wounded shapeshifter, fingers linking together. Aske feels a twinge in his chest. They're all in this mess because he brought Saga, Runa and Bragi here. He and Agnar might not have seen eye to eye on many things, but if Hildegard perishes here, the other man will never forgive Aske. He will be heartbroken, Yngvi too, with the loss of their lifemate. Aske doesn't think he will ever be able to forgive himself either.

"I'll get them back to safety," Agnar groans as he moves to push himself up on his feet, though he stumbles as he does so. "Yngvi has got most of us on the retreat, we'll meet up with them on the way back. Finish this."

Aske nods and turns, shifting into his beast form, slithering quickly through the swamp. The final group might have taken the shapeshifters off-guard, but it doesn't change the fact that it is only that one last group left, and even amongst them, few are left.

And Aske is a very angry and focused individual now. The quicker this end, the sooner he and the others still on their feet can get the wounded to safety, to Bragi.

"*Aske!*" He stops short at the harsh whisper, and cautiously he raises his head. There, just slightly off to the right, on a well-hidden branch, Aske sees flashes of Balder's harrier form.

"They're up ahead, the three remaining." Aske slowly lowers himself down again. As far as he knows, only he and Balder are left to fight, or at the very least, they are the only ones close enough to coordinate together now. He mulls over the situation, tries to come up with a plan that will give them the greatest chance of victory.

"If you blind one, I'll take the other two." Balder nods, beak clicking together before he takes off. The movement causes the branches to creak and the leaves to rustle. The three intruders turn swiftly, but with their eyes up towards the sky, they do not notice the giant serpent heading their way slowly. Aske finds a spot where he'll get the two closest to him in one fell swoop, and waits for Balder to make his move.

Time passes, to the point Aske very nearly wonders if Balder have abandoned their objective. Then, there is the sound of something cutting through the air, a bird's cry, and Balder is suddenly in the face of one of the humans, talons digging into his target's face, gouging the flesh. The man screams, the other two turn towards them swiftly, crossbows raised.

Aske strikes.

He launches himself forward, fangs ready to sink into and skewer the leader, who is the primary target. For what he has done for years, for what he did to Saga and her family, for what he did to Bragi and his home, for what he will continue to do if he gets away. He must die here.

The other hunter, however, reacts quickly, shoving the leader away, out of Aske's reach. He is not quick enough to dodge himself, though, and Aske's fangs pierce through flesh and skewers the man. His sacrifice is in vain, as well, because Aske is used to fighting several enemies at once, so even though his jaw closes around the wrong prey, he reacts immediately.

He ignores the thick coppery taste in his mouth as he locks his jaw around the body and turns sharply, shooting forward like an arrow and coiling around the leader, dragging him along and away so he can't cause trouble for Balder.

Aske drops the one in his mouth along the way as he drags the leader with him a few paces away, before a sharp stinging sensation followed by a searing heat makes him uncoil and drop him. The hunter is quick up on his feet, disorientation leaving him quickly as he turns his attention onto Aske. The shapeshifter shifts his upper body back to resemble that of a human, hands covered in scales, hard and sharp. A quick glance down along the length of his tail offers the explanation to the pain.

A long cut, thankfully not too deep to be dangerous but bad enough to mess with his concentration, runs along his tail. He will have to end this quickly, end this one last threat and get the wounded back home. He coils his tail beneath him to push himself up enough to tower over the human. It does little to intimidate the man, who appears to strengthen his resolve in the face of his adversary, raising his sword.

"You're the last one, filth! You've lost!" Aske hisses, but it doesn't discourage the man. In fact, he appears to stand prouder, a smirk gracing his features. It infuriates Aske, he nearly sees red as he prepares himself to lunge.

"At the very least we have managed to get yours too, beast! The Goddess will reward me in Utopia!" His conviction would have been laughable, if it isn't for the fact that the supposed great deeds of his which he will reap rewards for is the murder of many innocents. Whatever little shred of patience Aske has been so desperately clinging to slips through his fingers.

"When my time comes, I can at least boast that I never purposefully killed innocents!" He snaps, finding no small amount of satisfaction in seeing the smirk slip off the hunter's face.

Aske lunges, lightning fast, but the human rolls out of the way. Aske is undeterred and takes a sharp turn, the powerful muscles in his tail propelling him forward again with great speed and force. The human barely manages to bring the blade back up between them to block Aske's claws from digging into his chest. The shapeshifter's momentum causes them to fall over, the human on his back, struggling to keep Aske away. The shapeshifter pushes forward, letting the weight of his massive form help add pressure on the man, inching ever so closer.

This is it. He has him, he finally has him. This is the end, he can see it in the man's eyes. Fire flickers to life between his fingertips, the human's eyes widen as he notices, feels the steadily building heat from the flames Aske will use to kill him, this is-

Aske tumbles sideways, as the human rolls them both. The shapeshifter cannot stop his massive shape, can't turn around quickly enough to stop the human from darting around and slamming the pommel of his sword into the wound on his tail. Aske screams. He tries to stop it, tries to fight to keep his shape, but the pain muddles his thoughts as he trashes on the ground.

He fists his hands, blunt nails and all, in the wet muddy ground as he tries to get his breathing under control. His thigh is burning, he can't move the leg very well, and he glares at the edge of the water he is laying close by. He should have just drowned him, less risky. Should have just dragged the human all the way over. Aske underestimated him and fuck it all.

"That's just the way it is with you shapeshifters," the man brags. Aske can hear him saunter confidently over. "You rely too much on your powers, it renders you no better than animals." Aske turns with a snarl that tapers off into a choked off groan. His leg hurts so much. He crawls backwards, even though he knows it is futile. He has no weapon, and the searing pain in his thigh is interfering with his ability to shift his shape, his ability to cast magic.

The hunter, while seemingly enjoying his superiority in this situation, is not going to drag this out. He stomps on Aske's chest, forcing all the air from his lungs. The shapeshifter coughs and gasps, clawing at the man's legs with blunt nails. In a desperate bid at having the man fall to even ground, Aske forces fire into his palms. The man screams in pain, faltering if only for a moment, almost falling over, before he glares down, putting all his weight on the leg Aske is hurting. The fire dies out quickly, and it doesn't take long before Aske's vision is swimming, black spots dancing and beckoning him to give in. The human won't give him a peaceful end. He will drag it out and pull Aske under.

"Justice, beast, always-" the man starts off, only to be cut off as something snags him by the shoulders and lifts him up.

He yells in surprise. Aske heaves for air now that the pressure is gone from his chest. His lungs burn, his throat hurts. He pushes himself up on his elbows, searching frantically for the human, eyes tipping upwards, following the screams. He watches as the human is lifted high up in the sky by a hawk. A huge hawk. A familiar hawk.

"It can't be?" He rasps out, watching as the man is carried further and further up. It is a quick affair, but something is wrong, something nagging him. Just the day before, that person, she couldn't keep the transformation for longer than a few seconds, and-

It feels like his heart stops beating in his chest when suddenly Saga, in her human form, is free-falling with the human. Her hands grasp the man's collar, she is yelling something at him. Then, she curls her long legs between them. She plants them on his chest, manoeuvres them in the air so he is beneath her. Then she kicks. With an enraged shriek which pierces Aske's ears, Saga sends him hurtling towards the ground. The force accelerates his descent, and the human screams as he falls. Aske doesn't pay him any mind.

He is staring at Saga's falling body. His heart races like a hummingbird in his chest, willing her to utilize her magic to at the very least slow her own speed.

She doesn't.

He scrambles to his feet, only to fall over as his leg won't keep his weight.

"Fuck!" He tries to change, at the very least just his lower half so he can push forward, so he can catch her, but he can't.

"Saga! Saga, turn!" He yells, slamming his fist into the ground, splattering mud everywhere. She doesn't. she is hurtling downwards, and all Aske can do is watch in horror. She is seconds from hitting the ground. From that height, with that speed, she'll be crushed against the earth. Bones broken, flesh and muscle and sinew torn, blood splattering.

She looks resigned, and Aske screams again, throat raw, despairing. After everything, this is how it ends? He left her behind in the Sanctuary so this wouldn't happen. Because she can't use her powers properly, he left her behind for that reason. She's just a few metres above the ground when a harrier of considerable size crashes into her.

Both her and the bird are hurled sideways, and they skid and roll across the ground.

Nobody moves.

"... Saga?" His voice cracks. No one responds.

CHAPTER FORTY-FOUR

Bragi desperately wants to go out and look for Aske, for Saga. No one's seen her for quite some time now, and he is more than just a little bit worried. Runa is downright terrified. The moment Ylva was brought in, wounded as she was, it didn't take the little girl long to understand what was going on. And with both her mother and Aske missing…

Bragi does not have the time to comfort her, however much he wants to, because the wounded are being brought in, one after another. Despite being the only one able to conjure healing magic, the shapeshifters working alongside him are indeed capable of tending to the wounded. Thankfully, most of the injuries can be treated with medicine and proper care. Not many are in immediate need of magic, and can wait until he has dealt with the worst of it.

The one in the worst condition right now is Hildegard, and their lifemates Agnar and Yngvi, patched up as much as needed, watch over them from a distance. Bragi is expending a lot of magic, they do notice, and their fingers are woven tightly together, brows furrowed with worry as they watch Bragi work. Bragi would have assured them that everything will be alright, but he is honestly not sure, and he's got enough to contend with at the moment. And he has received no news! No news of his own love, of Saga, or the situation as a whole. Did they win? Did they lose? Are they still fighting out there? Are they alright? Are they hurt? Are they de-

Bragi shakes his head. He needs to focus on Hildegard right now. Information about the rest of the group will come in due time, right now he

has a duty to focus on the patients in front of him. These people are relying on him, he cannot fail them simply because he lost his focus worrying over things he cannot do anything about. He has never had trouble like this though, never once in his long life has he had problems focusing on the patients while other worries nag at him. He has always prided himself on being able to compartmentalize in such situations, but this time he can't always keep his thoughts from wandering. It is worrying.

Hours pass, Hildegard is out of danger, none have died. The severity of the injuries varies from person to person, but most will be out of the house of healing before a week has passed. Hildegard will be staying a while, though they too should be able to make a full recovery. Yngvi and Agnar are relieved to hear it, offering Bragi quick hugs in thanks before they move on to stay beside their lifemate.

Bragi is wiping the sweat away from his face and neck as he is overlooking the room. Only Aske, Saga and Balder are missing. Now that he is done, he allows himself to properly worry. No more holding back and shoving the thoughts away. He is drained, every last drop of his magic is gone. If Aske, Saga or Balder, or all three of them, are severely injured, he will not have any magic to help them with.

Only herbs, potions, medicine, water, bandages. He feels a bit lost. He has never once in all his life exhausted all his magic like this. He feels... helpless, for a lack of a better word. It is ridiculous, because most of the time when he is tending to patients, to the sick and injured, he has mostly used his knowledge of diseases and injuries and medicine to treat them, falling back to magic only if absolutely necessary.

Here, with so many wounded, gravely so too, he had no choice but to use his magic. And now it is all gone. He hopes the last three aren't too badly injured, wishes they aren't injured at all, but that is a fools hope, and he knows it. He must stay realistic about this, if not, he will not at all be prepared for what greets him upon their return.

Bragi gives instructions to the others before heading for the exit. He needs fresh air, he needs to get out of this building, away from the smell of blood, the groans and whimpers of pain, and wait for the return of Aske. Because he promised he would return.

So, Bragi opens the door, exits, and moves to lean against the wall on the right of the door. Now that he is outside, with no one yelling for him or asking for help, he realizes just how exhausted he truly is. He slides down and sighs, trying to keep his breathing steady. He feels himself drift in and out of consciousness, not fully falling asleep, but not staying completely awake either. It is like he has fallen somewhere in between. He feels warm, calm, nothing is plaguing him, no worry nagging at him. Just peace. Awake enough to be somewhat aware of where he is but gone enough that everything is fuzzy around the edges, as in when you are somewhat awakening in the morning, yet your body is trying to lull you back to sleep. The calm peacefulness, the in-between consciousness and slumber, that moment where-

"Bragi?" His breath hitches as his senses grow just a little bit sharper, enough to convince him he is waking up properly. He fears opening his eyes, wondering if it is just his mind playing tricks on him. He is scared that if he opens his eyes, no one will be there. That it is simply a dream his mind supplies him out of comfort. But the voice calls out again, soft and warm and exhausted.

"Bragi, are you sleeping?" Well, that is just odd. He cracks an eye open, only for both to open wide as he scrambles up on his feet, eyes roving over the many cuts, bruises and scrapes on his lover. The world narrows down to just Aske and Bragi.

"What happened?" Bragi can guess what happened based on the state of many of the others, but the question tumbles out anyway. Aske grins ruefully.

"Got the shit beaten out of me, is what happened," he snorts. "Can't even walk by myself." He nods sideways at the person whose shoulders his arm is slung over. Bragi had been so focused on Aske he didn't notice the others. Saga grunts as she adjusts her grip on her brother, Balder standing behind them with hunched shoulders and covered in dirt. Saga's clothing is dirty, she is too, and he does not doubt that she too has a bruise or two on her somewhere, but other than that, she looks content. Balder looks no worse for wear either.

"Are you alright?" Bragi asks her and Saga nods, slowly.

"Just a bit bruised. I mean, compared to this idiot who got stabbed with a sword."

"He what?" Aske glowers at her as Bragi begins a proper inspection, poking, prodding and pulling on his clothes.

"I have a cut on my thigh, I did *not* get run through," he clarifies. Bragi kneels down and pulls on the torn fabric, ripping a bigger hole in it, exhaling and closing his eyes. His right hand moves up to pinch the bridge of his nose as the siblings watch him.

"Let's," he exhales tiredly, "let's get you inside. Please help me with him, Saga. Runa is inside too, worried sick about you." Saga's cheeks redden in shame, but she helps Aske inside. It wasn't Bragi's intention to shame her like this, but perhaps she is just now finally beginning to think of the way she just disappeared from everyone. How would Runa, who had lost everything, react? It mustn't have crossed her mind at the time, in her hurry. She helps deposit him down on a make-shift bed, before she is nearly tackled over by her daughter who is both wailing and shouting and having trouble with deciding whether to be furious with her mother or hug her.

While Saga sits not too far away from them, assuring her daughter that she is fine, she is safe, everything is over now and that she is sorry she worried the little girl, Bragi rips Aske's trousers, cleans the wound and inspects it. Then he moves away to grab what he needs of medicine and supplies, coming back to treat the wound. Once he pulls out a needle and readies himself to sew the wound shut, Aske speaks again.

"What, no magic?" He aims to tease, but the way Bragi glares up at him from his position makes his mouth click shut audibly.

"Right, not a time for jokes. Sorry."

"I've spent the entire day worrying for your safety, tending to the very sudden influx of wounded, and now this. I am utterly exhausted, Aske, both of magic and patience." Bragi's never sounded so brisk to the shapeshifter before, it catches the other off-guard. He ducks his head, stays quiet to allow Bragi to focus on stitching him up properly.

"I'm sorry I-" he begins when Bragi rolls the bandage around his thigh, cuts himself off with a hiss, the area throbbing and Bragi stills.

"Too tight?" Aske nods, and Bragi eases up on the wrapping just a little bit.

"Go on."

"What?" Aske blinks.

"Finish your apology." The brunet sniffs.

"You absolute bastard," Aske says fondly, barely holding back a chuckle, his lips quirking upwards. "I'm sorry I worried you. I came back as soon as I could, but considering we're the last ones back, and, well," he gestures to the room full of wounded, "I'm sorry it took so long."

"You better be," Bragi mutters as he finishes up. He gets back up on his feet, ignores the aches all over that beckons him to rest, reaching out to instead cup Aske's face in his hands. With Aske sitting like this, on a low bunk, Bragi is the one towering over him for once.

"Is it over?" The question is so quiet Aske nearly doesn't hear it.

"Yes." He closes his eyes, relishes the feeling of the gentle caress. A stark contrast to the day's violence. No more hunters, no more persecutions, at the least for a while. Just time to recuperate, heal, and live. To figure out what they want and need.

Time to figure out where they want to go. Once Aske's leg is healed up properly.

"Once this has healed," Bragi presses a kiss to Aske's forehead, ignoring the mud, blood and dirt and taste of sweat, "I will be giving you a stern lecture." Aske grins, his own hands cupping along Bragi's elbows, rubbing at the fabric of his tunic with his thumbs.

"Oh, a lecture, is it?"

"Yes, that is what you get. I'll make sure to nag you until your ears fall off." Aske laughs, ignores the throb from the forming bruise on his chest by the action, and hugs Bragi close.

"Oh no, woe is me, how will I ever survive?" Bragi laughs too, a tired but earnest sound.

"You brought this upon yourself." He pulls back a bit to smile fondly down at the other man. "You legless lizard." Aske sputters, affronted.

"That *is* insulting!"

CHAPTER FORTY-FIVE

Andor is bored. So bored he yawns so hard tears spring to his eyes. Birger has his head either in the books of the town hall or in the garden left by the serpent. Halfdan is with him, tending to the garden the best he can. There is not much a fifteen-year-old can do on his own though, so it is fortunate that Birger is invested in keeping the garden as is until the serpent returns.

Signy, at this age, have been somewhat forced to take on duties such as sewing and cooking. Of course, in return she demanded to be allowed to be a part of their village's little hunting group. There's never been anyone more frightening when skinning dead animals in their village. Andor is careful around her, so *he* doesn't end up being skinned. Her knife is really sharp.

Andor, unlike the other three, has lessons. He hates them, but his father reminds him again and again that as his son it is expected of him to become the next head of the village. At first, he had been excited. Being the next in line to lead the entire village, being the chief, sounds exciting, yet as time had passed and most of the time was spent following his father around, watching and listening how he dealt with issues popping up as the days pass, he quickly grew bored of it.

Right now, Andor would rather be up at the caves and dig around in the garden. And when the opportunity presents itself, he slips away unnoticed, and sprints up the hill to the cave. Birger and Halfdan are already there, tending to the garden as best they can. Andor frowns at the sight. He doesn't understand why they're doing so much work to keep it as it was when the serpent left. He can understand the usefulness of the herbs and spices and fruits and berries, but they're putting in a lot of effort not to *change* anything. And that is a useless thing because everything changed when the serpent left.

Sure, they have been lucky enough to avoid any more bandit attacks in the years that have passed since the serpent left, but that is the only positive.

"Birger, Halfdan!" he calls out. The other two teens look up, smile as they see him advance on them.

"There you are. Got away again, did you?" Andor nods, settling down cross-legged next to Birger as the other teen tends to a herb plant. He seems to have taken an interest in medicine and is actively helping out the village doctor with gathering herbs and mixing potions and medicines. And all the books he reads…

"Are you going to be the next doctor, Birger?" Said teen grins at Andor, mischievously, scratching at the tip of his nose.

"Well, you're going to be the next chief. This way, I can support you." Andor pauses, before a wide smile stretches across his face. It is good, to have friends on your side, friends who'll support you.

"Birger-"

"The Goddess knows you'll need it considering all the trouble you get into." And the smile slips as he punches the other in the arm, hard.

"Hey!" Birger complains, rubbing the tender spot, before he launches himself at Andor, causing the both of them to roll across the ground and over both bushes and flowers. It is not actually a *real* fight. Andor knows that Birger is just pulling his leg, is just trying to cheer him up in his own way. This is just playing, like when they were kids. Still, Andor is not about to just roll over and hand the other the win.

So, of course he fights back. He is the leader of their group after all, and the next to be chief of the village, as his father continuously reminds him of from the moment he wakes up in the mornings until he goes to sleep at night. He must-

Someone grabs him by the scruff of his neck and lifts him up. Andor blinks several times in confusion, mind not keeping up with what is happening at present, sees Birger being held similarly in front of him, appearing just as confused as he is.

"Why are you rolling over and crushing my bloody daffodils?" Both of the teens look up and see a tall, redhaired man staring down at them. He appears rather unimpressed with their antics, a brow raised high above yellow eyes-

Yellow eyes!

"Snake!" Andor yells, and the man drops them both before crouching down to inspect the flower bed they've crushed. Most of the flowers are shredded and crushed to the ground, stems broken, the earth trampled down. He does not look best pleased.

"Oh dear, can they be saved?" Another man appears, brown curls streaked with solid grey. The teens recognize him from years ago, when he appeared and ascended the hill to the serpent's cave. Recognizes him as the one who came to the village just before the serpent left.

"Magic man!" But his name they do not recall. The man startles and looks at Andor. Then it clicks.

"*I beg your pardon?*" The redhaired man barks out a laugh at the affronted tone of voice from the other. He gets back up on his feet with a bounce and wraps an arm around the shorter man's shoulders.

"It has been years, Bragi, you can't fault them for not remembering your name."

"It is just plain rude! They could have just asked!" The redhaired man just laughs harder. "It isn't funny, Aske!" But Aske just continues to laugh, shoulders shaking so bad he needs to lean on Bragi to not fall over. It only tapers off as he looks over the garden. It is not as lovely and vibrant as it was when he left, and something is missing. Wordlessly, he walks around, carefully pulling on the plants, bushes, flowers, branches, whistling quietly all the way. Bragi just watches.

"What's snake doing?" Halfdan has made his way over, curious as to what is going on.

"His name is Aske, dear boy. Learn to use it. You wouldn't like it if people went around calling you 'human' or 'boy', would you?" Halfdan silently agrees, trying again.

"What's Aske doing?" Bragi's eyes turn somber as he follows his lover's movements.

"He's looking for the spirits he left with the garden. But I am afraid they might have ceased to be since they have yet to show themselves."

"Oh." Halfdan blinks, before reaching into his coat's many pockets and pulling something small out. "Like this one?" Bragi stares for several moments, standing in stunned silence, before finally finding the ability to call out for Aske to hurry over.

"Aske! Aske, over here!" In the blink of an eye, Aske is there, retrieving the little spirit gingerly from Halfdan.

"Daffodil," the shapeshifter murmurs. The spirit is cold, looks weak, yet happy to see their friend. They look like they are on the brink of disappearing, truly.

"They started disappearing a year ago," Halfdan explains, Andor and Birger brushing the dirt off themselves as the they move to stand beside their friend, watching curiously as Aske inspects the little spirit.

"This one is the only one left."

"Oh no," Bragi whispers, leaning closer as Aske holds Daffodil up close.

"I'm sorry I took so long," the redhead mutters, brows furrowed as an apologetic expression passes his features. Daffodil whistles, smiling gently, finding comfort in their friend's gentle hold.

"Do you think you've got enough in you to go on a little adventure with me and Bragi?" The spirit struggles to sit up properly in the palm of Aske's hand, but nods. They look a little better, at least a little, as if being close to the one who willed them into being is giving them strength again, slowly but surely.

"Will they be able to do so?" Bragi is worried, but Aske smiles, cooing a bit at the spirit.

"Sure they can. They were willed into being by me. If they were all still here, I planned on us staying for a little while to make sure they would be able to go on, but since Daffodil is the only one left, well, we'll just take them with us immediately."

"You're leaving again?" Andor exclaims, startling both his friends and the adults.

"Yes," Aske answers. "I've got something to do."

"Didn't you leave the first time because you had something to do? You're finally back, so why are you leaving immediately?" Aske and Bragi exchange a look before turning back to the teens. None of the three appear particularly happy with this news.

"I did have something to do back then, but I am not done. I just came back to check on this place."

"But this is your home!" Andor very nearly yells. Aske remains calm despite the boy's sudden outburst.

"For a hundred years it was," the shapeshifter acknowledges, and the teens stare. *Was.* "But a home can change, and right now, my home is here." He cradles Daffodil in one hand alone, while the other comes to rest above Bragi's heart.

"My home is where my loved ones are."

"But…"

"You'll understand one day, I'm sure. I've got something to do now, first, but I will return again someday, alright?"

"Do you promise?" Birger asks. Andor's expression has morphed from distress to a rather adorable pout. He has overcome the crisis thanks to Aske's assurances, but he is still not pleased with this outcome.

"I promise. It might take some time, you might even have kids or even grandchildren of your own by the time I return, but I will." It seems like an impossibly long stretch of time he's hinting to, but even so, it is better than him not returning at all.

"What is it that you need to do, then?" Halfdan asks, the important reason as to why the shapeshifter has not returned for good but is just stopping by. Aske looks around the garden, eyes roving over every little nook and cranny, turning to take in the sight of the cave as well. His eyes glaze over as he falls back into memories of this place. He appears almost wistful, lost, even a little bit sad, until Bragi squeezes the hand still resting on his chest, gently pulling Aske back to the present.

He looks down the hill then, at the village and a small smile graces his features again.

"My time here, even though I didn't know it then, was the safest I had been in a long time. None of you cared that I am a shapeshifter. There aren't many safe spaces in the world for my kind. There's only one that I know of, but it cannot house all of us. I aim to find as many shapeshifters as I can, and create a second safe space before-"

"This place can be a safe space!" Andor calls out, startling everyone with his eagerness. "You said it yourself; you were safe here! And you know the area! The garden is yours, and, and-" his rant tapers off as the teen breathes heavily, trying to come up with more reasons for the shapeshifter to agree. Everyone stares at him, and blood rushes to his face out of sheer embarrassment. For many moments no one says anything, before Aske releases a quiet chuckle, which grows into a great booming laugh. It doesn't make Andor feel any better, being laughed at, but the shapeshifter calms down, wiping at his eyes where tears of mirth have gathered.

"It sounds lovely, Andor, but who is going to make this possible?"

"Me!" The teen exclaims, slapping his own chest, wincing only slightly at his own enthusiasm. "I am going to be the next chief! I'll do everything I can to make this a safe space for shapeshifters!"

"We'll help!" Birger chimes in, Halfdan nodding eagerly beside him. "I'm going to be a doctor, I'm already an apprentice, Halfdan is well on his way with understanding how to take care of your magic garden, Signy is part of our defence and hunting squads! We can make this work!"

"Besides," Halfdan rubs his arm awkwardly, looking up at Aske with wide eyes, "everyone here misses you." That causes some pause on the shapeshifter's behalf, then he exhales loudly, running a hand through his hair. He doesn't appear displeased, rather, he appears perplexed and a little bit touched. Then he steps forward, bowing down so he doesn't tower over the three teens. He scrutinizes them, staring for several heartbeats, but the teens do not back down, they stare resolutely back. He comes to a decision.

"Fine. I'll send my people your way, so you'd better make sure to keep up your end of the deal. Just to be clear, most of them will most likely be suspicious of you." Andor grins and sticks his hand out for the older man to shake.

"It is a deal, and we'll find a way to end their suspicions, we're good at it! Now, you've got to come with us back down and tell my dad!"

"What? No, I've got-" Aske begins to argue, knowing that if he is trapped in a room with Gunvald to explain everything, he will have to listen to the man's incessant chattering for hours on end. The three doesn't let him get away though and begin bodily shooing him down the hill. Aske casts a desperate look at Bragi, who is covering his mouth to hinder the laughter threatening to escape him.

"Bragi! Tell them! Don't *laugh*, stop them! We don't have time for this-*Bragi, you bastard!*" Aske realizes that Bragi has no intention of stopping the pushy teens from absconding with him.

The four disappear down the hill and Aske's half-hearted shouts dwindle away, and once Bragi gets himself under control, he releases a fond sigh as he looks around. He smiles, before following the others.

Yes, this could become a lovely Sanctuary. He hopes he will be able to see it.

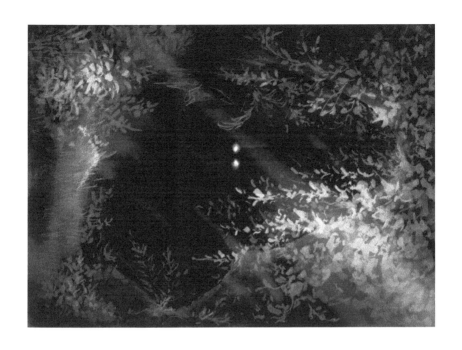

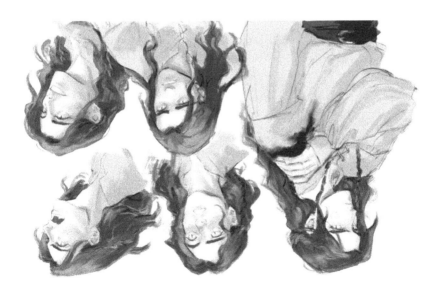

Milton Keynes UK
Ingram Content Group UK Ltd.
UKHW010007240823
427351UK00004B/254